Joel Foote Bingham

The Twin Sisters of Martigny

A Story of Italian Life Forty Years Ago

Joel Foote Bingham

The Twin Sisters of Martigny
A Story of Italian Life Forty Years Ago

ISBN/EAN: 9783337140335

Printed in Europe, USA, Canada, Australia, Japan

Cover: Foto ©Andreas Hilbeck / pixelio.de

More available books at **www.hansebooks.com**

THE
TWIN SISTERS OF MARTIGNY

A Story of Italian Life

FORTY YEARS AGO

"What Shadows we are, what Shadows we pursue."
— EDMUND BURKE

By

THE REV. J. F. BINGHAM, D.D., L.H.D.

Lecturer on Italian Literature, Trinity College, Hartford, Conn., Author of
Francesca da Rimini, Canova's Bonanza, etc.

BOSTON
LEE AND SHEPARD
M DCCC XCIX

What Heart

DURING AND ENDURING

THE CHANGEFUL YEARS

ALIVE AS THE WIND-HARP TO MUSIC

WITH MINE

Has Quivered

IN HOPES AND IN FEARS

WHOM BEST OF WOMANKIND I KNOW AND LOVE

To Her

IS DEDICATED

This Remembrance

LIST OF VIEWS

LIST OF VIGNETTES

CHAMOUNY AND THE AIGUILLES.

I.

THE trumpet rang clear and the notes rolled in echoes from the mountain-sides. My ear trained to the voice of the military bugle could not be deceived.

"*Ubi terrarum sumus?*"—Where am I?—What troops can be here?

The long, last note was hardly over, when I had gained sufficient consciousness (though still somewhat clouded in mind and memory) to leap from my bed with an eager anxiety to reconnoitre the situation. Peeping over the short curtain which screened the lower half of the casement, I saw a squadron of dragoons formed in line across the greensward in front of me.

They wore the French uniform of the second empire. In front of the line was an officer, whose dress showed him to be of very high rank, superbly mounted and attended by a numerous staff, which remained stationary, except the trumpeter who clung to him like a shadow, and a junior officer who followed exactly behind him, as he presently turned and rode slowly up and down the line, occasionally halting to examine a carbine or look into a knapsack, and now and then wheeling so as to face the line and speaking, apparently in an inaudible voice, something which was immediately translated into ringing notes of the horn, and instantly obeyed by the men.

The manœuvres being presently over, the old officer turned toward me, and I could distinctly discern a weather-beaten face, a snow-white mustache, and a breast covered by the decorations of many orders. I had seen, I afterwards learned, a marshal of France. Was it Canrobert? I never certainly knew. He retired, followed by his staff and the prolonged salute of the whole command. The junior, who until this moment had been merely tracking the steps of his superior, now dashed up in front of the line with the trumpeter at his side, and gave a few orders, which were trumpeted and obeyed as before. Then, with a spirited flourish of the trumpet, all started off at a gallop, and a moment later the whole vision had vanished.

I wondered much that French dragoons, in a time of peace in this part of the world, should be in Switzerland and on the frontier of Italy; and not much less, at so high an officer being so far outside the apparent route from France to the seat of war in the East.

I afterward learned that the great officer had a mission from his Emperor to meet Cavour at Turin; that the squadron of dragoons was an escort of honor which had been detached from a large body of the same which, in fact, a few weeks before I myself had seen at Lyons on their way to a transport-ship at Marseilles, whence they would touch at Genoa, receive on board the marshal and his escort and sail direct for the Bosphorus.

He had come from Lyons to Geneva by the *diligence*, had passed the time, till the arrival of the escort, at several Alpine resorts, and now met them for the first time at *Martigny*, whence he and his staff would immediately cross by the Great St. Bernard and meet them again at *Aosta*. There he and his staff would join the escort and they would thence proceed together to Turin.

The events just described happened on Sunday, August 6, 1854 (according to my diary), when I found myself at the *Hôtel de la Tour* at *Martigny*. I had arrived in the darkness on the evening before from *Chamouny* by the *Tête Noire*, after a nine-hours mule-ride, which included a thorough drenching in a tremendous shower. Unusual fatigue had prolonged my slumbers well into the day. When the bugle awoke me, the glare of a midsummer sun was pouring into my little chamber through the slightly curtained casement, and the pillows about my head were bathed in a brightness with which they glistened like the mountain snowdrifts of which I had been dreaming.

One of the most wonderful of the many wonders of dreams is, I think, the extension of minutes, or even seconds, into a seeming consciousness of hours' duration. This dream seemed to me to have been going on for an hour or two, at least, though I have reason to think that it did not really occupy five minutes.

During a week's stay at *Chamouny* I had been reading, in the intervals of my own excursions (one of which was a bootless chamois-chase with the old hunter, *Tairrez*), Albert Smith's romantic description of his ascent of *Mont Blanc*, two years before. My fancy was full of his pictures, many of which I had myself just verified.

The *Glacier de Bossons* rose before my mind with its scenes of "splendid desolation and horror." Its huge and ragged icebergs glittered, I thought, like pale emeralds in the rays of the broad moon which was just setting behind the *Aiguille du Goûté*. These emerald-mountains were perforated by lofty arches overhung by pendent icicles and opening a distant perspective of fantastic masses beyond. Some of these distant masses

GRANDS MULETS.

seemed to be stupendous bridges crossing awful gulfs below ; others rose like embattled castles on projecting cliffs and commanded, in the view still beyond, valleys and gorges of boundless ice.

At one moment I seemed to be sitting on the top of one of the *Grands Mulets*, searching with the chamois-glass for game under the distant cliffs to right and left, and on the ragged edges of *Montanvert ;* and then to be scanning the villages in the *Val de Chamouny*, which appeared like white atoms scattered along the spotted ground.

At another moment, I was making the grand ascent, and was passing. around the precipitous flanks of the *Rochers Rouges*, with the *Jardin*, *Monte Rosa*, and the *Col du Géant*, successively spreading out before me ; and then came that stupendous vista—the vast undulating field of ice looking down the *Glacier du Tacul* toward the beginning of the *Mer de Glace*.

Finally, after incredible fatigue and dazed with glory, I thought I stood on the *Calotte* itself — the very cap of *Mont Blanc*, where there was nothing higher around me. The sun, coming swiftly up, was already tingeing the top of the *Aiguille du Goûté*. The mists in the valleys were spread out like a "filmy ocean" on every side, and, pierced by the glittering tips of the higher *Aiguilles*, the *tout-ensemble*, tinted by the reflected sheen, lay before me and around me like an "archipelago of gold."

The growing brilliance went on brightening at the horizon into a transparent crimson, merging away toward the upper sky through every color of the bow—into the deepest violet at forty-five degrees, and a dark azure at the zenith. The living snow reflected in a paler tint every overhanging color; and the *Dôme du Goûté* stood in awful white with a rosy scarf around his waist.

At the moment when the sun sprang above the horizon, and an indescribable conflict of direct and reflected rays confused me with a commingled and overpowering brilliance, I thought a strain of celestial music burst on my ear, as if ushering, with a flourish of angelic trumpets, the arrival of the king of day. This music awoke me; and I recognized, as I have described, the notes of a bugler of French dragoons.

II.

Hark, the Sunday-morning bell,
  Sweet music making,
Ringing clear o'er wood and dell,
  To worship waking ! [1]

AS I finished my toilet a sound of many voices was becoming more and more audible abroad. I went again to the window and now threw open the casement. The dark-blue sky was unflecked. Trees, rocks, and sod, and even the unsightly houses of the poor town, after being washed by the shower which had drenched me and my beast the evening before, stood in Sunday dress and seemed to be shining with a keen holiday joy. As often a woman, whom the world accounts plain, will brighten under some pleasing excitement so that we forget the disparagement of her attractions and declare that she is beautiful still, so I could not then help admiring homely *Martigny " en état du plus beau jour."*

At this moment the bell of the little church was started, and began to send out its clanging peals. Under its magnetic influence, the scene soon became stirring and picturesque. The main road and several mountain footpaths grew alive with country-folk and village-folk. Man and maid, mother and babe, rollicking childhood and old age creeping on its staff, came converging toward the sanctuary. At a little distance in front of the leather-curtained door, on the green borders of the highway, or where a building, tree, or mossy bowlder offered a shade from the August sun, were ever-increasing groups in holiday attire.

Waists and petticoats shone in all the hues of the Alpine bow. Ribbons as bright and varied floated from broad-brimmed hats of *Livorno*. Under these broad brims, oval cheeks, olive with Italian blood and dyed yet deeper by kisses of wanton wind and ardent sun, but faintly disguised the roses that bloomed and withered there, and eyes, black as ravens' wings, shot out their sparkling rays — dangerous enough within their humble range. Often these jaunty *sombreros* hung swinging from dusky wrists and forearms which no further exposure could darken. Below the bright petticoat, also, sometimes a dark-blue stocking, but oftener a sun-browned ankle, appeared, and then a queer, stout shoe.

The males of all ages were clad of course in the infamous "*Martigny* brown." It was clean, however; and many a young man, and often an older, sported a jaunty ribbon on his hat.

The bell ceased. The group about the church door disappeared. Other groups and individuals approached and entered. A few, however, remained without, absorbed in conversation, or even in some quiet amusement.

CAPPELLA E CAMPOSANTINO.

III.

The grave is still and deep ;
    Frightful its portals stand,
The secrets safe to keep
    Of the unkennéd land.

No songs of Nightingale
    In those deep chambers sound ;
And Friendship's roses fall
    Lone on the moss-grown mound.

There Brides will wring and wound
    Their hands in helplessness ;
Nor through the cold, deep ground
    Can plaints of Orphans press.'

AN hour later, after my frugal *colazione*, I was seated in the neighborhood of these groups with my book in the attitude, but hardly in the act, of reading. The worshipers were now issuing from the church and scattering in all directions toward their homes. A few turned their pensive steps toward the cemetery. These, of whom, as far as I remember, there may have been a half-dozen, were all females. My attention, it is hard to tell why, was so earnestly arrested by the figure and bearing of one of these that I followed and quietly, and I think unobserved, entered the open gates of the "*Campo Santo*," consecrated ground, where mortal bodies are planted for the harvest of immortality.

After passing some time in respectful examination of the very various and though rude yet often exceedingly touching memorials of the departed, I came upon a chair, *e naturalibus*, which stood beside a grave on which many flowers were growing. The spot at that hour lay gratefully beneath the shade of a wide-spreading beach-tree that grew outside the wall. I occupied that chair, not without a twinge of conscience in making a convenience of a seat evidently sacred to mourning love and consecrated by sad and solemn meditations, I could not doubt, of death and immortality.

All considerations of myself, however, were soon drowned by an absorption in the scenes transpiring around me. All or the most of those whom I had seen enter the enclosure were now kneeling at the head of one grave and another telling their beads. Among them I saw the figure that had interested me before, and had been the attraction which had drawn me to the spot.

Motionless as a statue, it was kneeling at the head of two comparatively recent graves — or, to speak more exactly, a double grave: The mounds were barely distinguishable as two, so nearly did the adjacent sides coalesce in one curve. The headboard (for it was of wood), was painted white with lettering of black. After an old fashion, common enough in rustic graveyards, it was one piece, but divided at the top into two tangent semi-circles, each, in this instance, surmounted with a rudely cut cross. Properly speaking, there was no inscription. But on the right side was the letter L, and on the left, M. The letters were so large (I should think two feet in length) as to reach nearly over the whole height of the slab; and there was no more, whether of epitaph or ornament, there.

My position being directly in front, the face of the figure at first I could not see. But the cut and tone of apparel bespoke youth in the wearer. Her head also was uncovered, and an intermittent zephyr would now and then play with some fugitive lock which had broken loose from the glossy, black cable of braided tresses which it seemed certain could not yet have buffeted the storms of twenty Alpine winters. Besides, there was an indescribable apparent suppleness (though without any real movement) in the figure which seemed to express beyond mistake the trembling tenderness of still lingering girlhood.

The forces of nature, however, seemed to sympathize in my interest, and helped partially to relieve my curiosity. The sun, now past the meridian, soon began to encroach on the shade of the fir which had sheltered these graves during the morning hours; and the kneeling figure, turning to escape the advancing rays, offered unconsciously to the scrutiny of my glass,—for I sat at a distance quite sufficient to forestall any scruples of improper intrusion on my part or any notice on hers — a profile of strangely commingled and strangely attractive loveliness. With due allowance for the rudeness of the environment, a fairer vision I never beheld. Religion, simplicity, beauty, sorrow were blended in that picture in a fascination which captivated me, soul and body, and which I had no inclination left to resist.

My heart palpitated with emotion. I can feel its throbs at this moment. I used my glass industriously many minutes, till every outline of her figure and every thread of her attire became indelibly registered in my memory.

Upon the grass at her side lay a pair of clean but heavy shoes. A flat-brimmed hat of coarse black straw, trimmed scantily but very neatly with lusterless black ribbons, depended by the tie-strings from a corner of the headboard above described and swung gently in the intermittent breeze which ever and anon puffed over the silent mounds and toyed with the tufted grass.

Her eyes were closed. The long silken lashes lay trembling on the lids. Occasional crystal drops darted out, chased one another by leaps and starts across the olive cheek, and fell to the ground.

Her face was sharply cut in features of a striking outline and of exceeding beauty. Her hair of the deepest black was parted on a broad, low forehead, and drawn smoothly back to be confined behind by one of those curious silver combs which are so often found among the better class of peasantry in most of the countries of Continental Europe — inherited and handed down through many generations.

Her feet were bare — a matter, however, of no great note or significance, at that period, in her sphere of life and in that quarter of the world,— though, I believe, the march of civilization and artificial life has now arrived and changed much of these primeval habits even there to-day.

Notwithstanding this, her attire in general was distinctly above that of her class,— that is to say, of the class to which I took her to belong,— more subdued and refined in taste, with a nearer approach to elegance, or, at least, to a suggestion of it in both cut and finish, even where the material was but the common stuff of the country. She wore a sleeveless bodice of some thin black fabric, deeply *décolleté* over a *chemisette* of white dotted muslin, with sleeves of the same, frilled at the wrist. Upon the heart-shaped top of the bodice in front lay a curious rosette of black crape. From the waist flowed a narrow black skirt of a thicker material than the bodice, and longer than the usual habit of peasant-girls in Switzerland and Italy, just revealing, as she knelt, the soles of unshod feet.

Her hands were clasped in front. On a pink coral rosary, which depended from them, ever and anon a bead would drop — the record of a prayer recited.

All the other figures except the object of my curious concern one by one disappeared from the consecrated spot. The worshiping congregation had long since vanished. Along the highway and on the far-off footpaths of the mountain-side the diminishing, twinkling, fading bright dresses had all dissolved away in the blue mist of empty distance. Only we two of living beings were in any quarter visible; and she was absorbed and unconscious of my presence.

The village street was now noiseless and empty. High noon had taken possession of the world. The intermittent zephyr was dead. Not a leaf fluttered. Not a blade of grass nodded at my feet. Not a ripple passed over the golden surface of the neighboring grain-field. Not a cloud floated in the deep, silent sky. Changeless and motionless the kneeling girl kept on with her voiceless prayers, and steadily the recording beads kept dropping.

In that universal silence, time seemed to join hands with eternity. Sitting thus under the glittering stillness of that summer Sunday noontide, amidst a congregation of unknown dead, in speechless company with that young, beautiful, sad, saintly stranger, who, unconscious of my presence, was conversing with heaven, I thought dreamily, yet sadly, too, of another graveyard, far away beyond the dreary ocean, where bodies dear to me also were sleeping their dreamless and unwaking sleep.

Presently my reverie was broken. The scene assumed a more earthly but not less interesting aspect. The *religieuse* became again a *séculière*. The haloed saint, hedged about by the sanctities of death and prayer, became again but a sweet, sorrowful girl, with a pitiful story, no doubt, to tell, and a woman's heart most assuredly hungry for sympathy.

The figure moved. The rosary was replaced. The red crucifix rested on the white muslin that covered her rising and falling bosom. She crossed herself above and on either side of the sacred emblem, then arose from her knees and sat at the foot of the fir-tree. Presently she reached after the suspended bonnet, with a slow precision fixed it on her head, and, taking the discarded shoes in her hand, arose and passed with hasty steps toward the cemetery gate.

To her surprise and mine it was closed; and though not locked (as it would not be till sunset, the great padlock hanging loose on the post), some ignorant or careless hand had turned a clumsy fixture which could be undone only from the outer side.

To force the heavy timbers was impossible. The enclosing wall, built of rough but firmly cemented stones, might, with difficulty, be climbed. Indeed, there was now no other way of egress.

I saw her turn and look anxiously along the line of the stony barricade to discover if there were any spot more feasible than another for such an ascent and the still more perilous descent on the opposite side. I had wished for a decent occasion to accost her. That opportunity had now appeared. I sprang up and ran towards her.

She had already laid her shoes on the top of the wall, and set one foot on a projecting stone, when I was near enough to exclaim:

"*Mon enfant!*"—for although I was convinced by what has been already mentioned, that she had passed a good way into the experience of the graver cares and sorrows of life, yet she seemed so tender and young that I could not force myself to give her a maturer title—

—"*Mon enfant, pardonnez-moi, mais certainement vous me permettrez de vous y aider*" [Pardon, my child, let me help you.]

"*J'en vous remercie, monsieur, merci de bon coeur,*" [Thank you, thank you, sir, with all my heart] came back in timid but sweet tones.

Nerved by a pleasurable excitement, I leaped or climbed (I know not how) over the uncouth wall, released the gentle prisoner, replaced the bars, and received a repetition of sweet thanks with an added '*Adieu,*' as she started briskly forward. But desiring to prolong the agreeable meeting, I walked on by her side on the grassy bank of the highway. She observed my movement and gave me a sad smile, but nothing more. I knew not what to say to start a conversation that would be agreeable to her, and so for a little time we walked on in silence.

At last, thinking I might be more sure to buy her favor and open the avenues to a genial acquaintance by a little gentle flattery, I said:

"*Mademoiselle,* it seems to me a strange thing

to see one so young and beautiful, whom everybody must be ready to please and make happy, looking so sad and lingering in so gloomy a place."

But she only glanced on me another sweet smile and said nothing.

After revolving it several times in my thoughts, and computing the probable consequences, I ventured to risk the question point-blank :

"*Mademoiselle*, do you often come here?"

"Yes, *monsieur*, on Sundays when it is clear."

"And to these same graves?"

"Always, *monsieur*."

"Dear ones must be sleeping there?"

"The dearest, *monsieur*."

"Father and mother?"

"It is not they. Dear mother lies elsewhere. *Babbo vive ancora, grazie a Iddio*" [Papa lives yet, thank God]. Only the last part was in Italian, the rest in French, as usual. This surprised me, but afterwards it was explained. To my further questioning, "One is my sister," she replied, "the other—I cannot tell—I do not know who it is."

"What!" said I, "each of those graves holds one dearer to you than all the world beside, yet one of them you do not know who it is!"

"It is so."

"That is very strange."

"Alas! it is too true. It is the saddest part of my sad lot. Oh, if I knew who it is!" Her cheeks flushed crimson and tears stood in her lustrous eyes.

Not without a sentiment of pity at the evident distress of the beautiful stranger, mingled with some alarm at the delicate ground on which I was treading, my curiosity pushed me on to insist:

"Do explain to me this riddle, *mademoiselle*."

"I am pressed," she replied, hurriedly, with her free hand brushing away the great teardrops that glittered in her eyes.

No doubt, by all the rules of politeness and propriety, I ought to have been satisfied with this and bade my interesting companion a courteous '*Adieu*.' A thousand times since, at the recollection of it, I have felt twinges of mortification at my reckless impertinence. But I was young; the girl was not only beautiful, but with that peculiar charm which instantly and powerfully inflames the masculine heart. The fact was, that I was unwilling to leave her. It would have cost me too severe a pang to break away from her magnetic presence.

And I did, also, vehemently wish, for its own sake, to get this revelation of the secrets of her sweet, maiden soul. For mystery was always very attractive for me; and I could not believe that in this instance it shrouded any guilt or shame on her part. In short, I selfishly resolved, by mere force of will, to overpower her resistance and ravish her secret for my own gratification.

Assuming an insinuating gentleness, I persisted :

"Your secret will be very safe with me, *mademoiselle*, for we shall never meet again."

She merely replied, in an agitated tone: "I have far to go."

"Whither, *mademoiselle?*"

"Four hours towards the *Hospice.*"

"Of St. Bernard?"

"*Si Signore.*" Then, as correcting herself, "*Oui, monsieur.*"

It now flashed into my mind that she had made this slip again, unconsciously, into her vernacular, and that, as her complexion and the fire in her eyes seemed to show, she was certainly an Italian—perhaps an exile, and God only knows for what reasons—perhaps political—perhaps criminal. Who can tell into what a network of suspicion, arrest, imprisonment, I may be foolishly running? Then a momentary vision of daggers and cups of poison and a grim phantasmagoria *a la Cesare Borgia* shot through my soul. But a look into her pure and gentle face reassured me, at least sufficiently so to make me adhere to my purpose. Yet I was not quite at ease. Such thoughts rushed through my mind as these : 'Is not this the way the Syrens always allure? Am I not utterly alone here? If I should be made 'away with,—dropped into some fissure of a glacier—which she or some hidden accomplice could so easily do—who would ever know what became of me? Or, if left stark at the roadside, and picked up and buried in the strangers' lot, or put into the *morgue* of the *Hospice*, who would ever be the wiser as to how I met my fate?'

In this way the courage of my passionate desire failed me a hundred times, and was a hundred times restored by another look into her dear face, which was always convincing, satisfying, irresistible.

There had been some moments' silence, while this internal scuffle of ideas had been going on for me, when at last I dashed across the Rubicon with :

"I was to go to the *Hospice* to-morrow. I would go to-day. Mightn't we walk in company?"

"As *monsieur* pleases, but I must go quickly."

"I think I can keep step, *mademoiselle*."

"I think *monsieur* has never raced with an Alpine girl."

I noticed the word and thought with myself,

for an instant, 'Is it possible that this sad creature is coquetting with my interest in her, and is verging on fun? is she preparing, perhaps, to play me a practical joke?' I could not believe it, but shaping my answer to meet her seeming challenge, I replied:

"If I succeed in the race, will you then tell me the riddle? Shall it be the prize of my victory?"

"I do not know if I shall be able," she said in a tone, I thought, of commingled indifference and sadness.

"I will take that risk," I replied, and with a gay '*Au revoir*,' to which she responded with another, I flew to my lodgings to make the few needful preparations.

HOSPICE OF ST. BERNARD, A. D. 1854.
Coming from Aosta.

IV.

"She sings the wild song of her own native plains,
Every note which He loved awaking,
Ah, little they think who delight in her strains,
How the heart of the Minstrel is breaking."
MOORE'S IRISH MELODIES.

IN a short half hour my brief arrangements were completed, and I was *en route* for the *Hospice*, hastening at my utmost speed, for together with the advantage of the start, I knew that the girl had shot on at a rate I could hardly hope to exceed.

Leaving *Martigny* for the south, the road presently parts into two great routes — one leading to Geneva and France, the other to Turin and Italy, over the Pass of the Great St. Bernard. I took the latter, and with a few bounds, leaping like a boy, crossed the wooden bridge over the *Drance* and proceeded at a brisk pace, with the gurgling ice-waters on my left. The scene around me was grandly picturesque. In the stillness of the hour, the voices of nature, unmingled with artificial sounds, were melodizing in a kind of awful symphony that was enchanting. Elevated with a delicious excitement, in sympathy with the environments, I passed swiftly on, leaving the outskirts of the village quickly behind me.

The road here is comparatively direct, yet numerous minor turns, suiting to the broken nature of the ground, or to the windings of the stream, continual sinuosities of the smoother parts of the surface, intervening bowlders, and occasional patches of larch, beech, or fir-forest, render the perspective of the passenger, in this part of the route, limited and uncertain.

As I turned each bend of the way, or rounded a huge bowlder, or escaped some interposed bush or tree, I stretched my sight to catch a glimpse of the flying maiden, but in vain. And worse than this, I often imagined that I saw her in the distance before me, only to be deceived and disappointed. The object presently proved to be a rock, or bush, or shadow, or some other optical illusion.

After many such little eminences had been surmounted in vain, many such turns in the road passed without discovery of the object of my search, many illusive hopes even, raised only to be dashed, at last my spirits began to sink, my courage began to fail. Was it not becoming evident that I had been deceived by that strange girl? Was it not more likely than otherwise, that this lovely, sad, and apparently so ingenuous creature, had started me on a false track to escape my annoying importunity? Was n't she an Italian? Shades of the Borgias! What better should I have expected?

My brain swam. The still summer air, the lonely highway, the silent landscape, the long vista down the valley of the Rhone, the stupendous gorges on either side, the amazing *Galerie de la Monnoye*, ever and anon the roar of distant *avalanches*, the reëchoed sounds of falling or rushing waters, the presence of the snow-capped, glittering, unspeakable mountains standing so near and yet so far on every hand;—all these mighty inspirations, which ought to have invigorated my soul, and contributed not more to my wonder than to a sentiment of serenity and joy, now operated, on the contrary, to disturb my peace, disorder my memory, excite my forebodings, bewilder my thoughts. I began to doubt whether the maiden and her concerns had not been the phantoms of a dream — or, if she were a reality, she had not put herself where I should not meet her again.

Should I then proceed a step further? I cannot fully describe my deliberations; but with the

HOSPICE OF ST. BERNARD.

Coming from Martigny.

suddenness of a thought, I faced about and began slowly to retrace my steps.

As I repassed a *détour* in the highway, around a sparsely-wooded cliff, where the dismantled Castle of the old Bishops of Sion comes into view high on the mountain-side to the right, I became conscious of an indistinct musical cadence which seemed to be floating in the air around me. I fancied that I could distinguish the higher notes of a female voice, though, except at brief and infrequent intervals, it was quite drowned in the multifold echoes from the distant mountain-sides, and in the absorbing immensity of the vast chasms.

For a time this faint melody seemed to grow nearer and clearer. Then it suddenly ceased altogether ; and my own footfalls were painfully audible in that vast stillness, unbroken save by the soft twitter of some little bird sheltered in a neighboring bough, or the faint tinkle from a goat feeding hundreds of feet towards the sky on some well-nigh inaccessible rock, each dropping in with a melodious monotony upon nature's own soft, low, tremendous, eternal diapason.

What was it to me, then, that I was surrounded by enrapturing prospects, and fanned by the breeze that had been cooled on the Bernese Alps, and brought to my ears, like perpetual minute-guns, the soft thunder of the distant *Jungfrau's* incessant avalanches? What was it all to me? I lacked the mood to listen or to look, to be charmed or distracted. I was uneasy, disappointed, disconsolate. I sauntered slowly and wretchedly along on my mortifying return. Suddenly the full, clear notes of a wild song burst, like a mountain-torrent, on my ear. The words I could not retain. The cadence and substance was as follows:

> At dawn I drank the breeze
>   Gentle and clear and cool,
> Flowing beneath the trees,
>   With soft refreshment full.
>
> I walked at midday there;
>   The blazing sun was hot,
> And through the sultry air
>   His withering arrows shot.
>
> Ere fell the shades of even
>   Dark storm-clouds downward poured,
> And through the dreary heaven
>   A fierce tornado roared.
>
> Is this, is this the breeze
>   That soothed me at the dawn,
> That whispered in the trees,
>   And rippled o'er the lawn?
>
> Has the soft zephyr, given
>   For morn's refreshing breath,
> Before the fall of even
>   Become the blast of death?

> Still blacker grows the storm,
>   Reddening with Fury's flash!
> Woe, woe! a noble form
>   Falls lifeless in the crash!
>
> When, when, like breeze of even,
>   Soft flowing o'er the lawn,
> When, from a gentle heaven,
>   Shall rise the changeless dawn?

I sank softly upon a bowlder at my side, and listened till the melody was over. Then, as I could not doubt who the singer must be, nor could she be far aside from the beaten track, nor from the spot where I was sitting, I quickly arose, and, again reversing my steps on the highway, began a careful examination of every plausible by-path, every shelving rock, every nook and corner that seemed possible to hide her from the notice of a careless passenger.

I was at that moment at the top of a gentle eminence where the *Val de Ferret* opens into the *Val d' Entremont.* I had not taken twenty steps towards *Osières* and the bridge which crosses the *Drance* for the third time to one coming from *Martigny*, when, looking always on this side and on that, I saw in the shade of a huge black bowlder, a few paces on the left of the traveled path, and almost concealed behind a clump of evergreens, my lost maiden sitting deeply absorbed on a kind of moss-cushioned sofa.

V.

Oh, do not dry
Love's endless tears ;
To the half-dried eye
The world appears
Empty and dead.
For aye let tears be shed
O'er love untasted ;
They are not wasted.[3]

AT the discovery of the maiden, one need not be told, my discontent was instantly gone ; and not only the end of my solicitude, but as well the interesting picture before me, would of itself have been sufficient to fill me on the instant with new cheer. She had sunk far down into the mossy seat, and, resting on her elbow, her face partly covered by her hand, she was gazing intently as in a reverie, far adown the village and the scenes we had left behind.

Such was the tortuous winding of the road, that, as I approached from the opposite direction, she did not perceive my presence till aroused by the sound of my steps. Turning then, she saw me not six paces from her and cried, in a cheery and almost playful tone, at which I was surprised :

"*Ecco il mio vagabondo!*" [Ah, my runaway].

Tear-marks were still on her cheeks ; nor had the moisture, from disappointment, anger, and shame, yet left the corners of my own eyes. She quickly rose and partially extended her hand. It may have been only an unconscious gesture of surprise or enquiry, but I seized and pressed it with the ardor of a sympathy as powerful as any other that ever touched my heart.

The mystery of my losing her on so direct a route, which had been to me so strange and so annoying, was soon explained.

She had hurried on and retired into this secluded nook to eat her slight luncheon and drink of the ice-water that trickled from a neighboring *glacier* into the little cup which she carried in her pocket and still held in her hand. There were, indeed, other reasons, faintly adumbrated in her song, why she chose to command the spot, for a time, alone. Fatigued and heated, she reclined upon the mossy bank and unexpectedly fell asleep. During her slumber I passed unobserving and of course unobserved. Awaking, as she supposed, from a momentary forgetfulness, she still awaited my coming, but wondering and uncertain at my delay, was on the point of going on without me.

She resumed her seat and I sat down near her on the same natural sofa. Presently she looked up wistfully into my face and said:

"*Ella è inglese?*" [The gentleman is English].

I noticed, now for the third time, that when taken by surprise or carried off her guard by excited feelings, she spoke in Italian, as if that were her vernacular; and from this I was more than ever convinced that she was at least of Italian stock. With a view to furthering my own purpose, therefore, of drawing as deeply as possible on the secrets of her heart, from this time on, I used French no more, but spoke only in the language of Italy to her. She, too (but without seeming to observe the change), thereafter spoke to me only in Italian. To her question I replied:

"Yes, *Signorina*, and no."

"*È dunque americano!*" [He is American, then].

"Yes, *Signorina*."

"*Ah, America, terra fortunata!*" [fortunate country]. "I have heard that the people are happy there."

I toyed with her remark a little with the view of drawing her out upon the Great Republic. I found the "American idea" in full force in her soul. The "happy country beyond the sea" seemed to her not much less than actually "flowing with milk and honey." She had seen letters telling of the great wages received for labor there, and describing the dainty food, "white bread and flesh meat had every day," and the nice clothing common to everybody there, such as "the peasantry of the old country could never dream of possessing for one day of their lives."

To be sure, she said the letters might be romancing, more or less, but she had herself seen such-a-one, returned on a visit, who came "in a hat *alla moda* and a silk gown and shoes and gloves, like a lady." Such-a-one had told her that she had, besides, a great many *fiorini* saved up in the *Cassa di risparmio* [Savings Bank].

At last I replied: "*Mia amichina* [my little friend], sorrow is everywhere."

"Yes, I know that must be so; but is it not delightful to live in a country where the people choose their rulers, and make their own laws, and do in every way what they like?"

"Doing what they like, *Signorina* — whether it would be the best thing or not — is not quite true of America; and the science of good government everywhere is a very difficult one. The selfishness and the passions of men are hard to manage. And worst of all, it seems impossible to tell what the result will be of any combination of political forces until it has been tried, and —— "

" And it may be too late to mend it then."

" Not quite so, *Signorina*, but the old governments have been tried for so long that their faults are well known ; and I must add their advantages also —— "

"Advantages ? " she interrupted, with an incredulous tone, almost a sneer.

" Yes, strength, in itself, as far as it goes, is an advantage."

" 'As far as it goes' — yes, if it does not go too far . . . and goes in the right direction," she said, now mournfully.

" Perfection of administration is an advantage — a great advantage — the certain execution of the laws —— "

" No matter how oppressive ? " she interrupted again, with a sigh.

" Nobility has a certain advantage, both as a standard of taste and living for the lower orders, and as a glittering prize permanently held out to extraordinary heroism, or superlative benefit wrought for the country, or for humanity at large."

" Yes, high and permanent examples ! . . . not seldom, of flunkeyism in procuring and of base living afterwards," she added, almost fiercely.

"Painful exceptions must occur in all human combinations. A fly will be found in the sweetest ointment."

"Alas for humanity!" she groaned, twirling her hat on her thumb.

"The largest and most inspiring patronage of the fine arts, is a very notable advantage. Your glorious galleries in Europe are the fruit of ages of monarchical government. Under republican institutions as they exist to-day, these, it is by no means likely, would ever have come into being."

"Exactly, be it so. Is, then, the profit worth the cost?"

"We are only naming facts, *Signorina*, not deciding values."

"Is n't liberty worth every cost?"

"I think you mean home-rule for Italy," I said, somewhat nettled at the turn she had given the conversation.

"Yes, that is what I mean, *appunto*" [exactly].

"Then I think it is, properly limited and made permanent."

She repeated my last words, and in an almost peppery tone, said: "Why do you distinguish so against Italy as compared with America?"

"I do not mean to disparage, nor predict, but Italy gives me the history of ages to judge from.

America has no past. Our present is fairly satisfactory. We cannot say that there are not clouds hanging about in several quarters of our political horizon, yet the promise of the future seems bright."

"All good men hope so, *Signore*."

"We believe it, *Signorina*. But we may be mistaken. We are still an experiment."

"At all events, you have not and need not the dreadful army there."

"True, there is nothing like the great armies of Europe there — the registration, the conscription, the garrison-duty, the manœuvres, the camp service."

"And the people are safe enough without all this wretched, wretched thing?" she asked in a tone of heart-broken despair.

"The ocean is, to be sure, a certain protection for us against foreign foes."

"And the people have n't to be kept down with bayonets?"

"Not yet, *Signorina*."

"O happy people! What good luck to have been born there! How contented the young women must be who have true lovers there!"

"I have no doubt they are. They ought to be. But will you not tell me that story now?"

"Let us go on," she said, rising and moving

toward the highway. "I could n't tell you on that seat and under that rock."

"That rock?" I said, doubtfully.

Looking timidly over her shoulder, she added, "That rock has fearful shadows."

We walked on then for two or three minutes in a silence which I did not venture to break, when the boom of an avalanche in the direction of the Bernese Alps, echoing ever softer and softer, as it rebounded from mountain-side to mountain-side, seemed to waken her from a momentary reverie, and almost in a whisper she began:

"I was promised — or thought I was — to one I loved. I was married to him — perhaps. Perhaps I am a widow — his widow, now. 'Perhaps,' I say, for I do n't know what I am — or whether I am anything to him — or ever was."

Here she paused as if she would say no more.

"You do not explain," I said; "you do but increase the mystery."

She stopped, and turning, pointed backward and rejoined in that strange voice of hers, soft, sweetly mournful, yet deeply thrilling: "*Ecco*, [see] the shadow of that rock lies there, like a solid thing, on the ground, though it is n't anything. That shadow is n't anything, yet all the same it's there. It is n't a mistake, nor a dream. It's real — you know that — you feel that — though it is n't anything after all. You move about on the same ground as if it were n't there ; yet its chill may go into you and make you shudder, and its dark silence may make you afraid. So my life is in a shadow. I move about in a shadow — in three shadows. They are like what that black bowlder makes under the sun and under the moon and under the evening star."

Casting about for some cheerful remark that might contribute toward quieting her disturbed feelings and disentangling her confused thoughts, I said :

" Is there not much beautiful life in shadows — even though they are done in monochrome, and black crayons at that? What lines of beauty, what pleasing movements, what delightful phantasmagoria,—from the wiry figures of wintry boughs dancing in the moonlight, to the soft majesty of noonday clouds sailing over billowy grain-fields ! "

" Yes," she said, " they were once delightful to me, but they are so no longer. They are sad and painful — only sad and painful to me now."

" Yet, you linger among them."

" It is so. On the bright summer Sunday afternoons I come and sit there. I sit there and shudder and weep, till the shadow of the rock grows with the slanting rays and finally becomes one with the shadow of the mountain.

"Often and often of a summer evening while the moon was sailing clear down the valley, I have been sitting there within the gray, weird outline, musing mournfully, till the approach of the deeper darkness drove me home.

"And often, in the moonless twilight, when I knew that the evening star was drawing the shadow-pictures of ten thousand happy lovers, I have been there within the faint rock-figure, talking tenderly to my lonely heart, till the star of love has sunk behind the snowy mountain-top.

"And then I wonder — I wonder if, perhaps — perhaps — for they say these stars are worlds, too — if, perhaps, there are heart-broken ones there — if we could see and hear their tears and sighs."

"Would it comfort you to think so?" I asked.

"Perhaps it would," she replied, "but I should be almost ashamed of it, if it were so. I never thought of it in that way before."

"You would not be alone," I said, "in that. I have had the same longing, as I have gazed upward and seen these beautiful orbs looking always so serenely down on me."

I had in mind a strain which I had originally composed in my own vernacular, and afterward, though long before, turned into Italian

and then recited, appearing to her, I suppose, to
be improvising :

> I saw the Star of even
>> Sail down the paling west
> And from the verge of heaven
>> Drop to her silent rest.
>
> How peaceful moved she through
>> The soft, decaying light,
> How lovely, pure, and true
>> She looked her sweet " Good-night ! "
>
> Doth thus our planet move
>> Through the high walks of space ?
> Is thus unmingled love
>> Still mirrored on her face ?
>
> Do the still spaces bar
>> The sounds of human woe,
> Doth Earth shine soft afar
>> As stars shine here below ?
>
> Ah, silent, silver orb,
>> Sailing in peace along,
> Doth naught but joy absorb
>> Your happy nations' song ?

" How beautiful to think so," she said, "and if
it be true — what Dante in the Vision says " —
here she recited, in a soft swift monotone, a
dozen lines from the *Paradiso* about PICCARDA,
happy in the Moon — " but we are still here and
the gloom is so sad."

" *Fanciulla carina* " [dear little maiden], I said,

"if these earthly shadows are so painful to you, why look at them, or even go where they lie?"

"Ah, that, that is the great misfortune of it," she replied. "The explanation is not to be told in a word; and I fear you would think me weak or mad. But——"

Suddenly stopping and looking up again wistfully into my face, she added:

"Tell me more about *America beatissima* [most blessed America]. Are there no such crazed, or foolish, broken-hearted there?—who——"

"No, *mia buonina*" [my good little creature], I interrupted, "I do not, cannot think you mad, or despise your grief. I, too, have been touched by the finger of the dark angel. I have been robbed of the being dearest to me in all the world."

"Tell me about it, *Signore*. Tell me how it happened."

I did not fail to observe that she was always postponing her own history, while endeavoring to draw out mine, or filling up the time with matters of far less interest to me. But I felt that the recital of my own sorrow, however painful to me, would be short, and that in my own interest it would be wisest to follow her humor. I therefore yielded and began:

"I did not see her fade in my arms, like a wilting flower. I did not hear her whisper in my ear a last 'adieu.'   She did not give me a parting look of love, ere I closed her eyes forever.   To my burning kiss her lips did not respond."

"Alas! how was it, then?" she softly sighed.

"I led her to the altar in angelic beauty.   The happy march which was to introduce us to the supreme felicity of earth closed its rapturous measures in one long, delicious wave of melody. Twice our hands were joined by the holy man. I feel the thrill this moment still.   Her sweet voice made herself my own.   I set the ring, sign and seal of our unending union, with ecstasy, on her fair finger.   How soft and snowy-white it was! How glad and proud I was to bestow on her all on earth I had to bestow!   We knelt for prayer and for the blessing of the man of God. Our heads were bowed upon the consecrated rail. The last 'amen' was said, and all was still — ah, yes, how still it was!   I feel that stillness yet.

"She did not rise. She did not move, and seemed at prayer. The priest stood motionless with closed book, and eyes raised to heaven. The company waited in patient love for the dear girl to finish her virgin orisons. Alas! they were already finished forever. The friends around her became sensibly disturbed. The assembly began to rustle. Every instant augmented the painful suspense.

"At last I stooped to lay on her lips the bridal kiss. Her lovely form sank gently upon my bosom ; but, when my lips met hers, I perceived that they did not move ; and they never moved again. Her heavenly eyes were closed, and they never again were opened. Her dear bosom rose and fell no longer. Her sweet breath had fled. Her pulse was still. No heart-throb fell upon my bosom. Her angel-life had gone out. She was in *Paradiso*.

"But I was here — here alone — here with her dear but lifeless body. I saw nothing else. I cared for nothing else. I bore it in my arms through the amazed and silent people. The organ, lately so loud in triumphant joy, and ready for a new triumphant peal, began softly to wail that tearful psalm :

Dirige gressos meos ;

and, as we rolled so sadly homeward, the bells, chimed for a marriage-peal, tolled out instead a mournful march ; and the crows in the tops of the old elms under which we passed, cawed down upon my head a funeral dirge. At last the dear body was laid in its deep bed under the oak tree in the old *Campo Santo*, where, as children, we sat and pledged our love with many a childish kiss.

"The robins build their nests overhead and sing in the boughs as they do here to-day. The breeze roars softly in the top, like the waves of the sea far away. Sweet all this was, while she sat on the sod at my side. But can I go there now? Can I sit there alone? No, indeed, I cannot. The sky seems so very high and open. The rattle of vehicles and the noises of busy men distress and frighten me. The roar in the tree-tops makes me tremble, as if the world were rushing to destruction. Even the birds seem now to be singing mournful elegies, and the neighboring waterfall pours a perpetual dirge.

"They tell me that this dread will pass away, and that the time will come again when I shall love to revisit the spot. They tell me that I shall even find a solace for my loneliness in lingering among these buried memories and in courting the company of the 'empty shadows,' as you call them, of my vanished joys.

"If this will ever be, I know not; but surely I cannot bear them now. I fled across the ocean to escape from those reminders — those duplicators of my grief. It is for this that I am here, *Fanciullina* [dear young lady], to-day. My heart is the heart of a child — a sorrowful child. I could n't laugh — I could n't smile at your sentiments — whatever they were. But I can weep with you, and find comfort in your sympathy; and it would console me to hear about your sorrow."

"O, how sorrow makes us all partners!" she said.

"It is so," I replied, "and on this ground partly I urge my claim to know the secret of your grief."

"Perhaps, then, you have a certain right; but how can I bear to speak aloud this sad history?"

"How can telling me make it more sad to you?"

"Ah, to speak it aloud — to speak it aloud — it will make my wounded heart bleed again."

"Even so, perhaps it would go to lighten your load, *Poverina*" [poor little one].

"May be — may be, it would," she almost whispered.

"I'm sure it would; and surely, it would go to console me."

"I should, indeed, be glad to do that. But I fear — " I saw the suggestion of a shudder pass over her frame, and interrupted:

—"Why should you fear? Would I betray anything? How could I, if I would? The ocean will soon be rolling between us and all our affairs."

"I did n't mean that," she replied, now with a calm and solemn voice. "Duty and sin are everywhere the same. May be I was not —was not without blame."

"We are all human, *Buonina mia* [my dear, good girl]. We all have to be forgiven in heaven.

Whatever it is, surely *Maria Beatissima* will intercede. I will tell the girls in America whom you think so happy. They will be sorry for you. They will pray to Our Lady for you."

This last word proved to be the "efficient straw, etc." Did I do wrong to say it? I did not know that one of my female friends in America prayed to the Blessed Virgin ; but I knew that she did ; and I was carried away with the desire to console a beautiful young creature, sobbing before me in heart-breaking sorrow, and pleading often in secret before the aureolated picture of the ever-sympathizing *Madonna*.

LA MADONNA SISTINA.

VI.

" Can the Ethiopian change his skin?
Or the Leopard his spots? "

BIBLE.

FEELING for a rosary of scarlet beads which hung about her neck, and remaining silent a few seconds, as if conversing with heaven, or meditating how to arrange her thoughts, she started forward with a slow and pensive step, and entered upon the following curious and pathetic history.

Her paternal ancestry, she said, was Italian of the Italians ; and as they had good cause to believe (not only from certain physical peculiarities, but as well from a line of historic reasons), even Roman of the oldest stock.

"My father," she said, "is of that tall and well-shaped frame — as all his ancestors have been — which we know is still found in the *Trastevere* at Rome. He glories in, and has taught us to speak with the Trasteverian accent and to know so many of those dear old words which have come down to us, though we lived for centuries within the dukedom of Tuscany. For our ancestors never would bend their tongues away from the masculine language of their fathers to babble in the lady-speech of Florence. So that I can have no doubt that the blood of one or more of the stolen Sabine wives flows in my veins."

She went on explaining that during the perpetual political convulsions which kept poor Italy in ceaseless commotion throughout the middle centuries, when, too, the fearful names of Attila and of Cæsar Borgia mingled terribly with the sad traditions of the family, political dangers — for, at that time, they were of equestrian rank, and so exposed to all the buffets of civil strife — drove them, stripped of nearly all but their lives, from their hereditary domicil in *Umbria*, on the sunny banks of the *Anio*, to the vine-clad hills of Tuscany. Here, ousted from official life, yet, in the culture of the vine and through commerce in wines, for hundreds of years they greatly prospered and acquired considerable Tuscan estates.

" But," she said, "having espoused the losing side of the Medicean quarrel—for the unquenchable flame of the Roman and especially of the Trasteverian passion for *libertà* has always been the undermining influence upon the worldly fortunes of our family—they were glad to escape from suspicion and arrest, from the prison, the torture, the gallows, and leaving almost everything to be confiscated behind, to come with their lives and a scanty property to the valleys of *Lombardia* — still, though in a less notable degree, dealing with the vine. But, when in *Babbo's* [papa's] early days the Austrian tyranny there became so accursed and diabolical, his Roman Trasteverian blood could endure it no longer, and he fled with his wife and almost empty hands to these bleak but free Alpine cliffs and valleys.

" So, moving ever northward, from under the very walls of the Eternal City, and from Magistracies with landed estates in *Umbria*, we came to be movers of commerce and vine-dressers in *Toscana* and *Lombardia*, and finally, from desperate necessity, mountain-shepherds here."

" It must have been dreadful tyranny," I said, " to drive your proud ancestry to make such sacrifices of rank and property in such a descending scale for themselves and the prospects of their posterity."

" It was, it was, indeed," she said, " and I am not sure whether it were greatest (considering the general rudeness of the earlier times) in the days of the Guelfs and Ghibelines, the *Neri* and *Bianchi*, the *Piagnoni* and *Palleschi*,' etc., through all the sad ages of poor *Italia's* history, or in comparatively recent years."

"The world well knows," I said, "that the Austrian rule in Lombardy has always been severe. The gentle Silvio Pellico has given us a blood-curdling specimen of it in his *Le Mie Prigioni.*"

"Ah, do you know that?" she said, "but what would you think if I should tell you that in the days of *Babbo's* flight hither, not only men were so treated, but the infamous Austrian had come, not seldom, to use the rod upon the naked backs of reputable ladies who were guilty of nothing beyond entertaining and speaking sentiments of generous and honorable patriotism!"

"I never heard of such a thing," I said.

"I will give you, then, an instance, if you care to have me do it."

"I should be desirous, yet sorry to hear it, *Signorina.*"

"Many are *troppo brutto* [too ugly] to be told of. Here is one far from being the worst among many of the like. In *Milano* two young girls, one a visiting *Fiorentina* [girl of Florence] of eighteen years, the other a girl of twenty, from *Cremona*, were each condemned to fifteen stripes for having reproached a renegade Italian female who made an ostentatious display, in one of the windows of her apartments, of the colors of the Austrian flag — black and yellow.

"And when the poor girls were brought out

into a public square, stripped for punishment, and bound to the whipping-post, and while innocent patriotism and virgin modesty were undergoing the shame and torture of the executioner's strokes, all the proudest Austrian society in *Milano*, from their windows and carriages, looked on with jokes and laughter at their fright and screams.

"And for putting the greatest possible contempt on the Italian people, the Austrian authorities caused it to be announced in the newspapers that the rods with which the two girls were whipped were bought in *Vienna*, and, together with all the other expenses of this wholesome and beautiful show, were to be paid for by the city of *Milano*."

I expressed the utmost horror and amazement that such barbarities could happen and had happened in the heart of a Christian civilization and within the memory of men still living.

"It was necessary that you should know this," she said, "in order to understand what I am to tell you of my own history and my fortunes. Even our name must be explained to you for the same reason.

"During some of those earlier centuries of our Italian life (it is uncertain which, or where), one of those terrific storms with lightning and thunder which occur in the heats of late summer, burst with unparalleled suddeness and fury through the valleys of the Appenines.

"So suddenly did it arise that our ancestor and his young wife, who were abroad at some distance from their home, were unable to gain any more available shelter than a shelving rock, over which hung a clump of firs.

"The storm raged with violence for hours. Sheet after sheet of descending water, hurled by the fitful gusts, drenched and drenched again and again the forlorn young couple. The terrible intensity of the lightning and the terrific thunder threw the young wife into paroxysms of alarm. At last the skies cleared and the storm was forgotten.

"A long time after, when their eldest child came to them, it bore on its breast a mark which was thought to resemble a fir-tree overhanging a dark rock. The same mark has appeared from time to time in successive generations till now. According to one tradition —less credible, indeed, than another which has been more generally adopted — it was supposed to be this incident that suggested our family name — *Ombrosini* [shadowy ones]."

VII.

Stat nominis umbra.

"IT was long, long ago," my companion proceeded, "though many centuries later than the earlier story. *Milano* was then entirely surrounded by the *Naviglio Grande*. The suburbs beyond this artificial and navigable water-course were a favorite quarter for the palaces of the great nobles. The lord of *Milano* had a superb villa outside the *Porta Vercellina*. The gardens of this *villa* were extraordinary even among the surrounding sumptuousness. Many statues of classic models, and many busts of distinguished Italians and especially of Lombard celebrities were interspersed among rare exotic trees and stretches of forest curiously trained and trimmed.

"When the famous *Giovanni Visconti* became archbishop and lord of *Milano*, he summoned my ancestor and induced him to leave his own estates, which had now become considerable in *Lombardia* and come to the Milanese Court as Master of the Park.

"His name, in the dialect of that region, is lost, but — apparently from his very brown complexion (which mark of southern descent had been handed down through so many generations)— in *Milano* he was called *Brunetto*.

"He was a man of great but exceedingly eccentric talents. Perhaps the greatest of his many oddities, was a passion for evening landscapes, and his astonishing management of moonlight shadows.

"The prince, charmed by his genius, entered at length into his plans and caused a chamber which he named *il Teatro* [the Theatre] to be elegantly finished and furnished in one of the palace-towers. The front of this 'Theatre' was one vast window, looking out upon a portion of the landscape which he called the *Spettacolo* [stage].

"Here and on every side, nigh and far, according to designs furnished by *Brunetto*, trees were trimmed into a thousand imitative, or beautiful, or wonderful shapes. Huge statues were reared and arranged in a thousand ingenious ways. Many other objects, in a great variety, were scattered about apparently, in unspeakable confusion and disorder, but really with the strictest eye to effect and in such a way that the *tout-ensemble*, under the moonlight, threw into view from the *Teatro* a stage-full, in life-like shadows, of strange and beautiful figures. And as the moon passed on, the shadowy actors moved and changed positions and shapes in such a way as to represent with striking effect many beautiful, terrible, and ridiculous scenes.

"These changes were provided for, not only during the hours of a single evening, but following the vicissitudes of the moon, continued from month to month, as the successive seasons went on. So that this *Teatro* in dumb-show offered a kind of endless 'season' of natural theatricals.

"It is said that the great poet, *Petrarca*, during his long residence at *Milano*, often witnessed these spectacles with great delight; and when *Bocaccio* visited him there he brought him to see the wonderful show. But it was after the death of *Giovanni* and the succession of his three nephews to his dominions that the fortunes of our ancestor rose to the zenith, and our name became fixed in the heraldry of our country.

"When the elegant and learned Emperor, Charles IV, came with his Empress into Italy to be crowned at Rome, he was for a few days the guest of the three lords of *Milano*. On the second day after his arrival, he was entertained by his hosts with a review of their troops, which passed before him as he sat in state behind the great

window of the *Teatro*. After dinner that evening, in the great hall, the gentlemen were
escorted into the *Teatro* where the ladies were
awaiting them. The Emperor in some surprise
asked whether they would ride to the play, or
whether perhaps they would walk through the
palace to the *proscenium*.

'We do not go to the play, your Majesty,'
answered the lords, 'the play comes to us to-
night.'

"At that moment all the lights in the *Teatro*
seemed to be suddenly extinguished by an invisible hand, except two or three concealed tapers,
which threw a dim glamour over the company.
At the same moment began as if in the far distance the soft music of a symphony, and the
curtains slowly rose upon the shadowy scenes
which were moving over the snow (for it was
Christmas-tide), in the vast *Spettacolo*. The royal
party, taken wholly by surprise, were wild with
excitement. Even the Empress gave a sweet
little scream of delight, which pleased the Emperor exceedingly.

"The fact was, that Fortune smiled on the
whole affair. *Brunetto*, having received some
weeks' notice of the coming event, had laid out
his utmost skill, had, one might truly say, out-
done himself, in the preparation. Even the as-

tronomers of the University, in view of the unparalleled honor of an imperial visit, had assisted him with the nicest calculations upon the hourly position, progress, and path of the moon. The night proved cloudless. The silver luminary was at her full. The figures came out with extraordinary distinctness and moved with elegance. The show was an unparalleled success. The Emperor was delighted; the Empress was in ecstacies.

"*Brunetto* had contrived to represent the whole long line of Roman emperors, riding in chariots, and passing on far away into the distance. Charles, with his lovely Empress, came last of all, surrounded with every possible sign of pomp and glory.

"Processions of church dignitaries and ecclesiastics of every degree, squadrons and columns of military escorts, multitudes of happy people making frantic demonstrations of joy, banners waving from windows and poles, navies dressed with innumerable streamers, senates and courts of law and schools standing in rapt attention upon the scene, seemed to be laying the world at the feet of the latest successor of the Roman Cæsars.

"But the most wonderful feat of all was the putting of the *Visconti* coat-of-arms, in colossal proportions, at the foot of the panoramic picture, like a seal of approval, from this powerful family, to the succession of the new emperor. This coat-of-arms was an extraordinary thing, and had been adopted by the *Visconti* from a Saracen banner, taken by one of their ancestors in Palestine during the wars of the first *Crociata*. The design was an enormous serpent swallowing a naked child, with the legend beneath, DEVORABIT [it will devour], which was understood to be a translation from the Saracen *Cabala*, and to indicate how voraciously and irresistibly Time devours the works and the race of men, who are as helpless before its power as a new-born babe.

"Gentle symphonies had been playing during the successive views, till, as the evening grew later and the more stirring scenes appeared, the music sympathized with the sentiment, growing ever louder, harsher, more daring, more defiant; and, finally, as the closing scene came brightening out, with its fearful legend, the cymbals crashed, the drums rolled, the trumpets blared; and when, at the last moment, a park of a hundred cannons was fired, and a thousand rockets of every hue were shot into the sky, the Empress fell fainting with excitement and fright into the arms of the Emperor.

"This last incident pleased his imperial Majesty beyond bounds. He called for the artist, but he could not be found. During the progress of the spectacle he had occupied a conspicuous seat, absorbed in the contemplation of his deploying figures. But now he had disappeared, whither no one knew.

"Messengers were dispatched for him in every direction. The palace within was searched from end to end, in vain. It was at last discovered that somebody had seen him issue from the palace and enter one of the serpentine walks which led toward the *Spettacolo*.

"Lanterns soon glistened along every alley, lane, and walk; for the moon had now set, and comparative darkness had settled over the witchery of the scene. Each exploring party carried a horn to be sounded on a discovery of the lost manager. The lights were long seen from the *Teatro*, flitting to and fro, and winding along the labyrinthian passages. At last the horn sounded at some point near the middle of the *Spettacolo*. The manager was found wandering among the figures, passing in front of one and another, murmuring now a word of compliment, now an expression of mortification or reproof, such as :

"'Ah, Juno, you stood every inch a queen. I was proud of you. His Majesty, too, I could see that he was impressed by you. Well, Venus, there's nothing to be said about you. The men stared at you finely. You always touch the blood. You, too, Psyche, and Daphne, and all you girls there — you were ravishing. Socrates, what made you keep so much in the dark to-night? Plato, and even Alcibiades, quite overshadowed you. O Hannibal! there in the swamp, how is your eye to-night? I thought you seemed uneasy, but perhaps it was the waving of that swamp-willow over your head. By Jingo! Julius Cæsar, what ailed your horse's tail? I'll have those grooms beheaded, if that occurs again. And you, Commodus, how could you break that chariot-wheel? It must be repaired at once. You Cedar of Lebanon up there, why didn't you nod lower when the Emperor went by? We'll trim your hair for you, to-morrow.'

"Rapt in his reveries, he did not seem to doubt that the statues and trees heard and understood his words; nor did he observe the approach of the messengers till they took him by the hand and began to lead him back to the palace.

"When the story was told there with great glee, and naturally created more or less laughter among the spectators, the dazed manager not even then comprehended the true source of the merriment; but, attributing it to some comic failure of the spectacle, he approached the Emperor with a countenance grave even to sadness, and knelt before him, with eyes cast down like a culprit awaiting the sentence of his judge.

"But, at a signal from the Emperor, there was a flourish of trumpets. Then came a discharge of the whole park of artillery at once, which shook the palace again; and again the ladies, headed by the Empress, uttered a little scream. Then the Emperor arose, and, receiving from an officer of the Court a sword with trappings, which had been provided for the purpose, gently tapped with it the cheek of the kneeling mana-ger, saying, 'Arise, *Signore Conte de' Ombrosini.*' Then, as the new Count arose, the Emperor threw the trappings over his shoulder, and or-dered the patent of nobility to issue, and that the crest should be 'a full moon breaking out of storm-clouds and throwing shadows into the foreground.' My ancestor then hardly awoke, as from a dream, under the congratulations of his friends; and, dropping again on his knees, returned his warmest thanks to the Emperor.

"The patent was issued, and has been relig-iously preserved and handed down. The blessed parchment is still safe in our cottage. The first Count' (*Babbo* is the thirteenth) was given estates near *Vercelli*, which were enjoyed by many gener-ations of his successors.

"But, in the troubles that followed, our family,

like so many others, became entangled, our property was confiscated, my ancestors were obliged to flee and remain unknown. Even our shadowy name was for long concealed, for, to reveal it in *Lombardia* or in *Toscana*, would have cost the head of the family his life, or a lifelong imprisonment. It is safe this side the boundary, and *Babbo* has revived it.

"In this way we have lost everything but our name and the memories and sentiments which belong to it. Yet we are not alone, nor singular, in this misfortune. Higher and older titles than ours and not only the estates but even the names to which they belonged have been utterly lost. So that among the vineyard and mountain peasantry hereabout, to-day, flows blood that was once historic, sunk now into an everlasting shadow.

"Ah, *Signor*, will you doubt it? There still dwell in our bosoms the same sentiments, memories, and aspirations which enlivened and ennobled the lives of our ancestors, though we have to feed our bodies with these coarse nutriments and clothe them with these poor garments, because and only because from our hands have fallen the slippery fortunes of their better days.

"*O Dio in cielo!* Where are now the jewels that glittered for centuries on the fair shoulders of my great great grandmothers and their daugh-

ters for twenty generations in the palaces of
Umbria, of *Toscana*, of *Lombardia*, and should have
been the heirlooms of sister and me? Where
are they now? They are glittering on the neck
of some English peeress.

"*Oh mia povera Italia sventurata!* [Oh my poor,
unfortunate Italy!] They were offered on the
altar of thy destiny! They were sold to bring
gold to carry on the patriotic wars of thy enslaved
sons and daughters! They were plundered in
thy defeats by foreign foes! They were wrested
from their gentle owners under the torture!
They were confiscated in thy internecine convulsions! But *O Italia*, thou art *mia Patria* [my
fatherland] still. I love thee, poor, fallen, abused
as thou art. I love thee as my life. I adore thee,
bella, bella Italia!" [beautiful, beautiful, Italy].

"No, no!" I replied, "you have retained much
more than you claim, *Signorina*. The witness of
those better days, as you call them, did not pass
away with those jewels. It is written on your
every feature. I could swear to you that the
patent of your nobility is engrossed on your
countenance as with an angel's pen. That precious parchment might be lost or destroyed, but
the sentiments indwelling in your soul — the
heritage of a thousand years of noble lineage are
always visible and are indelible."

Her lustrous black eyes flashed up in my face for an instant, and then sailed away into the distance. A soft, sad smile languished on her lips, and she was silent.

With a sudden impulse, I struck up the strain, America:

> " My Country, 'tis of thee,
> Sweet land of liberty, etc.",

in the well-known Italian version, and after singing one stanza ceased.

She was gazing far away as I sang, and when I stopped, she made me begin again, and then herself struck in. I was at first startled and wondered at this. But I instantly remembered that it is also the National Melody of Germany, and that she must often have heard it in her home on the borders of Deutschland. At all events, she was at home in it, and the effect on me was electric. Her ringing, sympathetic voice, and the peculiar timbre of it, added to her powerful emotion at the moment, rolled like a rattling musical fusilade into the echoing stillness of that vasty natural concert-hall, and sent a thrill through my whole frame, not unlike what I have felt in hearing the fiery Marseillaise sung by a crowd of Lyonese peasants; and when the last stanza was done, I was left in a kind of confused and indescribable mental exaltation.

VIII.

" I'll keep this secret from the world,
As warily as those that deal in poison,
Keep poison from their children."
WEBSTER (Duchess of Malfy).

THE ice being now pretty thoroughly broken, my companion presently went on to describe their home on the mountain side, the sheep and goat pens near the house, the patches of plow-fields scattered among the cliffs, the meadows for mown grass — one a half-hour away on the other side of the river, and one a half-hour further up the mountain, on this side, and called by the family the *Alto Prato* [upper meadow], and finally, the *Boschetto* [little-forest] which was situated on the hillside in one of the broken valleys about an hour from their home. The family drew a part of their support from fire-wood which the *Babbo* cut there and sold in *Martigny* and at the *Hospice.* The chips and small twigs (what were not made into faggots for kindling and sold with the large wood), and barks, especially of the oaks, supplied the family fire.

Many knots of firs and pines were shaped into tapers, for use in the house; and the bark of the birches was rolled into torches to be used outside on dark and stormy nights in winter. But perhaps the most profitable of all were the long, straight birchen twigs which, during the long winter evenings, the *Babbo* made into brooms and sold, a few in *Martigny*, but chiefly in *Aosta*, whither he went with several mule-loads of them every spring.

Her mother, she said, was of a family of similarly decayed fortunes from *Nismes* (as also the grandmother had been), and was a distant kinswoman of her father. "They were many years married without children; but nineteen years ago when the ground was white with snow, on the *festa* of S. S. MARIA AND MARTHA a pair of little daughters were born to them; and were christened *Maria* and *Marta*. I am *Marta*. People thought the babies exactly alike, and could never tell the one from the other. As we grew the resemblance became, if possible, still more perfect. Our size continued always the same. Our complexion, hair, and eyes were of the same shade. Our voices were so perfectly alike, that out of their sight, our parents never knew which of us was talking or singing.

"This resemblance was, of course, the cause of

AOSTA — GENERAL VIEW.

many entanglements; and in fact an insidious omen of sorrow yet to come. But it gave us no concern. We were rather amused by the mistakes occasioned by it. Even when one was rewarded for a good action done by the other, or punished for the other's fault, as sometimes happened, by a tacit agreement we accepted each alike, without explanation and without resistance. Habit so accustomed us to our lot, and we came to regard our affairs as so joined and mixed, that we retained no sentiment of pain or of injustice from it, whatever either of us enjoyed or suffered on the other's account. In short, we seemed to ourselves, as nearly as possible, one being in two bodies.

"Besides all, as I believe is not uncommon in such cases, our natural resemblance was pleasing to our parents, and, instead of being in any the least way opposed, was favored and completed by them with a studied similarity of dress and treatment. This natural and innocent turn of parental love and pride fostered, however, our childish folly to an incredible pitch. We could not bear, nor be persuaded to allow anything pertaining to us to differ in the least particular. This exaggerated whim often rendered us ridiculous, sometimes wretched. We would, for example, soil our faces, tear our frocks, bang our bonnets, even scratch our hands or ankles — the one by accident, the other voluntarily to complete the correspondence — both undergoing often, and always cheerfully, the punishment for the fault.

"But, notwithstanding all, there was a concealed difference between us, and it was such that we could neither escape it, nor exchange it. This, too, became the turning-point of my fate.

"I BORE, ALAS! THE INDELIBLE FAMILY MARK — THE SO-CALLED SHADOW OF THE FIR-TREE!"

IX.

And night for each must close the cheerful day,
The feet of each must tread the gloomy way.[5]

HORACE.

"OUR childish lives went smoothly enough on for the · first twelve years. There were moments and hours of childhood-grief, but the causes were trivial and the sorrow was brief. Our spirits were light and easily depressed; but, commonly, a word or a kiss would cure our sadness, and a breath of mirth would easily blow away the flying cloud that was darkening our little souls. We were busy and petted and happy.

"So our years flew by till our thirteenth birthday came. Our happiness had then risen to its zenith. But with it came our first great sorrow. It was winter. The whole ground was white. There came the *festa* of S. S. MARIA AND MARTHA—our festival day. We went to Mass then, as always, on that feast. This year it fell on a Sunday. The day was fine. The Bishop of *Aosta* was there. *Maria* and I were then confirmed;

69

and, by a special dispensation, received immediately our first communion. Dear Mother had been preparing us ever since we could read, and we had been ready and waiting since we were ten years old. But no bishop had been at our little church for more than four years. This had been a great grief and constant anxiety to dear Mother.

"Both she and *Babbo* received the communion also (as they always did at that *festa*), and we all went, on Saturday evening before, to Confession. It was very cold; and dear Mother had toiled very hard to get our dresses ready and to make a feast for us at home. Oh, how happy we were at church that day, and at our little banquet in the afternoon!

"When the dinner was ended, but before we rose from the table, dear Mother tapped gently on her plate — for sister and I were in almost a boisterous frolic over a funny picture on one of our presents and over the queer inscription under it. We instantly looked up into her sweet face and were still.

"Then, in her soft, lovely way, she began: 'My dear, dear children, it is your birthday into this world of sin and sorrow. It was a blessing to us when you came. It was a blessing to you to be born. It is right to make *festa* over it.

"'We have delighted to feed your bodies with the perishable bread of earth, which one day you will need no longer. But to-day you have come to the table of your Great Father, and been fed with the bread that came down from heaven, which will nourish your immortal life for ever and ever. How should we make *festa* over that! God and the *Madonna* be praised that I have lived to see this day!' Then she began, and we all joined with her in singing *Ave Maria*. I never felt so happy. But we were so near to Eternity!

"That night dear Mother was seized with dreadful pains, in a few hours became very sick, and never had her reason more. She talked wildly of 'dear, warm France,' and of her girlhood there; and said many times to *Babbo*, '*Ah, Jacques,* ramenez-moi à ma belle France!*' [Ah, James, take me back to my beautiful France], and *Babbo* constantly replied, '*Sicuro, sicuro, M'amie*' [I will, I will, my dear].

"In a short week the promise was fulfilled. She was carried to sleep with her kindred under the warm sun of her native sky. We all, except *Vigilo* — he was our great, dear sheep-dog — went with her dear body to *Nismes*; and we buried the precious treasure there in the *Champ du repos*, where a long line of her ancestors are sleeping by her side.

"This journey to *Nismes* for *Maria* and me was the greatest event of our lives. We had never been there; but from infancy we had heard so much about it both from our dear Mother and from *Babbo*. For was it not a foremost stronghold of the old Romans from the first Cæsar on? And was it not morally certain, then, that both her Trasteverian ancestors and his had seen service there under the world-conquering eagles,— had marched over those hills and through those ravines with the thundering host to the music of the trumpet and the horn,— had manned those old fortresses,— perhaps led as centurions, or tribunes, or even lieutenant-commanders, those old iron cohorts and legions, before the era of salvation?

"The thought of it made our child-blood tingle, and did something, even in our dreadful sorrow, to enliven the gloom of the sad journey. Dear *Babbo* availed of this motive to the utmost, and choking down his own unspeakable grief, spoke of every inspiring thing in this direction on the way, and planned to make the visit yield the most possible, both of comfort and of lifelong profit, to his dear girls. For, in addition to his tender parental love for us, he never for a moment forgot that our heritage was noble, though now enveloped in so deep a shadow.

"We arrived on the ninth day, and, approaching the city on the southeast side, were in the neighborhood of three convents — the *Dames de Besançon*, the *Dames de l'Assomption*, and the *Petites Sœurs*. At the latter house the family of my Mother was not unknown. For this and other reasons, our *Babbo* took us there and made known the sorrowful cause of our pilgrimage.

"We were tenderly received by the lady Superior and the sisters. The dear body was allowed to lie in the *Cappella* before the high altar; and, on the morrow, a Requiem Mass, at which all the nuns assisted, was said by the *padre* who was charged with the worship in the Convent.

"I had never heard such sweet singing as was done by the choir of sisters in the organ-gallery. I have since learned from travelers that such is heard when the nuns of the *Dames du Sacré Cœur* sing Vespers on Sunday nights at *S. Trinità de' Monti* in Rome. But I have never heard the like, before nor since. It seemed to waft our spirits on the bosoms of angels into the soft rest of *Paradiso*, where we hope the spirit of dear Mother is.

"*Maria* and I were lodged in the Convent for three days and in a room near to that of the lady Superior. It was called a '*cella*' [cell]; but as we had never been in a nun's 'cell' before, we found it a very different room from what we had expected to see when the good abbess told us with the sweetest tones that 'we should sleep in Sister *Angelica's* cell.'

"The good kind lady went on to tell us — what she thought would at once instruct and please us — of the good nun who had lived and died in that 'cell', fifty or a hundred years ago. But it frightened us and made our flesh creep, to hear how that holy woman went barefoot and prayed through the whole cold night and fasted and punished herself there; and when she was dead and her body lay there, how the sick and infirm people came and touched it and were made well and strong; and how it did not decay and they kept it there many months, doing such good work for the afflicted.

"When, after supper, and a long pleasant talk in her room, the abbess took a candle and led the way to that 'cell,' I think our young rosy faces must have turned white, and I know that our hearts palpitated so that we could hardly breathe. We followed her a few steps along the echoing cement pavement of the lofty corridor, and in a moment she turned a key that grated harshly in the lock, and opened, slowly and carefully and it seemed to us almost timidly, a great heavy door, entered in the same subdued manner and placed the little twinkling light upon a high mantel-shelf.

"We followed and stood in the middle of the 'cell,' looking about us with astonished eyes. What did we see?—whip and cord and hair-cloth jacket?—and we did n't know what other instruments of dreadful pain?—such as our terri-fied imagination had conjured up?—or even coffins and corpses and skeletons, the shadows of which were dancing a fearful rout in our fancy? Not at all. The opposite of all this.

"There was, indeed, heavy iron grating at the two tall windows, so that no one could get out or in, even if they had not been a half-dozen *metri* from the ground on the outside; and as we could plainly see in the clear moonlight, they looked out upon a large garden which was surrounded on all the three sides by a high and smooth wall. There was, also, a very large, strong lock on the door — all conspiring to the same purpose. But everything within was peaceful and pleasant as the parlor of a lady.

"The room was large and high. A little fire was burning in the chimney-place; over which hung a beautiful picture of the *Madonna*. Several more large and beautiful pictures hung on the walls around — such as a *Pietà* [the dead body of Jesus in the lap of His Mother or the like], a martyrdom of S. Antony, a Virgin exposed to wild beasts, and others which I do not now remember.

"There were many pieces of furniture, plain but good. A carved writing-desk, an armchair with leathern seat, a heavy chest, a square table, a case of book-shelves full of ancient-looking books, a candle-stand, a *prie-dieu*, a footstool, a large crucifix on one side of the mantel-shelf, a statuette of S. Peter with the crook and keys on the other. In the middle of the shelf, stood a very large wax candle in a heavy carved candlestick. All these articles were of black oak, as well as the not very broad bedstead, which stood in the corner farthest from windows and door and was hung around with white curtains. On the cement floor were several rugs of thick, nappy carpeting and sheepskin mats.

"The abbess saw us gazing around us with childish interest, but little divined the secret of our thoughts. Our child-idea of a holy nun's cell — the narrow closet, the rough plank bed, the wooden stool, and little else save the implements of bodily discipline, compared strangely with such a room as this. We were dazed with wonder to a degree, and our faces no doubt wore an expression to which she attributed sentiments more exalted and devout than had really entered our minds.

"'Yes, dear children,' she said, 'this is indeed a holy place. Think how many prayers, how many self-mortifications, how many painful but victorious penances, how many exalted and beautiful meditations, how many holy vows and unearthly self-consecrations, have gone up like a cloud of sweet incense to the Saviour's throne! None of the sisters, since *Angelica's* death, has been judged or felt herself worthy to occupy this room; and it has never been slept in since.'

"She meant it kindly, but this view of the case made us shudder. Somehow the sense of being the first to sleep in the holy death-chamber, coupled with the constant memory of dear Mother's body passing the night in the *Cappella*, came over our sore hearts with such an uncanny power at her words, though spoken so gently and with the sweetest tones, that *Maria* and I instinctively threw our arms about each other's neck, and burst into irrepressible sobs.

"The face of the good abbess showed that she was distressed for us, but she said no more; and going to the bed, kissing each of us tenderly as she passed, she 'made it down,' and added a hundred little pats and adjustments to the pillows and coverlets. Then she said sweetly, 'Blessed innocents, I am so glad you are to sleep here. I think holy angels will hover over you to-night, the same that carried the spirit of your dear Mother in their bosom to *Paradiso*. Prepare yourselves for your slumbers quickly.'

"While we were obeying, she went to a little recess at the side of the chimney-piece, which we had not before observed, and taking from there another tall wax candle, lighted it and set it upon the *prie-dieu* near the head of the bed. As soon as we were nicely between the sheets, she knelt at the *prie-dieu* and said some beautiful prayers for dear Mother and for us.

"When she arose from her knees, she said, 'You shall have this candle burning here, my dears, during the night. I shall lock the door, so you will be quite safe; and you will hear the footsteps of the watching sister in the corridor as long as you are awake. I shall come to you in the morning before *Ave Maria*.' Then she kissed us both like a mother, drew the bed curtains close, and went away. We heard the bolt and the footsteps of the watcher, as she had told us, and in a few minutes fell asleep till she opened the bed curtains in the morning. This was repeated each of the three nights of our stay.

"In the morning, true to her word, we were awaked by the loving abbess bending over us and singing softly, *Ave Maria*; and we heard the bells of the convents and of the churches in the city ringing it out. We ate at the table with the nuns, one of us sitting on each side of the abbess, who sat at the head. She did not speak to us then, for there was no talking at the table, but one of the sisters read aloud from the Book of Martyrs.

"We passed most of our time, when not at our prayers in the *Capella* (before and after the body of dear Mother was carried away), in the room of the abbess, who was all love and anxiety for us, constantly showing us interesting things in the house, and teaching us good and important things which we did not know before, both about religion and about the worldly life. In short, from the moment when she first set her eyes upon us, she was to us like a mother who has found her long-lost children. We wondered greatly at this, till one day, long afterwards, it was explained to us. Then, alas, too late, how we wished we had known that secret before!

"*Babbo* and the animals found lodging with the family of the gardener of the Convent a little further outside the boulevard. But, though he came into the Convent but once, and then only for a moment on our first arrival, yet he spent many hours with us outside.

"The first sad day was mostly passed in the

Cappella, after the Requiem Mass, which was said early, in prayers and tears around the bier on which lay the dear, precious body that we were going to put away from our sight till the resurrection morning.

"The *padre Cappellano del Convento* [convent-chaplain] staid there with us and would now and again say another prayer — sometimes for the dead, sometimes for us children, sometimes for poor *Babbo*. Oh, how dear *Babbo* groaned and wept! We staid on our knees around the bier a long, long time. *Babbo* trembled and seemed so feeble that the *sagrestano* [chapel care-taker] brought us chairs, and we sat there silent and so sad till, as the bells were pealing evening *Ave Maria*, came the *Compagnia della Misericordia*' to bear away the dead.

"*Maria* and I had never before seen their snow-white dress, with hood and veil of the same which covered them completely down to their feet, with only two small holes for their eyes. They came marching in a column, like soldiers, and chanting the psalm:

*Miserere mei Deus.*⁸

"Four of them, taking up the bier and placing the poles upon their shoulders, (the rest, each bearing a lighted wax-candle, following in the

LA COMPAGNIA DELLA MISERICORDIA.

same order as they came,) all went off chanting together to their measured tread :

Ostende nobis Domine.

" *Babbo* and the *padre* followed to the *Campo Santo* and saw the deposit made and finished there, but *Maria* and I took our last look as the procession vanished from the door of the *Cappella*, and returned to wait and weep in the room of the abbess.

"On the morrow, with the approbation and advice of the abbess, although in our overwhelming grief and melancholy we ·both were disinclined to see or think of anything but the memorials of our sorrow, *Babbo* took us to visit some of the beautiful and wonderful things to be seen in this very remarkable city and its environs.

"On the morning, then, of this second day we went through splendid squares and passed fountains, some with ancient Corinthian pillars and fragmentary remains of old Roman aqueducts, and came to the old amphitheatre with its very, very high walls and rows and rows of seats, where they told us more than twenty thousand people could sit, and its hundreds of arches and hundreds of exit-gates—the whole built of huge, unmortared rocks, and all as sound and perfect as if the poor gladiators had been butchering each other yesterday there, and the spectators had gone home but yesternight.

"We went to the *Maison-carrée*, which, we were told, was the finest and best preserved of all the old Roman temples anywhere now in the world, with its lofty steps, its Corinthian columns fluted and surmounted by exquisite capitals which, in the days of old Roman glory, stood, no doubt, in a forum surrounded by many other edifices of equal or greater splendor now gone forever.

"We went to the Temple of Diana, with its arches and vaults and corridors and niches, filled now with sculptures and antiquities found there, and surrounded by ruins of aqueduct and reservoir of which old Julius and his horses must have drank.

"We went to the *Tour Magne*, the old, old, octagonal Roman ruin, built for a mausoleum, and twice as lofty still as *Cæcilia Metella's* on the Appian Way — but, by whom and for whom was it built? What thoughts it awaked in our childish souls!

"We went to the *Porte d' Auguste* [gate of Augustus] and gazed with wonder on its two large and two small archways — built in that splendid reign. How many of our dear mother's ancestors had looked daily on that same sight for two thousand years! How many of *Babbo's* had marched under it, clad in bright armor, with shield and lance, in all the pomp of old Roman warfare! And with many, many other such-like scenes and thoughts, we passed the day.

"On the morning of our last day, while *Babbo* went to the *Campo Santo* to finish the last things about dear Mother's grave, the kind abbess sent two sisters with *Maria* and me to the *Musée de Peinture* to point out to us the more noted and important pictures and sculptures and engravings treasured there.

"From our books and from *Babbo*, we had learned the names of some of the very great artists of the world, especially those of poor, dear, glorious *Italia*. But here with wonder and delight we saw for the first time, and were dazed to think we were looking on the very work of their own hands. We trembled with wonder and surprise before the Holy Family by *Rubens*, the S. Agnes by *Tintoretto*, the Magdalen by *Guido Reni*, the Christ in Gethsemane by *Correggio*, the *Madonna* by *Titian;* and I have a more indistinct yet beautiful memory of many, many more which I cannot name.

"The last hours of the afternoon of this last day we spent in the *Campo Santo*. The day was clear, and the air, though it was winter, was soft and balmy there. *Babbo* had erected at the grave's head a cross of wood, heavy and well-lettered. We hung three wreaths of *immortelles* upon it — one for the love of each of us.

"We spent much time in prayers beside the grave. But at last we must go away and leave her alone — in her own dear, 'warm France,' indeed, but so far, far away from us whom she so loved and who loved her so.

"Oh, the pang of the last look! I believe I could never have returned, but that I was brought away by *Babbo* aided by *Maria*, whose face was streaming with tears. I was tearless with agony.

"When the abbess put us in bed that night, she lingered and kissed us over and over again and said many prayers, so that we were asleep before she left us. In the morning when *Babbo* came for us, in saying '*adieu*' to the abbess we saw how his chin quivered and his voice trembled; and when she embraced us for the last time, her tears dropped upon our cheeks.

"It was after dark on the tenth weary day when we arrived at our home; and dear *Vigilo* was crouched outside the door ready to spring with a howl of delight into each of our faces, in turn."

X.

"Nor last, forget the faithful dogs ; but feed
With fattening whey the Mastiff's generous breed,
And Spartan race, who, for the fold's relief,
Will prosecute with cries the mighty thief,
Repulse the prowling wolf, and hold at bay
The mountain robbers rushing to their prey."

VIRGIL GEORG. Dryden's translation.

"REMEMBER," said my companion, "that if heirs of such ancestors, and getting some such great opportunites, yet *Maria* and I were real shepherdesses from our birth — brought up with the flocks, and more intimately still with our dogs. So that I must say something of these, since they came to play a much larger part with our own destiny than with that of the flocks.

"The first which I can remember was dear old *Vigilo*. He was a large, white, thoroughbred Calabrian sheep-dog, and was always with us children. While we were little, as soon as I can remember, Mother used, in summer, to take him and us with her to the upper pastures around and beyond the *Prati* [meadows] to tend the sheep during the day, and, at nightfall, he drove them home. The outgo in the morning was commonly without difficulty, but often the return was not so. In fact, in this matter without him we should have been helpless.

"*Babbo*, having released our five or six goats with a bell on the neck of each, to take care of themselves on the rocks and steeper mountain-sides during the day, was busy with the mules in the fields or in the forest, or in going to the markets. On our return, we commonly found him at home ready to receive the sheep; and while he milked them (with mother's help and often with mine), the dog went after the goats. They, especially if the kids had been kept in the fold, were usually not very far away, and in a short time, also, came trooping into their pen, to be milked and protected for the night."

Being much more concerned to get on in the story than to know the particulars about sheep or goats or even dogs, I should have felt impatient under so many details, if I had not already seen that she was unlikely to waste any words on matters not intimately connected with herself, and necessary for understanding what else she had to say. But I was not conscious of feeling, much less of showing, any sign of uneasiness at the drift of her discourse. Still, something of the sort must have appeared on my countenance or in my manner; for, stopping in the chain of her narrative, she said:

"It is true that it is a common thing for Alpine shepherds and herdsmen—more especially in the Eastern Alps, where more cows are kept—to send away the flocks and herds, often for a whole summer, among the upper valleys. I have known a young girl like me go with them, only with a a dog, and not return from early summer till the the frosts and snows of autumn drove her home.

"They build a hut for her there, and she milks night and morning, and makes butter and cheese during the day, and pens the creatures at night. Her brothers, and often other young men, visit her every week or two, commonly of a Sunday. They go with the mules and carry to her loaves of bread, possibly some berries which grow in the lower valleys, sometimes a jug of broth, or part of a boiled fowl, or piece of mutton. They spend the day chatting, helping her in some bit of heavier labor, eating their simple dinner with her at noon, and at evening they return carrying with them the accumulation of butter and cheese to be marketed by the *Babbo*, or added to the stock in the buttery at home."

—'But the long week through!' I could n't help but exclaim, 'and the loneliness!'

— "To be sure," she said, "if she were a giddy thing, or had nothing better than thinking her own foolish thoughts to do; and even so, loneliness is but one of the many *dispiaceri* [unpleasantnesses] that must be endured in a life of poverty and toil. But work is a great alleviation of it. To be busy with hands and thoughts upon necessary or useful things makes the hours fly swiftly; and to see what has been accomplished at nightfall, or at the week's end, to an earnest person is a great reward."

—'No doubt this is true, and the remark does you honor, *Signorina ;* but still that sentiment is, I think, not so common among the young as among older persons, and grows with our years.'

—"*Signore*, you are a man. Pardon me, if I tell you that women, young and old — of course I speak only of those I know — French and Italian women — are more earnest and take life more seriously than the men."

—'I never thought of it before, but a moment's reflection makes me think you are right, *Signorina.*'

—"*Si, Signore*, the more you reflect on it, and the more you come to know of the Italian women especially, and indeed of French women, too, the more clearly and certainly you will see that it is so. We have, alas, too many careless men, but the careless woman is an exception.

—'So far as my knowledge of the people of France and of Italy goes, I believe, *Signorina*, you are right. But connected with the loneliness I spoke of, there are dangers. What of the wolves? —and, worse than all, of the human . . .

—"We never knew or heard of any bad accident happening to such a girl there. Around the great sheep-yard in which the hut stands the men make a fence of rocks or logs meant to be high enough and strong enough to keep out wolves and robbers at night. At all events, the dog will give notice of their coming, and she has a gun always loaded and a long sharp knife. Between them the wolf does not often come a second time for the best of all reasons; and a robber (if there were any hereabout) knows the Italian woman too well not to think three times before provoking her last resort.

"But *Babbo* did n't and could n't use this plan. Our Upper Meadow was not so far away as to make a night stay necessary. Then, our pastures were small and scattered; so that there was no convenient common center for them, and not one nor two huts would have answered for them all. Even otherwise, *Babbo* would never have consented to the exposure. His hereditary pride forbade it.

XI.

"Go abroad to hear news of home."
OLD PROVERB.

"AFTER four years, the longing to revisit dear Mother's grave had become so strong in all our three hearts, that *Babbo* took us there. It was early in the month of September. The expense by *diligence* for 500 *chilometri* we were unable to bear. We went on foot, carrying the greater part of our food with us; and it was for us a nine-days journey.

"We renewed the cross and wreaths and rebuilt the mound, and the season now permitting, we planted violets on it.

"It was a great satisfaction to be there again and to do this. We grieved no longer as children. We knelt together around the grave and recited prayers for the repose of her dear spirit. Then, much comforted, though in quiet sadness, we started, on the third day after our arrival, upon our return.

"But, beyond this mournful satisfaction, the visit was remarkable for revealing some very tender memories, and, to us children, some very interesting incidents in the lives of our parents, of which we had never before heard ; and now was cleared up for us a romantic mystery which had always hung around the name '*Cecilia*' (which was the second of my baptismal names, the first being that of my Mother), but, often as we had put the question, never before could we get it satisfàctorily answered. Sometimes dear Mother had seemed to be beginning an explanation, when a look from *Babbo* made her silent. Now we heard it all, and wondered and rejoiced and pitied and wept.

"Among the changes which four years had wrought at the Convent, was the passing away of the abbess whom we learned to know, and whose so tender kindness we enjoyed with wonder on our former visit.

" She was now lying in the *Campo Santo* and not two steps from dear Mother's grave. It was, in fact, the nearest available space except that next dear Mother, bought and reserved for *Babbo* when his hour shall have come. And when that shall be, he will be awaiting the great sunrise with dear Mother on his left side, as they stood at the altar, and the good, kind abbess on his right.

The abbess herself chose and secured this spot for herself immediately after dear Mother had been laid to her last rest. The mound was only distinguished now by a frail cross marked in black letters: SORELLA AGATA [sister Agatha].

"Our first wonder was why she should be laid, from choice, just there. The next was to see the inscription in Italian, instead of the language of the country, and especially of the Convent. This certainly showed that she was of Italian blood, and of a patriotism that could not bear to be separated forever from her dear *patria* — not even by a foreign word over her body after her spirit was in *Paradiso*.

"But the third and the greatest wonder of all was to see that her departure — a stranger to him, so far as we knew — should make our *Babbo* so very, very sad. For, when he first discovered the grave, he uncovered and bowed his dear white head, and kneeling before that little rude cross, whispered some prayers while big tears ran across his cheeks and dropped upon the ground.

"Another thing that we wondered at for a moment was, that there was no date on the cross. But we presently remembered that on our former visit, when we happened to ask one of the sisters how long she had been in the convent, or how long she had lived the religious and secluded life, we were astonished to hear her say 'she did not know.' And, not daring to press the question, nor being willing to show our surprise to the good sister, we reserved our enquiry for our evening talk and the teaching of the kind abbess, when we should be alone with her in her room.

"Her answer, though it met the case exactly, was new and strange to us. For she said : 'We keep no memory of years. These belong to us no longer. Time measured by sun and moon with us is no more. Our existence is merged in God. Eternity with us is begun. The past is forgotten ; and there are no mile-posts on the road in the endless future.' '*Grazie a Dio*' [thank God], she added, with a soft, sweet sigh.

"*Babbo* also caused a heavy cross, exactly like dear Mother's, to be put in place of the frail board that was there, and to be marked below the sister-name :

Her name in the world was
CECILIA MARIA ELIA ATTILIO.
Loveliest of the Lovely.

F. O.

"Then we wondered still more, and most of all, how he had known her worldly name.

"When we returned to the convent for the night, the new abbess called us to her own room and conversed with us till the early hour of retiring came. Her manner was very gentle, and she asked us many things about both our secular and our religious life — more especially, if we had ever contemplated leaving the vanities and sins of the world and becoming *réligieuses.*

"She told us then that the late abbess had left a written request that, if ever we came there again (as she expected one day we would, to revisit our mother's grave), we should be received 'with especial kindness and consideration.' These were her own words.

"The abbess thought from this that perhaps, on our former visit, we had talked with her about taking the vail. The more so, since she had made no such request for any others, though many visited there ; and even some of these were rich.

"We explained that we were the stay and comfort of our *Babbo*, most of all since our Mother's departure ; and frankly confessed that we hoped one day, a great while in the future, to have husbands and children.

"To this she replied with a sigh, 'So have many, many before you, and found the men untrue, and themselves deserted and broken-hearted ; and then fled from a wicked and vexing world to a pure and peaceful life of religion, and found in the Blessed Saviour a lover who will not deceive, and in Holy Church a refuge where the misfortunes of this world cannot reach.

'But,' she added, after a moment, with a sad emphasis, 'this life is not for all — alas! it is not suited for all. Be sure of yourselves — be sure, *mademoiselles*, before you leave all worldly hopes behind.' As she uttered these last words, we saw her lips quiver and tears twinkle in the corners of her eyes.

"I saw tears standing in *Maria's* eyes, and felt them starting in my own as I looked into the sweet, sad face of the abbess, and said in my thoughts, 'Who knows what heart-sorrow you have had, and whether, perhaps, too late, you found you had mistaken your refuge?' But that secret we never knew.

"The third day after our arrival we started early on our return. We had left our home on a Monday and with our utmost endeavor had barely reached *Avignon* on Saturday evening, had been lodged over the Sunday at the Convent *de S^{te}*. *Ursule*, and had arrived at our destination in *Nismes* on Monday evening. So that it was Thursday when we set out to return and could only reach *Grenoble* on Saturday evening. We found the usual welcome at the Convent *S^{te}*. *Marie* and passed the Sunday there.

"*Babbo* would not under any circumstances less

than imperative, continue our journey on Sunday, since he was always more careful than many are in the observance of the day; but now, with all our hearts so serious with fresh thoughts of dear Mother in *Paradiso* and our bodies so fatigued by travel, we were but too glad of the occasion to rest and hear high Mass with the heavenly music at the Cathedral.

"The day was fine, and we did not return directly from the Cathedral to the Convent on the other side of the *Isère*, but after Mass sauntered away from the church into the *Cimetière St. Roch*. Here we spent a long while, wandering among the tombs and reading so many strange names, so many curious inscriptions, and some very touching ones, which made us feel what a world of sorrow this is, and in every country alike.

"As the hours wore on, we withdrew to the adjoining *Promenade de l' Ile Verte* and sat in the shade of those grand old trees, eating the light lunch which the kind nuns had provided and endeavoring to console one another with our conversation.

"That morning, before *Babbo* came to the Convent for us (for he lodged with an acquaintance of his boyhood, near the swimming school, on the other side of the river and of the town), *Maria*

and I had agreed to ask him about that name
'*Cecilia*' which had been a mystery to us all our
lives — why it was put into my name, since we
had no relations called so — how he had known
that it belonged to sister *Agata* — in short, to tell
us the whole story, while we had leisure, and
were in a mood to hear it and to be comforted by
it. For that there was a story we had long been
sure from snatches of remarks we had heard
between *Babbo* and dear Mother even from our
infancy; and still more so by what we had seen
and heard on this visit.

"During our lunch I proposed the question to
Babbo and *Maria* pressed it in her own gentle
way. Taken by surprise, he at first tried feebly
to escape it, saying :

— 'Why, children, I never thought it would be
to the honor or benefit of anybody to rake up old
follies of bygone days, but to let the dead past
be buried decently and forever.'

"But *Maria's* great soft eyes looking so plead-
ingly into his he could not resist, and presently
he said:

— 'How can I, dear children, deny you any
pleasure that is in my power? — and at best you
have so little !'

— 'We have you, *Babbo* dear, and that is everything,' we both cried in one breath.

— 'You are angels from heaven,' he said with a tender trembling in his voice, 'but I don't know if this knowledge will make you happier.' Then, after a little pause, he began

The Story of CECILIA ATTILIO.

'Forty-five years ago *Cecilia Attilio* was a *fanciulla* like you. Her father, *Roberto*, possessed a little property on the edge of the *Val d' Aosta*, ten or twelve *chilometri* from the Little St. Bernard. He used often to come to *Aosta* with the product of his garden and orchard and a patch of chestnut and walnut forest, and on days of the fair he often had a *baracca* [stall or booth of boards or cloth or both] where his pretty daughter sold cakes and honey and milk and walnuts and boiled chestnuts and the like.

'There was always a crowd around this booth who paid their money quite as much for the pleasure of talking with her and of being served in her sweet wonderful ways — which made the men frantic to take some little playful liberties with her, as they used to do with many of the handsome girls at the fair, but which she never for an instant allowed to anyone.

'She was always light-hearted and bright as the morning, but never foolishly frolicsome. She came to know hundreds of young fellows and older ones from all the country round; and when she met them again after the year or six months, since the last fair, she would recognize each one so sweetly and enquire after their health and luck in their affairs (their sheep, or cattle, or vines, or silk cocoons, etc.), and even in some cases, where she knew it would please, after the betrothed (whose existence she only conjectured), and then would exult with the accepted and condole so comfortingly and inspiringly with the jilted—'' 'T is a shame for such a nice fellow as you! but never mind, there 's a much prettier and better *fanciullettina* [sweet, pretty little maiden] waiting eagerly for you in her hiding-place—hunt her up at once and come to me laughing next fair.

'Or, as she handed the glass to some demure lad, 'Well my fine fellow, how tall you are growing!—I think you 've gone up half-a-span since the last fair—there must be a *Signorinetta* in the case by this time I know—I congratulate you both.' Or to a rough, sturdy *contadino* [country 'chap'] with a broad-brimmed slouched hat, badly banged and brim turned up in front, holding a long, heavy whip stifly upright *à la* shoulder arms, '*Ecco, il mio padrone!* [Well done! here is my honorable landed proprietor] I hear you are growing rich—well, I'm glad of it—you deserve it all—only do n't get proud, and pity the poor!'

'Or to one newly married (of whom she knew nothing, but only guessed), 'Is it a *bambino* [boy-baby] *Michele?* — kiss him for me — does he look grand like you ? — or like his beautiful mother ?'

'And so on and on, something different to each, always nice and pleasant to the happy, and always hitting the mark.

'Or if it were one whom she knew to have been struck by misfortune, or to be in trouble of any kind, she had a soft mournful word that went straight as an arrow carrying a thrill of sweet comfort to his heart; and as she spoke, her beautiful lips would tremble, and often a tear would start in the corners of her great lustrous eyes.

'In short, no matter who he was, or what joys or sorrows he carried in his heart, the neighborhood of *Cecilia's* booth was always the pleasantest spot in all the fair.

'She and I used to meet regularly at the fair and often at other times from the time that I was twelve and she two years younger. At this early age, while our two fathers were busy, each with his own affairs in the market, we sometimes strayed together along the great central street looking at the shops; sometimes we wandered into the suburbs and gazed with wonder and childish remarks on the ancient wall and tower and the remains of old Roman days; or romped

AOSTA.—OLD SOUTH GATE.

for wild flowers in the meadows on the banks of the *Dora-baltea*.

'In many ways, as the years went on, we came to know each other so very well. We called ourselves by our Christian names, and "gave the *tu* to each other." [10]

'She grew to be strangely beautiful. Her figure was perfect, her step as light as a gazelle. Her features had no irregularity, yet did not remind me of any other person. The quintessence of sweetness lay upon her lips, and her skin wore the flush of roses reflected on snow.

'But it was, I think, the fiery softness of her coal-black eyes, coupled with her flaxen hair (which, when unbound, flowed in native ringlets far below her knees) — a combination so rare as almost to be an unheard-of thing — which so immeasurably exalted her beauty and distinguished her from every other woman I have ever seen; and wherever she went, drew upon her the gaze of every eye.

'Of course, she began to have many and many admirers; and, in her circumstances, it could not fail that she should be more or less exposed to designing and wicked approaches. But the breath of flattery passed over her like the blasts of winter over the drifts of snow. She seemed both unconscious and careless of her marvelous loveliness, and advances of that sort were as ineffectual as efforts to climb *Mons Buet* in icy December.

'But, as I grew older and came to know more and more of the world, she was more and more in my thoughts, and I became more and more anxiously concerned for her safety.

'One day, during the time of the fair, when I was nineteen and she seventeen, it chanced, as had often happened before, that I had a *baracca* beside hers. We had met and talked together, for the snatch of a moment, at least, almost every hour, during the three days of the fair. It was early afternoon of the last day, when the *scirocco* sprung up with a sudden gust and whirlwind, which, in a moment, overturned both her booth and mine in a mingled heap of indescribable confusion.

'Happily, no one was injured. But I saw her falling, through fright and by the prodigious force of the wind. I leaped from my own tottering booth, and, seizing her in my arms, carried her to a place of safety. An instant later a heavy board fell upon the place where her head would have been.

'The gust was soon over. I helped restore her effects to order. Her sweet voice filled my ears with thanks and praises, till my soul was overflowing with emotion such as I never felt

before. She seemed to me an angel of heaven.
She did not seem heavy in my arms ; but then
and afterward, during the remainder of the day,
I trembled from head to foot, as if I had been
over-strained with too great a lift ; and the feeling of having her in my arms continued for several hours.

'That evening, when we all were packed and
on the point of starting for our homes, feeling as
if it would kill me to let her go out of my sight, I
ran up to take leave of her, as on such occasions
I always did, but instead of the usual "*a rivederci*"
[good-bye till we meet again], I brought her hand
(which trembled more than mine) to my lips and
said, "*io t' amo, io t' adoro !*" [I love you, I adore
you].

'God only knew what happened. Her sweet
countenance instantly seemed to change to anger. Her rosy color fled, and her face became
snowy white. She dropped my hand without
a word and ran from me.

'I know not how I reached home. I expected my vitals would burst in my bosom
from the thundering convulsions there, I knew
not whether of rage or despair.

'After all these years of encouraged love, —
all these years of silent yet real and accepted
heart-worship — had I at last been jilted ? — jilted

by her?—by *Cecilia?*—the angel?—nearest of mortal women to the *Madonna* in heaven?

'Was is possible that she cared nothing for my love?—despised the adoration of my soul?—hated my presence?—wished me out of her sight?

'Must I believe—could I believe that she had been deceiving me all these years? Had it not been, in a manner, taken for granted that we should one day belong to each other? What had appeared to change it now? Was there, perhaps, somebody else in sight? Was her so rare beauty a fortune too big to share it with a mere shepherd?—no matter what blood ran in his veins?—or—oh Hell!—had its market value become too apparent not to refuse to sell it for less than a mountain of ready cash! Could my *Cecilia* be a flirt—a false coquette? I could not believe it—but I must believe it!'

'Like one worn out with labor, or smitten by disease, I barely found my way with difficulty to my bed. For many nights and days I neither slept nor received nourishment. My Mother (may *Iddio* and our Lady shed light and rest upon her spirit!) nursed me incessantly in every best way her love could invent. She made no troublesome inquiries. It was not her way. Whether she suspected the true cause of my malady, I never knew. But one may suffer much from this disorder and live. It was so with me. My distress was extreme. Life lost its charm for me. Hope was dead in my breast. I was ready to die. Yet I lived. By slow degrees my strength returned. Again I slept and ate and worked. Still, it is true, like those diseases which can visit a man but once, and appear to consume from his constitution the aliment on which they feed, since the experience of that tremendous inflammation, I have never been quite the same. That unspeakable glamour of love never returned to me.

'Meantime, while this agonizing transformation was going forward in my soul, and my sadness and despair were subsiding more and more, to eventuate in a less jubilant, certainly, yet not less real and worthy life, there came a visitor to our home. My orphan half-cousin, *Marthe Helène Marie Manivet* from Nismes, came to my Mother, her only surviving aunt, and in fact only near relation in any degree, to spend an indefinite time. She had a little property in the *Rente* [national loan] but no home; and my Mother, as her nearest of kin, and with her mother-heart always open, invited her to come to us.

'You know the result for me. I loved again. Not with the frenzy of amorous madness. That, as I have said, was for me forever impossible, but a soft and peaceful flame was kindled in both our souls. A sober and steady affection, built on a true and firm friendship and an ever-growing mutual esteem, united our humble and chequered lives in one happy current, till it was struck by the Great Divider; and the chief comfort of my life now lies in looking forward to the reunion never again to be broken on the other side.

'But what of *Cecilia?* Ah, children, this is the cap-stone of my monumental grief. I was consoled in my misery, but not to the degree of being willing to revisit *Aosta*—the field of my misfortune—for many months.

'I was at length betrothed and I felt no desire to meet *Cecilia* again. In fact, my prevailing sentiment was decidedly the opposite. There were, however, some reasons which occasionally shook my resolve to avoid her forever. My anger at my assumed injury had gradually passed away, I was contented,—why should I retain a grudge? Besides, though perhaps not meaning so, had she not thrown into my arms a prize?

'During these months, after my perturbation had passed away, as I calmly reviewed these events, my conduct came up to me often in a ridiculous light, and more than once I caught myself laughing aloud at my folly. Once this laughter in a dream awaked me from sleep.

'At last, one day it was suddenly borne in upon me, like a flash of lightning, What if it is *I* who have wronged *her?* Had I not acted wholly on conjecture,—and that most hastily taken up? Was not my only ground, my own interpretation of her action—one single act? Must I not admit that a different interpretation, if not probable, was, at the least, possible? Had I not cut off all opportunity from her to explain? Perhaps an explanation would have healed my wounded self-love, if it did not satisfy my desires, and have saved my crimination of her, whom, surely, I would always wish to think incapable of wrong doing to me, or to any one.

'Remember, children, that I was then calm and happy in my love and betrothal of your lovely and blessed Mother. God forbid that I should ever say or think anything but thankfulness that His gracious Providence led her and not another to my heart and my home. But, I say, when the perturbation of my mind and heart was over, and I was safely moored in a sacred and happy haven of love, a desire arose to see *Cecilia* once more, and tell her of my new-found joy.

'If she had never felt for me (as I had, till the fatal day, wrongly supposed) the same passion which I felt for her; and if, as I now hoped, she felt kindly toward me, at least as an intimate friend and playmate of childhood, I thought it would be an agreeable thing to her to meet me again and hear my story, and congratulate me on my fortune.

'Full of this thought, which, however, I concealed in my own bosom, at the time of the August fair I went again to *Aosta* and sought for the *Attilio* booth. I could not discover it, and I wondered at this. But it was still early in the first day. I conjectured that some hindrance had occurred that would be removed, and the stall would appear before the evening. It did not appear that day, and I went home with my errand unaccomplished.

'I could not rest satisfied, however. There was now another problem to solve. Some important change I felt sure had occurred. Perhaps she was married — perhaps to some rich man, or nobleman — or in some other way had sold her glorious beauty and gone — God knows where, but probably never to meet my eyes again.

'I was too much interested to abandon my purpose, and on the following day, I was there again making the same search. Hour after hour I moved among the crowded stalls, and once and again had perambulated the principal street of the town, and peered into every lane and shop; but it was in vain.

AOSTA. — PRIORY OF S. ORSO.

'The forenoon was already nearly passed. I
had visited every quarter and tried every means
of search in my power; but all without success.
I had left the market-place and sauntered into
the suburbs, meditating whether I would not
give up the bootless chase and return home.
As I approached the old tower, accidentally lifting my eyes, I saw before me a female figure
which seemed to have issued from the Priory
of *S. Orso.*

'Of course, my heart instantly throbbed with
a new excitement. I seemed to recognize the
figure as that of her whom I sought. She was
moving slowly from me. There was the slender
height, the fine proportions, the step — no, the
step was not hers. The grace, the life, the elas-
ticity, so marked in her I sought, were not here.
Then, as I came nearer, I observed that the dress
was black — a color I had never seen her wear.
But, coming nearer still, I found a surer test.
The hair was black, or else it had been drawn up
close under a black silk cap. It was useless to
follow further, and, under some hidden impulse,
I changed the direction of my steps, and wandered to the south gate and the tower of *Bramafam* of uncanny memory.''

'I was resolved now to give up all further pur-
suit; and started by the nearest course for the

highway and my return home. I had reached the crumbling walls of the ancient *Teatro* and the arcades of the *Anfiteatro*, and, making an abrupt turn to the right, I came suddenly face to face with the slender black figure, standing under an umbrella to shield her from the August sun ; and, at the instant that this vision met my eyes, a little scream smote my ears :

"*Mio Iddio in Cielo! — Filippo Ombrosini !*"

'I stopped, stunned as if struck by a thunderbolt. That voice ! — yes. Those eyes ! — Ah, yes, their own indescribable languishing fire. That heavenly face !—yes, but as white as the sheeted snow, only, for the moment, by the shock of surprise, tinged on the checks with just a reflection of the flush of dawn.

'All else, how changed! The plump roundness gone. The bones of the face and neck and hands projecting as from a skeleton. The whole figure so thin that the garments hung as on a skeleton indeed.

'I did not and could not speak ; nor did she utter another word. But, after a moment of silent gaze — it seemed an eternity to me — beckoning me with her free hand to follow, she turned and led me to the further side of a grove of aged chestnuts, which threw a deep shade over some moss-covered rocks on the

AOSTA.—OLD ROMAN BRIDGE IN THE SUBURB.

brink of a rattling brook which had almost ended its noisy, hasty chase to the *Dora-baltea.*

'Nature had prepared this retreat—it was near the half-buried old Roman Bridge—as if arranging it especially for us. Two rustic armchairs, formed by conspiring rocks and roots, stood *vis à vis.* The spot was in full view of the great highway, and within hearing of the hum of the busy fair; yet it was sufficiently apart for the freest communications, without fear of disturbance or eavesdropping. She threw herself hastily into one of these seats. I sank mechanically and silently into the other. The little brook rippled and danced as in mockery of me.

'She had not spoken, and for a little space did not speak nor raise her eyes from her lap, where her fingers were toying nervously with the handle of her sunshade.

'Suddenly she raised those great eyes full of awful love and looked squarely into mine, with a glance that sent icy chills thrilling up and down my spinal marrow, and said with a voice as clear as the *Ave Maria* bell on that Convent of *S*.*Maria,* yet that trembled and hesitated on every word: "So—you—did—not—love—me!—you—you you—deceived me!"

'I wished to say something, I do n't know, and I believe I did n't then know what, but a lump swelled suddenly in my throat and made it impossible. But she, seeing me trying to speak, signaled to me to be silent and went on:

"Look at me, *Filippo!* — See what the fever has left me!" Here she snatched off the black cap from her head. "*Oh, mio Iddio!*" I threw up my hands and cried, for there was n't a hair visible on her snow-white, shiny scalp!

'I did not try to say more, but sat in silent agony, my eyes riveted on that horrible sight. She went on — pausing a good while between her sentences :

"*Filippo Ombrosini*, were we not children together?.... Did we not chase one another through the streets of the fair?... Did we not pelt one another with wild flowers in the meadows?... When I fell, who but my *Filippo* picked me up... lifted me so gently... wiped the soil from my brow with the petals of wild roses... and... and kissed the spot to make it well?"

'Here she paused, replaced the cap, and hid her face in her hands. I dared not speak, nor lift my eyes. For, not being able to bear her glance, I had dropped my eyes, at the first, on the ground, and my heart fluttered and pounded my side, like the windmills of *Venezia* in the gusts of November. All was still again for a long, long time, which seemed to me would never end.

'At last she went on again: "As we grew older, how thoughtful you were of me — how modest — how careful — how helpful.— Then, that dreadful day when the *Scirocco* blew — and you — your arms carried me — away to safety.— Oh, how — how grateful I — I felt to you — I thought — I thought I — I belonged — I belonged to — to you.— Oh, how afraid I was — afraid I should say — should say — say something — something a maiden — a maiden must n't say.— And that evening — that evening when the great moon was looking down on us and — and you told me — told me and — and my heart — my heart was ready — was ready to burst and — and I was — I was so frightened and — and turned — turned a little — a little away and — and I thought — I thought you — you would — would follow and — and claim — and claim and — take your rights and — and you — you did n't — did n't love me — truly — and have, have loved another — so soon — oh, so soon ! — and are — are betrothed — yes, are betrothed — I have heard of it — are betrothed — yes, betrothed — forever — yes, forever and ever — oh, oh ! — what to a man — to a man, is a woman's heart? — a woman's — heart ? — a woman's — a woman's heart ? — oh, oh, oh !" Then she broke down in hysterical sobs.

'The truth was flashed upon me. How could I ever have distrusted her so? At all events, how could I have been such a coward, not to take her by force?—to take my kingdom of heaven by violence? I knew not what to say, or do. In fact, there was nothing for me to say or do, but to endure the torture of conscious guilt in shame and in silence.

'"*I had not loved her!*"—Good Heavens! God knows I had loved her with all the sentiments of my soul and all the energies of my body—that my mind and heart, entendered by the truest friendship, and the most unbounded esteem, were consuming in the fiercest flame of youthful passion. *Not love her!*—To save her from a pang, or to gratify her most whimsical wish, I would have risked my life in a moment—yes, I would have sold it, without a moment's hesitation.

'Yet I dared not—I must not tell her this—and how I had mistaken, in my mad love, the meaning of her conduct. The next thing would be to say I was sorry; and that, at all hazards and in any event, I must not do. It would be treason to your loving and trusting mother, betrothed by my solemn words, to say so, or to allow myself for one moment to feel so.

'But what had I done!—What an innocent

heart I had shamefully broken!—What an angel
life I had damnably murdered!—The remorse
of the *Inferno* rolled into my bosom. I felt the
pangs and the desperation of hell in my soul.
And the bitterest part of the bitterness was
that I knew, I felt that I deserved it all. Yes,
children, in all my happy life with your blessed
mother, here has been a wound in my heart
that never has healed. I have tasted the torture of the "undying worm."

'Oh, during those moments, while I sat under
her stinging words, how gladly would I have
thrown myself at her feet!—how gladly would I
have kissed the lowest hem of her garments!—
Or, rather, what peerless joy it would have been
to snatch her up in my arms and soothe her
like an infant! But alas, alas, I could not, I
must not show a sign of sorrow, nor even of
pity. It would, in a moment, have hurled me
into the whirlpool of actual infidelity to your
mother.

'I dared not remain a moment longer in her
presence. God only knows what would have
happened five minutes later. With a sudden
spring, I rose and fled from her—throwing
back, however, over my shoulder, these three
words: "*I did love you.—I misunderstood your actions.—I have got hell in my soul!*"

. 'I staggered home in the utmost anguish. My distress was far greater now than when I last passed over this track on my former sad return. Then I felt innocent, though injured. Now I knew and felt that I was a criminal. Every rock and bush at the roadside seemed conscious of my baseness and to cry out against me. Nor could I do anything to atone for my fault. I must carry my guilt through life. Yes, I must carry it into the other world — and how could I bear to meet her there?

'It aggravated my anguish, if that were possible, that I must bear it in secrecy and alone. For I dared not tell the facts to my mother, much less to my betrothed. The burden was again too much for my strength; and from the hour I entered my chamber, it was a month before I came out to breathe again the free air of heaven.

'Meantime my sufferings and the apparent danger that my reason would be unhinged, brought our whole family into great distress. My mother was nearly prostrated under her double anxiety — not only for her son but as well for the dear girl whose prospects in life were thus balancing between hope and despair.

'As I afterwards learned from your mother, the two women dimly but surely divined the true cause of the mysterious malady by which I had been twice brought so low, having been each time attacked immediately upon a return from the fair at *Aosta*. Many private consultations on the matter were held by them; and it was finally resolved that woman's tact should probe it to the bottom.

'This was accomplished. So skillfully was it done by masked approaches — chiefly while the two alternated at the bedside, fanning me during the hot afternoons — that I promised to tell my betrothed the whole story. This I did one Sunday afternoon while my *Babbo* and Mother were not yet returned from the Mass at *Martigny*.

'Did the dear girl upbraid me? Did she load me with accusations of my guilt and folly?— That angel?— No! On the contrary, she entered into my trouble even as her own. She took part of the distress upon her own heart; and so helped me to bear my load.

'It was at her suggestion that I wrote a letter to *Cecilia*, not so much to exonerate myself as to do all that a craving of her Christian pardon for my foolish and guilty mistake, and the expression of utmost devotion to her service and sincerest interest in all her future, could do to soothe and cure her bruised heart. Much, in fact, of that letter was the dictation of my betrothed — a dear woman's heart striving to console another dear woman's heart, with her profoundest sympathy and tenderest affection. Truly, they both were angelic souls.

'I received after many months, from the Convent of the *Ursuline* in *Aosta*, a brief but most Christian reply. "She was already dead to the world; and lived now only as Sister *Agata*." There were no accusations, in fact there was no discussion of her troubles. "The frankness of my letter comforted her. All was a leading of Providence. It was her duty and she hoped ever to make it her joy to delight in His will. My happiness was now her only earthly longing."

'"Her father's death before our last meeting had been the cause of the black dress which I saw her in; and which now she should never lay aside. Her little property she had given to the Convent. She made one request—that after our marriage my wife might be brought to see her through the bars, and afterwards, that she might be permitted to see our children, and lay her hand on the head of each with her blessing." Her removal to another convent soon after made it impossible to gratify this wish.

'I have never told you, for I could not before, without explanations which I could not give, why the body of your mother lay during the night in the Chapel of the Convent, rather than in some

Church nearer the *Campo Santo;* and that a requiem was sung there by the nuns, while you and *Maria* were asleep.'

"Hardly was this story done, while we were all three in tears, that *Maria* and I sprang up, and throwing our arms together around dear *Babbo's* neck, sobbed for some minutes in silence. We wept on, without another word, most of the way back to the Convent. On the morrow, we started early to finish our return."

VIGILO OMBROSINI.

XII.

"Who knoweth the spirit of man that goeth upward, and whether the spirit of the beast goeth downward to the earth?— BIBLE (Revised Version), ECCL. iii, 21.

"ARRIVED at home, no *Vigilo* was lying before the door, but we found him on a mat in the kitchen partly covered with rags. He faintly wagged his tail and turned his languid eyes towards us as we entered. *Maria* and I bestowed on him the gentlest caresses, and did for him everything that could be done, but in two days he died.

"This was one cost of our visit to dear Mother's grave; and it, in turn, became again the link that drew upon us the dreadfulest grief of all.

"We had been absent nearly three weeks. *Babbo* had employed a friendly old shepherd (who lived two hours from us, having a married son who could care for their own flock) to stay in our house and look after our affairs while we should be away. Age had crippled him so that the active care of the flocks rested mainly upon the poor dog. He was a noble fellow of a noble breed.

He seemed to understand and rise to the responsibility of the situation, and it was fidelity in the line of duty that finally cost him his life.

" Being mostly alone with the sheep during the day, just what his experiences with them were, we do not know. But the old man said that on the second day the dog came in at night behind the flock with bloody ears and limping on one leg. All went well, however, till the evening before our arrival, when there was trouble with a goat which had lost her kid and refused to be put into the pen. The old man was not active enough to give the dog much assistance. She finally leaped high in the air and shot like an arrow far afield. *Vigilo* was soon in front of her, however; and when she tried the same tactics again, she found the dog too quick for her. Their breasts struck together with a powerful shock ; but the goat being heavier than the dog, or standing on higher ground, the blow which threw her backward landed him on the edge of a loose bowlder which was balanced on the verge of a chasm. His weight and the shock dislodged the bowlder, which fell with him crushing him horribly.

" It was in a grave near the door that we buried this dear companion of our infancy with tears of real sorrow. Before anything was put to mark the spot, *Maria* and I often whispered together some strange thoughts — you and other people may think them strange — may be they were foolish — but they were real to us.

"We could n't help connecting together our two great sorrows; and the more especially since one was at least the indirect cause of the other. There was a cross on one grave, why not — would it be wrong to put one on the other? Then the whole mystery came up to our minds. Do the dumb animals commit sin? Certainly some seem to be very malicious and naughty, and others as benevolent and good. If not, why do they suffer? If they do, did n't perhaps the Great Sacrifice suffice and atone for them, too, — especially if they try to be faithful and good, as *Vigilo* did? If so, what harm, or rather, how suitable to put over him the Great Sign! But we did n't feel very sure of our ground; and one day *Babbo* took out of the bed of the *Drance* a stone which we had often fancied looked much like *Vigilo*, as he used to lie crouched and sleeping on his paws, and brought and placed it on his grave. This became his monument; but I have thought often and much about the other."

XIII.

What if I choose to weep alone?—
For flowing tears are sweet—
Is not the secret pang my own?
The secret guerdon meet? [12]

AFTER this introduction—she had called it so—of the parting with her canine friend, during some parts of which her lips quivered and her voice trembled, my fair companion became silent, changed her shoes into the other hand, then presently removed her hat and set the shoes deftly on her head, all without turning or altering her gaze, which was fixed on the empty distance ahead. I did not speak, for I seemed to see a shadow rising over her countenance which, like the black summer thunder-cloud, foretells a coming shower. I was not mistaken. The shower of tears came. Silently, but copiously, the drops fell upon a dress-front that rose spasmodically to meet them with very soft yet audible sighs. Silently we moved on for some minutes, I surely being unwilling, by a word or a look even, to infringe on this tribute to a sorrow still unknown to me.

But I was not at ease. Much otherwise. My feelings, however, were confused. I dreaded that which I desired. For I was sure we were entering now into the penumbra, at least, of that deep sorrow, the shadow of which hung so dark over her young life, and which she had been so backward to reveal. I was sure that before those eyes so steadily fixed on vacancy were passing shapes and doings which I was impatient to hear of, though I thought likely the recital would thrill me with a painful sympathy.

I felt sure, however, of one thing, and I was much calmed and comforted by it; namely, that, whatever the source, her sorrow was not the fruit of vice or crime; that there was no illicit love in the story, no fruits of an unchaste passion, no vengeance wrought on a seducer, or traitor with dagger or pistol, etc.,— the everlasting staple of stories which in our day so many moral men and virtuous women strangely regale themselves with in secret. On the contrary, I was sure that the moral atmosphere about her was as pure as the clear, cool zephyr from the snowy top of the *Jungfrau* that was then playing with her unbound locks. In short, that the cause of her woe was of that class which may truly be called " an act of

God," and justly claim the sympathy of every good man, and receive every consolation which the Church can offer, or Divine Revelation afford.

Ere long her calmness returned. Her silent emotion had subsided. With bonnet swinging free on her arm, she quietly resumed: "It was in September that *Vigilo* died — the month when *Babbo* carried wood to the *Hospice*. He started early for the forest, loaded three mules — two were our own and one was hired — and arrived at the *Hospice* before noon.

"He ate the luncheon (commonly a good piece of black bread and a nibble of goat-cheese), which he carried from home, and baited the mules with the bundle of hay which was tied on the top of the load of each; and after about two hours' rest, started on his return and was home again before dark.

"One day while eating his luncheon in the *cucina* of the *Hospice*, as usual, he met there a young man from the Mantuan district who had brought up for the use of the monks some cases of choice wine. Divining from his accent whence he came, *Babbo* told him of our loss and enquired about the prospect of getting a dog of the Mantuan breed.

—'*Buon, buon per noi! Benissimo per tutt' e due!*' [capital, capital for us both] replied the young man. 'I have exactly the dog you need; and what is more, we are compelled to part with him.'

—'Compelled to part with him!'—interjected *Babbo*, 'has he made some acquaintance that must be broken off?'

—'No, nothing of the kind. He is the most orderly of animals.'

—'Nor mastered and hurt some neighbor's dog?'

—'No, *sicuro*, no! We are too retired for that, and he never goes off the place.'

—'Nor killed some nobleman's fox or boar making havoc among your vines?'

—'He has n't; for no such occasion has offered. I can't say what he would have done in such a case. He is a terrible fighter with wild beasts, and the most watchful and faithful of guardians when on duty.'

—'And yet you will part with him?'

—'We must. *Mamma* is dead, and *mio Padre* is too old to care for the sheep. I —' here he hesitated, *Babbo* said, and the color of his face came and went, but presently he went on,—'I have been conscripted, and shall be taken in two weeks into the barracks.'

" *Babbo*, with his tender, fatherly heart, was so touched by his tones and manner that he forgot for the moment about the dog in his interest in the young man and replied:

—'As the dependence of your father, have n't you good ground to press a claim for exemption from the service?'

—'Probably not, for, since *Mamma* is gone and we have a bit of property, and *Padre* is not confined to his bed'—

—'But you might try'—

—'If the cost were not so hard to bear, and the result so doubtful—or hardly doubtful.'

—'What, then, will you do?—what is your plan?'

—'There's but one course we can take. When I'm gone, the rents must be given up of the vineyard and pastures and everything but the cottage; and *Padre* will have to live as carefully as he can on the little we 've laid by. It may last a year if there 's no rise in house rent or maccaroni. The war, they say 's likely to carry everything up.'

—'What afterward?'

—'I do n't know, if he lives, what will become of him — unless to die *allo spedale* [in the hospital]. Here it is. Here it is. We would n't think of letting the dog go, if it were n't necessary to have the *scudi* for *Padre* to live on. For they are great friends; and *Padre* will be less safe and very lonely without him. But the dear brute must go, and we must find for him a good home. That is all we can do.'

"The gentle manner and amiable face of our *Babbo* appeared to captivate the young man. He said that that day week he should go with wine to *Martigny*, and enquired if *Babbo* lived near his route. *Babbo* told him that we did; and explained that there was at the roadside, opposite our home, a *piccolo santuario della Madonna* [a little shrine of the madonna] which on that day would be decorated with fresh flowers. *Babbo* also requested him, if he felt so disposed, to bring the dog with him, for which, if we kept him, *Babbo* agreed to pay fifty *scudi*."

"The young man having promised to be there with the dog at the appointed time, the conversation turned to other matters and the business arrangement was not again referred to.

"Another thing seemed to *Maria* and me exceedingly strange and unaccountable. *Babbo* had not asked the name of the young man, nor told him his own. We were amazed at this, especially since it was so totally opposite to *Babbo's* usual scrupulously careful way. We could not and never did give ourselves a really satisfactory reason for it. But it seemed probable to us then and afterward, that *Babbo* was from the first

smitten with such an admiration of him, and con-
ceived such an unquestioning trust in him, so
like an old and tried acquaintance, as not when
in his presence, to think of his name.

"But every way, the prospect of possessing the
dog delighted us, and we were anxious that the
young man should be so well pleased with us as
to make the prospect a certainty.

"Besides this, there was another very important element in our excitement which we did not
confess even to our own hearts; and of which,
probably, we were then really unconscious. This
visit, though ostensibly and truly an affair of
common business, would be a new adventure to
Maria and me.

"From the moment when *Babbo* came home
with the news, our pulses quickened, our hearts
pounded stronger and faster against our sides,
and our breath sometimes seemed strangely
choked. ·Our fancy at once became busy in
drawing a picture of the young man's looks.

"That he was handsome was certain from
Babbo's description of his 'tall, straight figure, his
abundant dark hair, his soft yet brilliant eyes, his
broad shoulders, his deep chest, and his step as
light and spry as a panther.'

"That he was as brave and kind as he was
strong, was plain enough, also, from the story

which he told *Babbo* in explaining about the dog.

'About a year ago,' he said, 'three sheep had disappeared, one by one, from the flock in the mountain pasture, though they were always folded at nightfall and guarded by dogs during the day. No signs of wild beasts were apparent, and no unusual tracks of any kind had been left; but the sheep were never found.

'At last a strict watch was determined on. There was on one side, commanding a view of the pasture, an old shepherd's hut, no longer used, but built, as usual, in the shape of a long, low beehive of reeds and mud, just long enough and high enough for a man to stretch himself under, with his head at the opening which looked toward the valley. Throwing bushes over this opening to give the place still more the appearance of disuse and neglect, the young man undertook to make a strict watch from this concealment till something should be discovered.

'Day after day and week after week passed by in constant watching, but without any important result. At last on the fourth week, one hot afternoon, when the flock was somewhat scattered, and individual sheep had strayed into the cooler nooks and shades of the hazel bushes and birches and projecting rocks, and when shepherds are

more often inclined to be dozing, or at least neg-
lectful, the dog, who had been quietly observing
the sheep from his sentinel-post, in front of the
bushes at the hut's mouth — except that now and
again he would dart off and drive in a sheep
which was straying too far into some thicket or
ravine, and then trot leisurely back and lay his
great head down again on his paws — came back
from one of these sallies in a state of great excitement, looking wildly every way, now holding his nose high up in the air, now coming
and looking through the overspread bushes into
his master's face with almost human enquiry,
all the while emitting a low, savage growl.

'Nothing unusual was to be seen, and nothing
heard, yet the shepherd knew too well the in-
fallible instincts of the dog, not to be roused to
the keenest suspicions. He immediately withdrew with the dog, in the utmost silence, to
a place among the rocks, where, without being
seen below, he could overlook every part of
the flock. For a considerable time nothing appeared, though the dog could in no way be
pacified. He looked constantly into his mas-
tter's face, and trembled in every limb.

'At last a slight rustle was audible, as if
in some thicket not far away. Still for some
minutes nothing could be seen. Later a clump

of hazel bushes seemed agitated by the wind, though there was not a zephyr blowing. The next minute, surely enough, the expected game hove in sight. Creeping on all fours towards a fine buck that lay quietly chewing the cud under a shelving rock, came slowly on a huge specimen of the mountain robber.

'He was bareheaded, and having stripped himself for work by throwing off his raw sheepskin coat, he was naked to the waist. The enormous muscles of his great arms puffed up, like a woman's bosom, on each shoulder. His bushy beard, which covered almost every part of his face, hung far down upon his dark-brown skin and hairy breast.

'He wore the common *calzoni corti* [shepherd's breeches] made of raw sheepskin with the wool outward, hanging loose at the knee and belted at the waist with a strong leathern strap, from which hung a long sheath-knife, a large pistol, and a short, knotty club.

'With his wool-coat on, which would reach a little below his belt, he would pass for a shepherd, and might even be seen on the road carrying a lamb or sheep on his shoulder without arousing suspicion in any he should meet, unless one should notice the heavy boots he wore, which reached to the knees and did not belong, surely, to a shepherd's outfit, but served to protect his lower legs from the briers through which his profession would cause him often to travel.

'Without making a sound, the young shepherd rolled himself over the side of the knoll on which he was lying, followed by the dog crouching like a feline beast in the act of springing on its prey. Having quickly cut a bundle of osiers in the valley, and fastened it with one of them upon his shoulder, he passed noiselessly around, out of the sight of the villain, and came with the dog at his heels, upon the top of the overhanging rock under which the thief was creeping for his prize.

'The dog took in the situation and awaited the motions of his master. Presently a slight disturbance was heard below. The next instant the accoutered thief emerged with the struggling, bleating buck on his shoulder. He was two *metri* below the shepherd and the crouching dog who lay motionless on the rock and ready for a spring.

'The next instant the signal was given. The dog leaped from his height down full upon the back of the robber. The force of the spring and the weight of the dog, coming with such an unexpected shock, in addition to the struggles of the buck, tumbled the scoundrel forward heavily upon his face, while the frightened buck ran away bleating toward the sheep.

'The robber had scarely uttered an awful blasphemy when the dog had him by the throat. The next instant the shepherd was on his back, and thrust his head several times violently down upon the rock. Having drawn the sheath-knife while the robber was still held by the dog, he threatened to sever his head from his body if he moved hand or foot except as ordered.

'The first order was to throw his hands behind his back. It was done; and he firmly bound them there with three withes made from the osiers which he had cut in the valley. Then he stripped his prisoner of the heavy boots and of the *calzoni corti* with all the artillery attached to them. Finally, having withed his ankles together in such a way that he could take very short steps, he made him rise, and driving him thus with a heavy mule whip (which he had brought with him, and which he had occasion to use many times with great severity on the obstinate but helpless and naked rogue), he arrived safely at the *Carcere di città* [city prison] in the edge of the evening.

'Women of the lower class were no longer in the streets to witness his humiliation and shame; so that the prisoner escaped, in this regard, a mortification which such villains in our country feel acutely. The gathering darkness which had also sent home most of the "small boys" of the street protected him from many indignities and little unmentionable outrages. As it was, only a little mob of a half-dozen gamins surged round him, like a swarm of wasps, pelted him with mud and even with small stones, and filled his ears with gibes and yells.

'The dog marched behind as a rear-guard, carrying the great boots in his mouth, and with his high-lifted head seemed to enjoy the triumph of the capture and punishment of the gigantic rogue quite as much as his master.

'The prison-gate at last closed upon the thief, and the young man saw him no more. But the next day his young wife was found in the street, with a babe at her breast, without food, without shelter, without a friend.

'It came to the ears of the young shepherd against whom the crimes had been committed. He knew very well how it often happens in such cases, that the woman is not only a concealed partner in guilt, but, being the more intelligent party, has been, in fact, the chief planner and promoter of the crime. But he knew, also, as well, that not seldom it is wholly different — that the wife is the unsuspecting victim of deception. Confiding in the false statements of her husband, whom she is taught by nature to trust and love, she becomes an indirect promoter and party to crimes of which she has no knowledge nor suspicion.

'How the truth lay in this case he could not with certainty know. But, save her intense interest in the prisoner, and her readiness to run into danger for his sake, to undergo suffering and to risk everything in order to see him and to try to save him from punishment — and what different from this, as a good wife, could she do, or ought she to do? — and she would not believe him guilty — or, even if he were, should she forsake him in his trouble? — aside from this, there was no evidence against her.

'He gave her the benefit of the doubt — he hoped of the certainty — of her innocence. While all others treated her and the infant with harshness or indifference, he who alone had suffered from the crimes of her husband, spoke kindly to her, brought her and the child to his house, gave her food and money, and sent them to her relations in *Urbino.*' "

Here my companion took breath and a draught of ice-water from the stream at our side. I had offered her — but she declined it — some *Lacrima Christi* out of my belt-flask. I had brought a few bottles in my luggage from Sicily. Though not superstitious, I was unwilling to drink to her happiness in water. So, after her draught, I borrowed her little cup and drank her health alone in that peculiarly Italian and, by those who affect such a wine, much-prized liquor.

TÊTE NOIRE.

XIV.

Why, now, Casella mine, I said,
Has so much anxious waiting fled? [14]

WHEN I heard of that expected visit, above mentioned, and thought of that fine young fellow, so worthy in himself, and enveloped in such a pity-inspiring environment of solicitude not unmingled with danger; and when I remembered the unspeakable tenderness native to the female heart; and in particular the evident unusual susceptibility of these two sentimental young souls — born, too, not of the stupid peasant races of the Swiss and Piedmontese Alps, but of a line drawing the hottest passions of central Italy from Sabinian *Trastevere* commingled with the infinitely piquant blood of Southern France — such native susceptibilities now harrowed and quickened by their own grief, and made still more hungry and thirsty for sympathy by the loneliness of their mountain-home; — my own heart could not but divine the possibilities, or rather imminent probabilities of the near approaching future, and was overshadowed by a haze of gloomy anticipations.

I foreboded, I know not what of uncanny circumstances. "Ah! what a fearful thing," I said to myself, "is that mysterious magnetism which slumbers in the bosom of every young son and daughter of Adam! Gentle and beautiful to see, yet as perilous as the terrible bolt of heaven!"

And from this moment, a new, undefined distress on her account came over me; and we walked on again in a pensive silence which I dreaded to break, though I desired as much as I feared to hear the words that were to come.

"Sister and I," she at last began, "did, as you will imagine, all that lay in our power to make our home look attractive and the luncheon pleasing to the stranger. We made everything as neat as wax within; and outside, not a little polishing was done.

"The space in front, around the pens and stable, was carefully cleared; the litter was piled in the best manner; every loose stone and stick, every tall weed and thistle on the way from the house to the road, was taken away; here and there an overhanging bough of the larch and chestnut trees was lopped off; and the footpath was swept.

"With our busy preparations and our busier thoughts the week wore away. At last the day of days arrived. The expected would appear. Would our fancies be verified? Would our trembling hopes be realized?

"We were up and at work before the light. Bread of wheaten flour was baked; cheese of the nicest was brought out; apples of the fairest were selected; the largest hazel-nuts were cracked; the brightest chestnuts were boiled; a foaming pitcher of goats' milk was set in the window of the mountain-ward pantry to cool.

"The table was covered with snow-white linen which dear Mother spun and wove while she and *Babbo* were only *promessi*. The bright knives she brought from France were laid beside her wedding plates. The silver spoons which were also a part of her dowry glittered near the various dishes. A flower-vase in the form of a group of S. S. *Maria* and *Martha* sitting at the feet of the Saviour (a copy of a marble in the *Uffizi* Gallery), cut in alabaster, which *Babbo* bought of a traveling artist from *Firenze* and gave to our Mother the year we were born, stood as a center-piece, and was filled with fresh flowers from our window-boxes; for the frosts had already begun outside. From the same source also we filled the vase of our Lady in her little chapel on the opposite side of the highway, as *Babbo* had promised, and before noon all was waiting-ready.

"*Babbo*, who helped us in everything, usually so calm and silent, was that day strangely excited. Could it all be caused by the not quite certain prospect of buying a new dog? Would it have been the same, if the dog had belonged to a different owner?—perhaps an old and married mountaineer?—or if *Babbo* were not the father of two marriageable daughters with hearts yet free?

"True, he said little, as was natural for him, but he bustled around in a way that was most uncommon. There seemed also to be a new expression on his face, which was able, we thought, to mean much or little. We could not decide what it meant, but neither *Maria* nor I thought it boded any ill. He did not appear worried. On the contrary, he seemed pleased with his own thoughts, and much of the time to be lost in a gentle reverie.

"But what was he thinking of?—what was it that so fixedly and not unpleasantly absorbed his meditations? We spoke of it to each other, but did not suggest any answer to one another, though perhaps the heart of each whispered a possible answer to herself. *Maria's* countenance looked to me wondrous wistful that morning, and it may be mine looked the same to her. Who could tell? 'Ah, the dear girl!' I said to myself, 'how truly and how much we all live alone in this world — even in the midst of our closest intimacies!'

"Soon after midday *Babbo* put on his Sunday clothes and sat in the shade of the great chestnut tree at the roadside, and Sister and I scampered up to our chamber to put ourselves in the best order we could. We braided and tied our hair with ribbons — *Maria* with blue, I with pink. We had silver combs which were quite the same to look at, but Sister's was far more precious to us, because it had been dear Mother's. It had been an heirloom of the eldest daughter for I do n't know how many generations. The other was a gift, we never certainly knew by whom.

"Some months before dear Mother left us, an unknown gentleman overtaken in a storm, had begged a lodging and had been entertained as best we could in our home. Sister and I gave up our chamber to him. During the evening we had playfully bantered each other which of us would get married first in order to be dowered with Mother's silver comb which happened to be lying on the table. The gentleman took up the comb and examined it; and when he laid it down, he looked at us with a curious smile, but said nothing. Who he was or where he lived, we

never knew ; but not many weeks afterward, it
was the next Christmas Eve, a match to the heirloom comb came with the post, and we guessed,
but this was all we knew. After dear Mother
was gone, by *Babbo's* wish we drew lots, and the
stranger comb fell to me. So the dower was
ready for each, but, alas, was never needed.

"We put our best gowns on, which were of the
same purplish-gray woolen cloth, cut alike and
not distinguished from each other, except by the
rosettes at the top of the bodice in front *Maria's*
was blue, mine of a pale rose color." Putting her
hand to her neck, and lifting the white kerchief
that was pinned at the bosom with a silver brooch,
she added, "I wore this pink rosary and sister one
of blue. *Babbo* gave us these the day we were
confirmed.

"Of course, each of us tried to make herself
look as agreeable, and to say the truth, as desira-
ble, as possible ; and we honestly tried to help
each other do it. It was a competition — certainly an unselfish competition, if there is such
a thing — and in our girlish hearts we hoped —
I do n't know what we hoped — and then we
descended together and sat down at the window, knitting and eagerly looking for the coming of the expected visitor.

"Needles rattled, tongues chattered, stockings

grew, but no visitor came. *Babbo* rose from his seat many times, walked a piece up the road, straining his sight in the direction of the *Hospice*, and returning sat down again to wait as before.

"After a time, enforced idleness became unendurable to *Babbo*. He pulled from his pocket a roll of strands cut from the tanned skin of a polecat, and having fastened one end to the rough bark of the tree, he began to braid them into the lash of a mule-whip. He worked on excitedly, his arms twitched nervously, and the work grew apace. He did not once look up, neither along the road, nor toward the house.

"At last our balls of yarn became small, our stockings became large, and *Babbo's* lash was finished, but no visitor appeared. *Babbo* trimmed the ends of the strands, cut his work loose from the tree, rolled and rubbed it smooth, and folded and put it in his pocket. The shadows were already growing long. The slanting sun was glistening across the *Tête Noire* upon the white top of *Mons Buet* and reddening the *Aiguilles* about *Mont Blanc*. *Babbo* started up with a spring and came briskly toward the house, with his eyes on the ground as if in deep meditation.

"As he burst open the door he exclaimed : 'Well, girls, we have been finely fooled. I don't even know his name — the slippery rogue. It may be a good joke for him. It will be a nice piece of fun, to make merry over with his comrades. But I would n't have believed it of him. I would have trusted him a hundred times as much. He seemed such a frank and earnest lad. Besides, there was just a little sadness in his manner, that made one pity and be the more ready to believe him. But — but — the Old Scratch is always ready to steal the other livery to do his own pranks in.'

"I had often heard of the practical jokes — sometimes very serious, indeed, — played by the Lombard travelers in their journeys on country-men and on one another, so that my intellect supported the suspicions of *Babbo*. But my heart, all the same, revolted against the thought. I could n't allow the pleasant pictures of my fancy to be so pitilessly wiped out — worst of all that my profoundest sentiments and serious interests should be turned into a comedy so ridiculous.

"'Is n't it possible, *Babbo* dear,' I said (for I must find some reply), 'is n't it possible that you mistook the day?'

—'I thought of that,' he said, but no, it is n't possible. The young fellow said to me plainly, "This is Tuesday *la festa della Natività della Beata Maria* [the feast of the Nativity of the B. V.].

Next week Thursday I shall be here again. That will be the *festa della Sacre Stimmate* [feast of the Imprinting of the Wounds of Our Lord on the body of S. Francis].[16] I am to bring here some special wine, as the Bishop of *Aosta* and the Prior of *St. Orso* are to visit the *Hospice* on that day. I shall get here the night before. On the day of the *Stimmate* I shall go to *Martigny*." Is n't it Thursday to-day, and is n't it the feast of the *Sacre Stimmate?* Did n't the priest say so, at Mass, last Sunday? How can there, then, be any mistake about the time?'

"I was silenced in that direction. 'But,' I persisted, ' he may be sick.'

—'I don't think so,' he replied, 'for the promised wine must be sent, in that case, by another; and if he were an honorable youth, the other would be required to stop on his way and inform us.'

—'The other may have forgotten it,' I still insisted.

—'That can't be,' he said, 'for I have sentinelled the road since eleven o'clock, and no such person has passed.'

—'Why, *Babbo* dear,' I replied, '*Maria* and I saw several parties go by, though we were too far away to distinguish who they were.'

—'To be sure,' he answered, 'two companies of English travelers with mules and guide went toward *Martigny* before I came in to dress, and three German men and a *Fraülein* went by together on foot toward the *Hospice* while I was sitting by the roadside.'

—'Could n't something have escaped you while you were dressing?'

—'*Sicuro no!* for besides that I have kept a constant watch with ears and eyes, I have examined the road for tracks. There are none, except those of the Englishman's party going toward *Martigny*.'

" This was unanswerable; and we stood awhile in silence around the hearth, looking at the smoking embers. At last *Maria*, who had n't spoken, though her cheeks were ablaze, and her soft, dark eyes, swimming with vexation and anxiety, had been lifted and fixed on me while I was pleading for the young man, but were now again staring into the embers, murmured almost in a whisper and without moving her eyes from the fire:

—'Could n't he have fallen into the water at the *Liddes'* bridge?—the flood, you know, about two days ago, might—'

—'*Mon dieu!*' I screamed, 'I had n't thought of that—he might!—he might!—'

—'Peace, child!' said *Babbo*, firmly. 'Of course, it 's possible, but the water there is n't above a *metro* deep — except, may be, in the holes and eddies — and he is an uncommon large, strong youth — though the mule might — yes, he might slip on the smooth stones, or catch his hoof between the rocks — one way and another, he might stumble and fall on his rider, and the load might come uppermost of all — *certo, certo*, the young fellow's head might — *sicuro*, it might strike one of those sharp rocks — and then to be sure, even at this season, he might get benumbed by the wetting — so near the glaciers of *Monte Velano* — the water there must be cool — yes, *Maria*, it is possible — the more I think of it, the more possible — I do n't know but I might say the more likely it seems.'

"The fact was, and we knew it well, though till then it had made no impression upon us, that two days before this it had rained for a day and a night and the melted snow had swollen the streams into torrents, and had carried away the bridge, about a half hour beyond our home."

The peculiar danger of this place at this time was (as my fair companion explained), that, in building the bridge, in order to meet squarely a bend in the channel, and to secure rocky buttresses at each end, the structure had been placed by its whole breadth up the stream-from the line of the beaten track of the road ; and during the drier parts of the summer, when the stream was low, only foot-passengers turned to go over the bridge, while all vehicles and animals went straight across by the ford.

The worn track, therefore, led directly down to the water on either side, and the stream spread out so wide there, and the banks had so gentle a slope, that it was sure to appear to a stranger, even when swollen to the highest, to be a safe and constantly-used ford, though it was, at such times, exceedingly dangerous, both on account of the jagged rocks at the bottom, and because of several deep fissures or pits just below the traveled path.

"As soon as all this occurred to our thoughts," she continued, "we all admitted the danger, and felt alarmed for the safety of our delaying guest. A moment of silence followed, during which we all mechanically strayed toward the window which looks up the road in the direction of the bridge, and *Babbo* repeated with much emphasis:

—'You are right, *Maria* — it is possible — it is possible.'

—'Could n't you? — could n't you go? — and — and see? — *Babbo* dear — before — before dark?' *Maria* stammered out, softly.

—'Yes, yes, *Babbo*, do,' I eagerly blurted in, 'do take —'

"But while I was speaking, *Babbo* suddenly laid one hand on my shoulder, and, with the other pointing up the road where, making a sharp turn, the track first comes into view, interrupted me with :

—'There!—there!—he's coming now, I do believe.'

"We looked and saw something coming, but the distance was too great clearly to distinguish what it was.

—'He can't get to *Martigny* to-night,' *Maria* whispered.

—'We can give him our chamber,' I added.

—'Hush, hush! girls,' *Babbo* exclaimed at that moment, '*Dio in cielo!* what is this?'

"At that instant we began to distinguish a man walking towards us at the top of his speed. As he came nearer, we could see that he carried his broad-brimmed hat in one hand, which he was swinging in great circles through the air, and with the other hand was making a huge walking-stick take three league strides along the path, while his unbuttoned coat sailed out behind him in the stiff breeze he was partly facing. A minute later, *Babbo* recognized the figure, and saying ''Tis one of the German men who passed here since noon,' hurried out of the house and down the footpath to the road, followed by us both.

"We were hardly arrived on the margin of the highway, when the stranger, fifty *metri* away, without any salutation, and panting heavily, jerked out to us:

—'*Es gibt — ein — unglüchlicher — Zufall — zu der Brücke*' [there's an accident at the bridge]—

"At this verification of our foreboding conjectures, our hearts rose into our throats. The truth was flashed upon us, and for the moment we were too dazed to speak.

—'*Sie müssen — fort — und Ihr Maulthier — mit*' [you must go there with your mule], he continued, in pushing past us, not waiting for permission or reply, making for the stable to get the mule.

"We all hurried back with him in silence, and amidst his frantic pantomime, harnessed and led out *Nicodemo*, our oldest mule, and driving him on before us, started with the stranger rapidly up the road.

"Walking on every side of him, pell-mell, we soon began to shower upon him answerable and unanswerable questions, while he was ever and anon goading and slapping the poor *Maulthier*, and himself puffing so powerfully that we made out nothing at first from his talk. By degrees he became more composed, and at last gave us an intelligent story. Of course, like every *Tedeseo*, he lingered on unnecessary details, while we were frantic to hear two or three important words.

"He and his companions, on arriving at the bridge, found it carried away. A temporary structure for crossing was in sight. But, since the passage for travel opened up to it was by a *détour* around a considerable bend in the stream, through a fir forest on a rather steep acclivity, it became a matter of some hindrance and difficulty to reach it.

"Accordingly, they went to the buttresses of the old bridge, hoping to find some way by which foot-passengers, at least, might get over without taking the long circuit on the hillside. While standing there, looking up and down the stream, one of the party observed something whirling in a frothy eddy and held from going down-stream by the stones and bushes on the lower side. Alarm was given. With much difficulty, being a heavy object and lying nearer the farther bank, it was at last pulled upon dry ground. It proved to be a case of Mantuan '*Rosolio*.'" The case was marked *Luigi Donati*. This name in itself meant nothing to us, for we had not heard it before. Nevertheless, it startled us and seemed to clinch our gravest fears. Searching now further down the bank, another similar case was found, and with it a piece of the strap by which it had been hung over the back of the beast.

"Curiosity now gave place to alarm. Searching up and down the stream, and shouting to one another from time to time, as some new sign appeared, or some new thought was suggested, a rustling was heard in the twigs at some distance from the bank.

"Thinking the owner of the wine had now been found — and possibly in some sorry plight — the men left the *Fraülein* below with the cases, and clambered up the hillside in the direction of the noise. Coming to an eminence which looked down into a little ravine, they saw a mule below them grazing. The beast was covered from head to haunch and from haunch to hoof with dried mud. It was plain that he had been drenched in the stream and had rolled himself in the dust of the road-track. But where was the rider, or rather the driver? — for the mule had been fully loaded.

—'We had n't suspected before,' said the man, 'that any really serious accident had happened — I mean,' he added, 'that it was a matter of life and death —'

—'*Mein Gott!*' I shrieked, '*ist er nun todt?*' *Maria*, meantime, sobbed and moaned softly.

—'I didn't say he was *todt'* [dead], continued the man, 'but the mule was all we found there—'

—'*San Martino!*' I exclaimed, 'you did n't give it up so!—'

—''*Scht! Kindlein*' [baby], said the man, gruffly, I was going to tell you that we went off searching again, *Fraülein* and all, looking everywhere, pushing into the bushes, and peering into every nook. Suddenly the *Fraülein* said :

'*Stille, stille!—ich bilde mir ein dass ich ein stöhnen gehört habe*' [I think I heard a groan].

'Then we all came close to her and listened for the groaning she fancied she had heard. But we heard nothing save the rushing of the water and a soft roaring of the wind in the tops of the fir-trees. Suddenly she cried out again :

'*Ja, ja! noch einmal habe ich es gehört*' [Yes, yes! I heard it again]. Still, neither of us men could distinguish anything of the kind. Presently she almost screamed :

'*Ja wohl, ja wohl, noch einmal!—Da geht es!— Es tönt drüben!*' [Yes, indeed, there it goes again over there], and pointing in a direction further back from the stream, she began to run thither.

"Then the man went on to describe how they all followed the *Fraülein* up a knoll sparsely set with mountain oaks and with many large bowlders lying around. Presently they all could distinctly hear a feeble groaning, but no one could tell exactly from whence it came. Sometimes it seemed to come from the tree-tops, and they went straining their sight up into the thick boughs, in vain. Again they were sure it came from among the rocks, and finally with this conviction they separated, each undertaking separately one part of the knoll to search thoroughly.

'It was not long,' said the man, 'before I heard the groans growing nearer and clearer at every step. I now felt sure of the game. Pressing on almost in a certainty of presently making the great discovery, I came to a very large bowlder. It was almost a cliff. Here the sounds died wholly away. I seemed to have approached and to be very near to the spot whence the sounds proceeded, but it was not apparent how I could approach nearer and I was perplexed.

'The rock on the side where I approached it was precipitous. The two faces on either hand slanted gradually to the ground, so that although the flattened top was very high, it could all be seen from a little distance away; and surely there was no hiding-place upon it. The rear, however, that is to say, the side most distant from where I stood, seemed to project far over like a shelf, but the ground in that direction was so steep and broken that I could not approach it directly. I retraced my steps, therefore, a considerable piece, and in making the necessary circuit, I fell in with a well-worn sheep-path which ran winding along in the direction I was seeking to go. Following this track, the sounds were soon renewed, and the growing distinctness of them convinced me that I was coming near the object of my search. As I turned a corner of the projecting rock, I saw in another minute that the groans did not proceed from a human voice —'

—'*Himmel sei Dank!—es ist ein verwundener wolf gewesen*' [Thank heaven! 'twas a wounded wolf], broke in our *Babbo*. 'How many times I've been cheated so by one of these wounded villains. These beasts will imitate the groans of a man to perfection. I've thought, then, may be 't was the soul of some scoundrel whom even DANTE did n't tell of. May be they hunted and worried the sheep of the Great Shepherd and have been put into the bodies of the beasts they imitated before they are shut down in the *Inferno*,— but did you kill him? — did you slay the rascal?'

"You may wonder how *Babbo* could so easily forget the anxious errand we were on and become so interested in the matter of a wounded wolf. The fact is, that there is nothing like the name or thought of a wolf — the cruel and ever-pursuing foe of the defenceless creatures his whole life is given up to feeding and protecting —no other idea which sets him so beside himself with fear and rage, as the bare suspicion that there may be a sheep-slayer, or a gang of them abroad in the neighborhood.

—'*Was für ein Wolf ist es ?*' [what wolf] rejoined the man, impatiently. 'What have I said about a wolf? I saw just before me a huge, shaggy, grizzly-white dog, lying with his head on his fore paws and groaning like a dying man.

'Just back of the dog, under the overhanging rock, the wind had piled deep windrows of leaves. Roused by the noise of my steps, the dog lifted his head, glared on me for an instant, then with a tremulous yell bounded over the windrows to the further end of the chasm ; then, throwing his head back upon his shoulder towards me, stood stark as a statue with nose pointed to the sky, emitting a swift stream of mournful, piercing notes that ran irregularly up and down to the extreme limits of the canine gamut.

'I had no longer any doubt that I had found the master, and I at once gave a shout that was answered by my companions, and ran to the dog, who with paws and snout was swiftly opening a windrow of leaves, which flew high about him in the wind, and ere I arrived where he stood, he had uncovered a man's body —'

—'Was he alive?—does he still live?' we all broke in together.

"Disregarding our queries, the man went right on: 'His eyes were closed and we could n't by word or touch get any sign of consciousness from him—'

—'Was he really already dead?—were you sure?—did you try?' we all broke in again together, but he went on regardless:

—'The body was still warm'—we interjecting:

—'Did n't he breathe?—did his heart beat?—'

"But the man quietly continued:

—'And we could n't certainly tell, but we thought he breathed very, very gently, and I was sure I felt a soft throbbing in his breast—'

—'*Himmel sei Dank!*' softly sighed *Marie* and I, while *Babbo* almost screamed:

—'*Aquavite!—Eau de vie!—Branntwein!*' or did n't you have any along?'

"The imperturbable German, without trying to answer our questions, or even seeming to notice our interruptions, proceeded:

—'The *Fraülein* was sent back to the luggage —that is, the knapsacks which we slipped off and left at the bridge—and charged to open and bring whatever she thought would be useful for the sufferer.

'We men carried the body quickly into a sunny nook among the rocks and laid it on the soft, warm sod. We stripped it of the wet clothing, and without waiting an instant for anything else, we swiftly set about drying it with our kerchiefs and chafing it with our woolen blouses; and as soon as the *Fraülein* returned with supplies, we wrapped it in a traveling blanket, put a spoonful of brandy into the mouth, put plasters on the bruises, and tied up with a kerchief the battered face.

'The greatest difficulty of all now stared us in the face — how to replace the soaked and muddy clothing with sufficient covering warm and dry. Neither of us had any extra clothing in our packs. We dared not carry the body merely wrapped as it was into the chilly wind that swept along the traveled road-track. There was no house within an hour's time going and returning. The slanting sun of the late afternoon warned us that whatever was done must be done quickly.

'While we were holding an anxious consultation, without saying a word, the *Fraülein* disappeared and in five minutes returned, waving in her hand a blue flannel petticoat, and saying, as she laid it at the feet of the body, "Could n't this be used in some way?" She presently added, "I have a warm hood in my pack," and again disappeared in the direction of the luggage.

'We men took a hint from her example; and before she returned, the patient was wearing an underwrapper and a cardigan with stockings and long, knitted leggins, contributed partly by my companion and partly by me. The petticoat was afterward put on and the blanket pinned tightly about from shoulders to feet. The *Fraülein's* hood was soon added, and the whole burden and outfit was laid on a bed of fir-boughs, with a bundle of twigs for a pillow.

'This extemporized hospital was put in charge of the *Fraülein*, with brandy and water to put a spoonful from time to time to the lips. It remained to gather up the scattered and broken parts of the harness, to make an ambulance of boughs, and put the demoralized mule in order for renewing the march. This I left *Dietrich* to do, and started after the first man and mule to be found for moving the poor fellow to some shelter.'

" After a moment's pause, while we were silent in the first shock of doubt, he added :

—'He'll need it, too —*ja wohl* [yes, indeed]— God knows how long —if ever he pulls through at all —which heaven grant he may.'

—'He must —he must be brought —to our home,' said *Maria*, softly, and with a little hesitation. I had thought the same, yet hesitated to say so, and *Babbo* now added with great emphasis :

—'Yes, surely, he must come to us.'

—'*Maria* and I, then,' I said, 'had better turn back now — for why should we go further — and get things ready there.'

—'*Ja, ja*, that's a prudent *Fraülein*,' said the man.

"Turning to *Babbo*, I asked : 'Put him in the *Salotto* [reception-room], I suppose?' This rather grand name we gave in playful irony to the tiny sitting-room directly under our bedroom.

—'*Sicuro, sicuro*,' said *Babbo*, 'where else? Bring down the cot from the garret and your blessed *Mamma's* French rocker from your chamber. You won't need it there while he is with us.'

—'Nor will he need it much below, I fancy, for some while yet,' I said.

—'But watchers may,' he replied.

"As we started to return, *Maria*, looking over her shoulder, said :

—'Where is the dog?'

"Her soft voice was n't heard, and I repeated the question :

—'Where is the dog?'

—'He'll be with his master, you may depend,' replied the man, throwing the answer over his shoulder after us, for we were already twenty steps away, and he and *Babbo* were swiftly hurrying on with the mule.

"We held it now for a certainty who the wounded master must be, and our hearts were full of conflicting emotions, but the matter even then was too sacred to each of us, even us sisters, to talk of ; nor had a word been said to the man, of our relations with the youth or his dog."

LEONCELLO DA MENTOVA.

XV.

"God hath chosen the things that are not to bring to naught things that are."   BIBLE.

"DISREGARDING, for this once, the hasty injunction of *Babbo* about the cot, after some deliberation we brought, instead, from our eyry-chamber in the roof, the bed on which *Maria* and I slept, and put it in order in the *Salotto* below. We had our own reasons for this which we deemed imperative.

"This bedstead was a beauty and had a history. It had once stood for many years in the *Salotto* with a small bureau and a little table. All were of beautifully figured French-walnut. A large ebony-framed mirror hung on the wall opposite to where we now placed the bed. All these elegant pieces came to my grandfather in a mysterious way which has never yet been fully explained.

"About the time the French King and Queen were murdered, an unknown gentleman came and lived for more than a year in that room with a glorious lady who was his wife. They came without any servant, and arrived in the evening after it was dark.

"The gentleman had plenty of gold in his pockets, and the lady many jewels. The furniture came as mysteriously as the persons. One morning when my *nonnino* [grandpapa] first opened the door to go to the flocks, these articles and some others were standing there on the sod.

"These gentle guests revealed nothing whatever about themselves. So far as was known, they wrote no letters, nor received any; and they never went abroad, except into the mountain glens on pleasant days. It has been fancied that the place was chosen both on account of its remoteness and because it was so near the frontiers of three nations. But why they needed to be hid was never known.

"At last, one morning in autumn, a messenger on horseback, in the uniform of a French officer of high grade, came with a letter and a packet. There came with him also a servant in a livery of black and silver, a pair of gray nuns in a covered *char*, and an empty-saddled horse caparisoned with the accoutrements of a general officer.

"Very quickly the great lady entered the *char* with the sisters, the man-servant sprang to his seat beside the driver, the gentleman and the officer mounted and rode behind. In this fashion the company started away, leaving everything behind them and never returned, nor were ever seen or heard of afterwards.

"The lady when she said '*adieu*' handed to our grandmother a little casket containing two rings, one set with a rose-colored stone, the other with a stone sky-blue. When *Maria* and I were born, after so many years, these rings remained still in the house, and, as they were going to be ours, dear Mamma chose these colors for her new-born babies—pink for me, and azure for *Maria*. When we were christened one of these rings was hung about the neck of each with a thread of the same color, and was christened with us. On the Sunday of our first Communion they were given to us for our own and we wore them on our fingers for the first time at the supper that evening and afterwards kept them preciously among our treasures.

"Among the pieces of furniture left by the strange gentleman and lady, besides a willow easy-chair in which the former slept, since, having a difficulty of breathing, he never lay down, and the lady's elegant French-walnut bedstead, curiously carved, there was a large picture painted by the gentleman at intervals during his stay and not wholly finished.

"It was a night scene. Far away on one side were the tents and banners of an army, partly hidden behind the hills. On the other side was a lake at the foot of a precipitous mountain. The moon, near her setting behind the mountain and just emerging from a dark cloud, threw across the whole foreground the shadows of two figures which were themselves hid behind the brow of the mountain.

"One of these was clad in mail from head to foot and had on a helmet with a plume. He stood very straight with arms folded across his breast and scowled under his deep eyebrows. The other who was speaking to him wore no hat nor shoes; and was scantily clad in a sort of sleeveless shirt, with something like a blanket wrapped carelessly about him. His hair and beard were shaggy and long, and blown out roughly in the gusty wind.

"We children, who from infancy well knew that our destiny as well as our name was shadowy and enveloped in shadows,—though we never could guess the gentleman's meaning in the picture — used often to stand gazing in silence before it, folded in each other's arms, and absorbed in our dreamy thoughts till our hearts would palpitate audibly, and not seldom tears would roll across our cheeks, while the real cause of these sentiments was as indistinct and uncertain to us as the shadows themselves.

"On the margin below the picture the gentleman had also written its name, or motto in English, the sentiment of which — having been explained to us by a visiting *padre* — exercised our hearts not less than the picture itself. We learned it by heart, and often discussed its meaning with one another. It was: '*Coming events cast their shadows before.*' Now we somehow connected, though very indistinctly, that past mystery with the coming one.

"We dressed the bed with the snow-white linen which our blessed Mother spun and wove during her young maidenhood before she came to visit our home, in her 'warm and beautiful France,' and brought to *Babbo* with her *dot*. We covered all with her famous figured counterpane.

"This counterpane was a curious thing which we held above all price. It was covered with scenes in the Siege of *Firenze*" and the other wars of the *Medici ;* views in old *Siena*" with her she-wolf-surmounted pillars and fountains, her black and white *Duomo*, her gorgeous annual *Palio*, the *Mangia* and the *Fontebranda*. *Babbo* bought it for dear Mother in the Fair at *Aosta* and brought it to her on their tenth wedding day. These things were all kept in the carved oaken chest in which they came with the other articles of her *dot*. This chest served for a seat in the eyry-chamber near our bed.

"As you may well suppose, the *Salotto* was a dear room to us, for all these memories and treasures. Here too *Maria* and I were born. Here dear Mother died. We had now kindled a blaze of fir-wood in the little fireplace. The tiny room looked lovely; and the fragrant fir-wood gave out an agreeable odor. All this cheered our spirits a little; but, alas, it was quite lost on the coming occupant of the room.

"The last rays of the setting sun were glistening on the peaks of the highest *Aiguilles* and the stars were already beginning to twinkle over the valley, when *Maria*, after having gone down to the road for the twentieth time, came running back and called to me, in her soft, sweet way:

—'They're coming *M'amie*, sure, they're coming now.'

"We both ran down to the road. Dark objects could be seen approaching over the brow of the hill. We did not go toward them, nor speak a word, but our hearts beat audibly, and we held each other by the hand and trembled in every limb.

"Presently, as the path wound along the hillside, we could distinguish *Babbo* by his hat and his gait, moving slowly along holding a bridle-rein. Two mules followed—one a long distance behind the other—with some kind of a cradle or litter swung between them. A large dog paced solemnly at the heels of the last mule. But neither Germans nor *Fraülein* appeared.

" *Maria* and I stood in silence till the cavalcade was within a few paces of our gate. Then without unclasping our hands we turned and led the procession up to our door.

CASA OMBROSINI.

XVI.

<blockquote>
" We will play no more, beautiful Shadows !
A fancy came solemn and sad,
More sweet, with unspeakable longings,
Than the best of the pleasures we had."
EDWIN ARNOLD. *Indian Song of Songs.*
</blockquote>

" WE three lowered the litter gently, gently to the ground, and lifting the body upon a sheet, *Maria* and I grasping each a corner, supporting the head, and *Babbo* the two at the feet, we laid the unconscious form, wrapped like a mummy, upon the bed.

" We proceeded immediately to undo the wrappings. Softly and silently we set ourselves at work in indescribable anxiety. Was he still living? We lifted the blue kerchief which had been laid over the face. There was the bandaged head done up in white kerchiefs. The eyes were closed. Some drops of sweat stood on the cold forehead. *Babbo* bent his ear to the breast. The heart was beating very, very softly. He touched the folded hands. The skin was warm. He felt the wrist and found a gentle, irregular pulse.

We administered brandy immediately and saw the chest rise and fall in respiration.

"We were all thoroughly exhausted, physically and mentally, yet thankful to be so far relieved from the strain of a terrible fear. But for me there was another shock awaiting far more shattering than anything I had met before. In the next few moments that prophetic shadow, which had followed me from infancy, must rise before me again, like a ghost from the *Inferno*. Alas! why must I, by this unwilling and unavailing presentiment, twice drink each bitter cup of my destiny!

"After we had arranged the patient in the bed as best we could, I went to stand for a moment in front of the fire. I laid my hand caressingly on the head of the great dog who had come into the room unbidden and unregarded, and seated himself at the further end of the hearth. He neither resented nor welcomed my caresses, turning his head every few seconds to and fro, seeming to be dividing a thoughtful regard between the merrily dancing blaze and the sad bed whereon his master was stretched.

"Presently I fancied that the dog looked more frequently and wistfully toward the bed. My back was turned in that direction, but accidentally lifting my eyes toward the mirror, I caught a sight which shot through my breast like a stream of fire.

"*Maria* was sitting at the bedside half-turned toward the fire. The jolly blaze, as if in grim mockery, was casting her shadow with that of the young man upon the opposite wall together. The mirror reflected the picture with an exaggerated glamour upon my horror-stricken sight. I shudder still at every recollection of her trembling profile resting upon the shivering shadow of his bandaged head. The fire in my bosom suddenly changed to a mountain of ice. A strange chill crept around my heart of hearts. I went immediately out of the room and endeavored ——"

Here the voice of my companion faltered and the shoes dropped at her feet. I saw that her face was deathly pale, and that she was beginning to fall. I seized and guided, or rather carried her to the roadside and supported her drooping head upon the grassy bank. In another instant I had filled my traveler's cup from the little stream at our side, and applied the icy water to her temples. The faintness was short. Her eyes soon opened; and raising herself into a more convenient posture, she said:

"Alas! I ought not to have spoken of this. Sometimes the thought of it makes me faint. But you will easily believe now—however it came about—that we are rightly named *Ombrosini*. It is not true, however, that all our family have had as much to do with shadows as I; nor that their business with them has always been as uncanny as mine.

"But are you not willing to believe, *Signor*, that our holy Mother, the Church, cares for us, her children, in this world as well as in the next? Are you not willing to believe that she works before us and upon us her perpetual miracles, and teaches us to see through the thin veil and recognize much that is going on in the world of spirits? But ah, *Signor*, do you Protestants, so rich and so learned, really believe in any supernatural world at all? For my part, I would die sooner than come to that—yes, sooner than flee from her protecting shadow. But stop. I am not trying to convert you to religion, but to give you a story.

"When I fled, unable to bear it, from the scene I have described, I continued saying to myself, notwithstanding, 'What can there be fearful in the shadow of a shadow?' But my only relief came in occupation and in other cares; and, happily, these were plain and pressing.

"On entering the common room, my first duty stared in my face. That table set out with so much anxiety and anticipation in the morning was now to be put away untouched. It was a gloomy task — that replacing by a pine torch-light those plates and bright knives — that re-folding of the white table-cloth and returning it to the dowry-chest in the loft — that removing of the uncut cheese and bread and apples and nuts, and storing them back in their places. In some circumstances, this would have been a pleasure, but doing it now, not as in the morning, thinking pleasant thoughts, and chatting gaily with *Maria*, but in silence and alone, and with that hideous shadow-picture, which I could not banish, hanging continually before my fancy — and — and *Maria*, dear *Maria* sitting at the bedside!

"When all was cleared away, I did not return to the sick room, but built a new fire and was busied for an hour or more in preparing the family supper. *Maria* refused to leave the young man alone, — though there was then really nothing to be done for him — or to allow me to take her place at the bedside.

"So *Babbo* and I sat down without her at the table; and *Babbo* then said that the cases of wine appeared to be unhurt, and he should carry them to *Martigny* in the morning; and he should, he believed, be able to bring back a surgeon, since there would surely be found more than one among the pleasure-and-health-seeking travelers who passed through there every day; and if not, on his return he would go over to *Aosta* and get one of the city surgeons from there.

—'*Ma Babbo caro*' [but Papa dear], I said, 'how can we bear the cost of that?'

—'In every way,' he replied, 'it must be done. But five *lire*, I think, will be ample from *Martigny* and ten from *Aosta*; and the wine (not to speak of my service in forwarding and delivering), will be worth fifty.'

"He looked thoughtful a moment, then he smote the table with his fist and exclaimed, as he rose:

—'There, there! by *San Martino!*— how strange I should have forgotten it — the young man told me, when we met at the *Hospice*, that he had an appointment to meet there to-day, yes, this very day, an Italian surgeon, *Dr. Carlo Ferrenti*, a distinguished *alunno* of the University of *Siena*, his own maternal uncle, who was at present attached to the household of the *Conte Crocini di Montepulciano* who had a palace in *Siena*, where he had by accident become acquainted with the young student, admired his talents, fallen in love with the qualities of his heart, and remained his friend and patron.

'This nobleman had been soaking for some months at the *Leukerbad*, and was now on his way to the hotter and stronger waters of *Aix-la-*

Chapelle. The party would be stopping for a week at the *Hôtel de la Poste*, because suitable accommodations could not be engaged with so short notice at *la Tour*. The wine was for the use of this nobleman by special prescription.'

"A very early breakfast was arranged and *Babbo* assumed the charge of the invalid for the night. After esconcing *Babbo* in the great willow-sleeper at the bedside, *Maria* and I made ourselves a bed in our own loft-chamber, and soon locked in each other's arms, both, as each believed of the other, fell asleep. But for me it was only snatches of unconsciousness and the night was filled with waking dreams, built of possibilities and impossibilities, pleasing and painful, which sometimes brought an involuntary smile to my lips, sometimes sent a cold shiver streaming over my whole body.

"Not long after midnight I awoke from a troubled slumber. The Moon, in her last quarter, hanging over *Monte Velano*, was pouring a flood of silver light through the room. I looked for *Maria*. She was gone. I sprang from the bed. Turning in the direction of the casement, I saw her, partly enveloped by a bed coverlet, reclining in an armchair near the dower-chest on which her feet were laid. Her head was leaned back upon a pillow, and she was soundly sleeping.

"It was a lovely sight. Her unbound hair streamed over the snowy pillow. Her deeply exposed bosom rose and fell with her slow and silent breathing. Involuntarily I stooped and softly, softly kissed her smooth, fair brow. Lifting my eyes, the next instant, I saw her beautiful profile clearly drawn on the opposite wall. But, under the pale, quivering sheen of the moonlight, growing every moment more faint and dim, as the sinking luminary approached nearer and nearer the horizon, and in the deep stillness, broken only by the soft *basso* of the mountain cascades, the sight fell on my excited fancy as another prophetic shadow of helplessness, disappointment, despair.

" Fearing on many accounts to leave her sleeping in that exposed and insecure position — which I had reason to believe, from her previous habits, she had taken in a somnambulistic state,— I led her gently back to the bed without awaking her; and soon myself fell asleep again.

"After another uncertain period of disturbed and unrestful slumber, I again awoke. Morning twilight had not yet begun. The Moon had set. The stars were shining in an unclouded sky. *Maria* was sleeping. I felt impelled to rise, and slipped softly from her side.

"As I passed our window, which looked toward

the west, I saw the Swan sailing down the Milky Way. Just below her left wing, ready to drop behind the *Col de Ferret*, glorious Lyra was shining so brightly across that snowy mountain top, as to throw a shadow — very faint, to be sure, yet a perceptible shadow of my loosely robed figure over my sleeping sister. The radiance of the constellations had brightened her countenance, and just the suggestion of a smile lay on her lips, as if she were in some pleasing dream, or, I thought, as if her spirit, while the body slept, were listening to the music of that celestial harp. But when the shadow of my form crossed her face, the smile disappeared; her brow was contracted, and it seemed to me that a spasm of anguish shot across her troubled countenance. I said to my trembling heart, 'Is this shadowy prophecy tripled upon her and upon me? What can it forbode? Is it that my destiny is fated to conflict with hers? Are the stars in the sky interested in us? — and informed, perhaps, of our future? — or is it true, as the story said, that there live our guardian angels?'"

XVII.

"Love is a pearl of purest hue,
But stormy waves are round it,
And dearly may a woman rue
The hour when first she found it."

MISS LANDON.

"AS the dawn was coming on, I crept silently down into the *Salotto*. The patient had so far improved during the night as to swallow readily, and *Babbo* was giving him, at frequent and regular intervals, milk and wine. There was a twitching about the eyes, though the lids were closed, a clenching and unclenching of the fingers, an uneasy working of the toes, and a low moaning which returned from time to time.

"*Babbo* now gave over the care of him to me; and proceeded to carry out his plan about the wine and the surgeon — expecting to have returned before mid-afternoon. *Maria* was to be out with the flocks — at that season, however, only during the few warmer hours of the day. *Velloso* [old shaggy], as from his shaggy coat, we then called the dog, not knowing his real name, would not go with her to the sheep, nor, in fact, could be persuaded for a moment to lose sight of the bed. If we attempted, however gently, to get him out of the room, he would growl horribly and gnash his teeth. When the moaning seasons came at intervals on the injured man, he would go and stand at the bedside looking now at his master, now up into the face of the watcher, whining piteously.

"*Maria*, having dispatched the indispensable duties of the household, departed with her charge up the mountain-side. Having been consoled by a good breakfast, *Velloso* stretched his great, shaggy body at full length on its side with extended legs before the smouldering fire. His suspicions now seemed to be quieted, his nervousness gone; and as I seated myself at the bedside, he seemed, as plainly as canine signs could express it, to entrust his master, without further scruple, to my care.

"After once and again repeating his survey of the surroundings, and appearing to find everything satisfactory, he laid his great head down on one of its ears, as for a secure and comfortable sleep, into which he presently fell.

"The door remained open into the larger common-room. All was still, except the ticking of the cuckoo-clock or its chirping out the hours, the loud breathing and occasional whine of the sleeping dog, and the heavy respirations and now and then the moans of the unconscious invalid.

"As the day wore on, the hours seemed to me to grow ever longer and longer. I became intensely lonely and at last alarmed — my companions an unknown, perhaps a dying man, and an unknown dog — the stillness, on which ever and anon rose the cawing of crows in the neighboring woods, the roaring of the wind through the treetops, the rattling of the autumnal gusts against the window-panes, and the moans at the crevices of the casements.

"My blood tingled and my heart palpitated with an undefined apprehension as I thought it must be another hour, perhaps more, before *Babbo* could arrive with the surgeon; and *Maria* certainly would not come till nearly nightfall. Who could tell what might any moment happen?

"It had been more than willingly that I assumed the duties of day-nurse. Nor was I, at first, alarmed or displeased at the thought of being left alone in the house with that responsible charge. I occupied the first hours agreeably enough, sitting with my sewing at the window, fulfilling from time to time the order about nourishment, now and again moving noiselessly about the room, replacing disorders, removing litter and dust, straightening the ever-gathering folds of the coverlet, smoothing out the wrinkles from the snowy linen, and returning to sew a little, but much more to gaze abstractedly up into the autumnal sky, where bright clouds were sailing swiftly along over the tops of the singing fir trees.

"Later in the day a strange thing happened to me, which, if it had not caused, greatly aggravated, my nervous distress and alarm. Several times, on returning to full self-consciousness from one of those musing abstractions, I had, with surprise, found myself standing at the bedside with a sort of pleased anxiety, gazing on the unconscious sufferer. I was alarmed and uneasy at it because I felt in my heart that, beyond my pity, which was really unselfish and keen, there was an attraction for me there which I could not extinguish, though I trembled while I was held fast in admiration of the noble form, the broad forehead, the gentle and lovely mouth — in short, a *tout ensemble* of manliness to ravish any maiden's heart.

"Oh, if I had had a mother then! — how I would have pillowed my head on her bosom and wept in silent relief! Nay, lone orphan as I was, how gladly would I have fled to our loft-chamber and buried my face in the pillows! But

I was pinioned and alone. I must stay. I dared not leave the room. At all hazards, I must regularly approach and administer the orders. At the price of his life, I must again and again direct my eyes where I should receive charge after charge of that mysterious magnetism which made me quiver in every fibre."

ALPINE SOLITUDE.

XVIII.

> " *Imogen.*
>   The dream's here still ; even when I awake, it is
>   Without me as within me ; . . . . . . "
>
> SHAK. CYMB. ACT IV, SC. 2.

AFTER a long silence, my companion resumed: "When I came to myself, I was on a cot in our loft chamber and partially bewildered. The surroundings were in general familiar enough, but the cot on which I lay, with head-and-footboards of polished walnut, certainly was not. There was also a stand of the same material, a rocker and a footstool which I had never seen before. These, as I afterwards learned, had been sent by the surgeon from *Martigny.*

"Although free from pain, my strength was gone. It was only with the utmost exertion of will that I could lift my hand to my head. I wondered what had happened to me. Gradually I gathered some scattered memories, but these were so faint and uncertain that I doubted whether they were facts or impressions of a dream. Excepting these, the intervening space was a void; nor, if these few memories had a reality behind them, could I tell whether they belonged to a day or a month or a year ago. But presently exhausted by these efforts, I fell again into slumber.

"When I again awoke, it was high-day. An unclouded sun was shining brightly over a dazzling world. The mountainside opposite the window glittered back from the tiny glacier-threads and the tinier rivulets. The casement was open. The soft, sweet breeze of a fine autumnal noon lisped in the leaves and blew gently over my brow. The fragrant air was filled with the droning of a few industrious bees who had been drawn from their snug quarters by the genial warmth of the noonday hour, and were now humming around some clusters of very sweet but late ripening grapes that still hung on a vine which sister and I had trained over our window with the view mainly of getting a grateful protection, especially during the midsummer heats, against the afternoon sun. The vine was almost leafless now, but the shriveled clusters perfumed our chamber, and afforded a little occupation to the honey-seekers who in these last days of the season hardly ventured into the vicinity of the glaciers, and found but scanty attractions in the valley.

"I found myself alone. Near my head on that polished walnut stand stood several phials, and beside them lay two or three ominous looking little folded papers. I knew then that a physician had been in attendance and wondered more than ever why and how long I had lain there.

"I endeavored to rise but was unable. The movement of the coverlet dislodged a spoon from the stand which fell on the floor with a sharp ring. Immediately *Maria* appeared at the door. Her soft eyes glistened and her face was wreathed in smiles as she instantly addressed me in French.

"The language itself had a meaning — a peculiar meaning for us, I mean — which I must explain to you. Like all the people here, living in this corner between the three nations, where there is no distinct national language, of course we knew and spoke, with exactly the same command and facility, the three languages of the nations around us — yet this, not quite indiscriminately. We always made a kind of instinctive and almost unconscious choice in using them. I mean that under certain conditions, one of these languages, under certain others, another, and again under others still, the third language would always burst from our lips, without any especial intention or thought about it. But in this involuntary and unconscious determination, there was a curious unthought-of motive guid- ign our tongues.

"The always acknowledged fact was that we venerated and loved, best of all, the language of *Italia, Italia carissima e sempre adorata* [Italy, dearest and ever adored Italy], the speech of our own nation, our home, our *Patria* — the mellifluous speech that bore to the breezes, through all the ages, the huzzas and the groans of her sons and daughters in the days of their glory and of their shame — the speech through whose rippling periods come down the thrilling pages of her tumultuous, heart-rending, unparalleled history — the speech whose sonorous and beautiful syllables name out to the world her own dear name, her rivers and lakes, her mountains and valleys, her cities and palaces, her villas and vineyards and unmatchable wines — the speech that was prattled in the mirth of their infancy, was filled with the glorious thoughts and visions of their manhood, and was whispered in the sighs and agonies of their departure by heavenly *Dante* and elegant *Bocaccio*, by *Petrarca* and *Ariosto* and *Tasso*, by *Copernico* and *Galileo* and *Colombo* and *Ricardo*, by *Raffaele* and *Michelangelo* and *Guido*, by *Manzoni* and *Leopardi* and *Foscolo* and *Pellico*"——

As the girl uttered these passionate words and whirled off a catalogue of which these above given are but the greater and representative names, she straightened up with a sort of mournful pride, her former almost childlike voice assumed a declamatory tone, and her countenance beamed with a lofty intelligence at which I was at once astonished and fascinated.

When this rhetorical flourish was over, and her countenance had assumed its normal expression, she added in her ordinary tones and with the first smile I had seen on her face :

"Of course, the very sounds were music to our ears ; and *Babbo* never spoke in any other language to us, nor we to him.

"But Mother, as I have said, was from France, and learned our Italian after she came to our home. The language of her own country always lay deepest in her heart. To her it was the language of love, of tenderness, of every private, domestic, family sentiment. Naturally, or rather necessarily, it was the lullabies of that language, sung by her over our cradle, under which we sank to our baby slumbers ; and our first infant prattle and our childish epithets of tenderness and affection, were taught us by her in her own tongue.

"Of course, the effect of this infantile training

was prodigious—one might say extinguishing—upon every other language in this field. Of course, no other words ever could sound to our ears so naturally tender, so full of meaning, so powerfully picturing every emotion and voicing every passion. With Mother we children never used any other; and generally in private, always in our tenderest moments, we used our Mother's language with each other. Its very accent to our ears meant love and passion.

"Of the German, I need only say that we spoke it only of necessity and with strangers of that uncouth nation.

"You will understand now how much meaning there was in it, and how sweet it was to hear, when *Maria*, coming now to the bedside, and seeing my eyes open, exclaimed, in great excitement, yet hardly above a whisper:

—'*M'amie, m'amie, ma chère enfant, est-ce-qu'il y a long temps que tu t' es éveillée?*' [dear child, have you been long awake?]

—'No, *M'amie*,' I replied, 'I have but this minute awoke. But am I sick? Have I lain here long? Who brought these phials and papers here and all these other things? What does it mean, *Maria* dear? Tell me—tell me everything.'

—'Yes, dear, don't you remember,' she said, 'when they brought you up here?'

—'No, certainly I don't—not a thing about it. When was it?—why was it?—what was it?'

—'You don't remember the *Medico?*'

—'No, indeed, nothing of the kind at all.'

—'That is very queer. You were talking to him all the time as fast as you could jabber.'

—'What did I say?' (for I was frightened at that).

"*Maria* made no other reply, but laid her hand softly on my forehead and smiled sweetly down on me, saying:

—'It's so good to look into your dear eyes again, *Marta.*'

"Though I was n't distinctly conscious of any chapter of secrets in my thoughts which I need be terrified at having unconsciously divulged, still there was a dark cloud hanging over my mind which seemed to me to envelop some piece of history—and, I felt, an uncanny history, too —but the particulars of which I could not at all recollect, and therefore my heart did tremble with timidity at what of proper or improper privacy that field of darkness without memories might have contained and exhibited. So I persisted:

—'What did I say?'

—'Nothing worth thinking of now,' she said.

—'But I must know now, now,' I insisted.

—'Well, dear, I can't remember it all, there was so much, I only remember that you seemed in great excitement and the words *l'enfant cher'* [the dear fellow] came over a good many times. But there was nothing for a good girl to blush at, dear. So be quiet, *Martettina* [dear little Martha], and tell me if you can take some *brodo* [broth] now.'

—'What am I to take *brodo* for? Am I sick? I feel as well as ever, only so weak.'

—'It's two days ago this afternoon that the *Medico* came and gave you one of those powders,' she pointed to the little papers that lay on the stand, 'and we've given them as he directed, and kept you asleep till now.'

—'But what's the matter with me?'

—'The *Medico* didn't say; but he will come every day till you are better. He came yesterday, felt your pulse, put his glass under your tongue, listened at your chest, asked me thirteen of the queerest questions, ordered one more powder, and said you should wake up 'to-day. He will surely be here this afternoon. Now I must bring the *brodo*. He told me to feed you with it as soon as you awoke. I made it this morning. It needs a minute over the fire.'

"With this she slipped quickly away to bring the broth. Being again alone, my thoughts wandered back to the events of my last remembrance, and became occupied with a hundred conjectures, wishes, fears. Then, I wondered *Maria* had n't alluded to the young man. One would n't have known, from her words or actions, she had ever heard of him. 'What had become of him? Was he already dead and gone? Or was he so much better as to be removed to the hotel in *Martigny* with his uncle? Should I never see him again? My heart was breaking to hear about him. But I could n't ask *Maria*. Why could n't I ask her? —Oh, oh!'

"At this point in my uneasy meditations, *Maria* came sailing in with the *brodo*. It was in one of dear sainted Mother's blue and white china tea cups which she brought in her *dot* from *Nismes*. Kneeling down at the side of my pillow *Maria* fed me very slowly with a bright silver spoon which the unknown lady had left, and it had the arms of France upon it. Between every spoonful sister leaned forward and gave me a kiss.

"When my meal was over, she remained for a time, moving softly about the chamber as blithe as a butterfly, as lovely as an angel. She spoke but little and her tread was as light as the step of a kitten. I thought I had never seen her soft eyes so bright; and her face seemed to be shining in a halo of sweetness, like Venus at her full.

This new radiance, thought I, whence comes it? It must emanate from some secret joy.

"When every little service of renovation and preparation throughout the room had been thus noiselessly accomplished, she came and knelt again at my pillow showering upon my hot cheeks gentlest kisses. That act of pity was too much. I could endure my silent thoughts no longer. My pent feelings burst forth like a new spring on an August noon from the foot of a glacier; and the tears streamed across my cheeks upon the pillow, like the torrents of the *Val d' Entremont,* with irresistible sobs.

" Distressed at this new symptom of my malady and ignorant of its real cause, my sister reached and took from the stand one of the strange phials and, gently wiping the tears from my cheeks, cautiously brought the loosened stopper near my nostrils. The sensation was new to me, delightful and refreshing. I was about to excuse my sobbing, and with some difficulty between the spasms, begun:

—'I did n't — mean — to cry, but '—

—'Yes, yes, *M'amie,*' she interrupted, ' I know it — how very weak your nerves are, but '—

—'No, no — not that — but '— I began again when she gently pressed over my mouth the *fazzoletto* [handkerchief] with which she was still absorbing the rivers that continued to overflow my cheeks, saying, hurriedly,

—'*Sta bene, sta bene, benissimo, M'amie* [It's all right, it's all right, dearest]. Don't talk now. Sobbing so will harm you. We must keep you quiet. The *Medico* insisted on this. I won't tidy up again till you are stronger. I see, I see that your poor nerves could n't bear my bustling round so.'

"Then turning her face up toward the window, she added, softly:

—'Oh look at the clouds, *M'amie* — how beautiful and peaceful they are now! It will soothe you.'

"I lifted my eyes and looked through the open casement into the soft, autumnal sky. Masses of bright white clouds of every conceivable form were sailing slowly down the valley. At this instant, I thought I heard a sound as of a slight movement below. *Maria* rose from her knees and slipped down the stairs, saying in a whisper as she went:

—'*Dans un moment, M'amie, je serai de mon retour.*' [I'll be back in a moment, dear.]

"I continued gazing quietly and pleasantly into those clouds. Wonderful figures presented themselves to my fancy. I saw there seas and islands, mountains and forests, fruitful fields and desert wastes, horrid battle-grounds and carnage and devastation, peaceful landscapes filled with the busy activities of animal and of human life, the bird twittering to his mate on a leafy bough, lovers in shaded grottoes embracing, mourners in churchyards beneath the sad cypress burying their dead — all noiseless as the step of Silence, moving steadily across the scene, in the van of other yet similar multitudes pushing them forward into the abyss of immensity. My brain finally swam, and before the promise of *Maria* was fulfilled I was again asleep."

ROAD TOWARD THE HOSPICE.

XIX.

Romeo.　　Peace, peace, Mercutio, peace;
　　　　　　Thou talk'st of nothing.
Mercutio.　True, I talk of dreams.

SHAKSPEARE.

THOUGH well nigh beyond the credence of our cold Teuton souls, stiffened by the chill fogs of the north, still the fact stands of a faculty of improvisation — wonderful improvisation — inherent in Italian blood; and what, for example, *Madame de Stael* has pictured in her *Corinne*, so far from being a touch of overcoloring in that brilliant romance, is a reality which can be matched not unfrequently to-day among that warm-blooded people. In fact, my young companion, with an exterior so rustic and an environment so bleak, yet with a thousand years of Roman equestrian blood tingling in her veins, was a genuine specimen of it.

"In a dream of that sleep," she said, "if it was a sleep — or was it a vision brought to me by my guardian angel? — kindly sent, perhaps, for my enlightenment and warning, by the august and

loving patroness of my sister, *Maria beatissma ?*—
in short, whatever it was, I seemed, at a wish,
to rise into the lofty air and to be borne swiftly
along, propelled and guided only by my will.

"Do you remember," she said, "the words of
our glorious *Dante*, in the beginning of the *Paradiso*, where he describes his own introduction to a
knowledge of the upper spheres." And then she
quoted:

> And suddenly upon the day arose
>   Another day, as with a second morn
> And second sun th' Omnipotent Dispenser chose
>   The heaven with double brilliance to adorn.
>
> Here where soft Luna's silver cycle reels,
>   Beatrice stood in glorious light embowered,
> With eyes fast fixed upon the eternal wheels ;
>   My own on her from heaven itself I lowered.
>
>   .   .   .   .
>
> ' Why wonder,' said she, that thou can'st ascend,
>   (Now free from fetters), as thou dost aspire ?
> 'Tis native, as the torrents to the valleys tend,
>   Or upward soars the flame of living fire.'[19]

In repeating these lines, which in common with
all the better class of peasantry throughout Tuscany and beyond, I could not doubt, she had been
familiar with from infancy, the feminine *timbre* of
her voice changed again into a full orotund,
declamatory tone, her figure straightened to its
utmost height, her step fell with a regular cadence,

and her countenance beamed with a subdued radiance of I know not what to say—of awe, intelligence, passion.

I was amazed beyond expression. She whom I had looked on merely as a specimen—certainly an interesting yet not quite wonderful specimen—of sentimental girlhood, now aroused in me something more than interest, more than astonishment, something rather like a mixture of Sibylline and angelic reverence.

"I seemed," she went on, in that strange, exalted strain, gathering new inspiration with every word, "I seemed in my flight to pass over cities, villages, hamlets, and wide plains sparsely studded with human habitations. I saw moving below me, as in a vast panorama, the multifarious occupations of mankind, the numberless varieties of existence, all the vicissitudes of human life.

"I heard—for my faculty of hearing seemed equally extended in compass with my faculties of sight and of locomotion and correspondingly intensified in delicacy—I heard the song of infantile glee and the wail of infantile woe; the shouts of youthful sport and the laughter of careless mirth; the coarse jests of swinish revelers; brawling oaths of the impious; the fawning and flattery of slaves, parasites, false-traders, and seducers; threats of hardhearted masters and defiant yells of the down-trodden; hurrahs of the full-fed and gasps of the famishing; lovers' pledges, wedded vows, the soft hum of domestic joys, the howling of the madman, the sighing of the deserted, natal festivities, burial obsequies.

"Over all these and over me, the twinkling stars looked down in solemn silence. The fickle Moon came and saw and went and returned perpetually her changing face, as if in cold unconcern, or in scorn. The glorious Sun, like a Monarch, mindful only of exalted duty, shone, with beams of health and joy, alike on the evil and the good.

"As I passed thus swiftly along, conducting myself I knew not whither, there hove into view a troop of etherial forms passing also swiftly in a direction to the front, but obliquely across my own. The leader was a short space in advance of his company, an old man whose snowy hair flowed far upon his shoulders; and an equally snowy beard fell far down his breast. His head was uncovered and a lofty forehead towered above the most benignant countenance I ever beheld. The whole company were robed in drapery that sailed far out behind, though so enveloped in a nebulous diffusion, that no more was clearly defined than I have described of the leader. Their uncovered heads were youthful and their beardless faces wore a look of seriousness verging on anxiety.

In a moment I was already so near that I involuntarily paused lest I should collide with them at the point where our paths were about to intersect. Even then the nebulous garments of the leader brushed my own; and as he passed, without turning his head, he said, in a soft and silvery voice:

—'Follow, if you will!'

"Without a thought or a reason, I turned my course and fell into the train, almost abreast of him on his left hand.

"Presently, without turning his head, he said again:

—'Whither bound?'

—'I know not,' I replied.

—'Seeking what?' he continued.

—'Knowledge and rest,' I answered.

—'Follow in my company,' he said 'and if worthy, you shall be satisfied.'

"A day and a night, as it seemed to me, we sailed on. The sun disappeared in a shadow and returned in glory. The moon sank behind the mountains and rose again over the valley. The stars, ever above the horizon, glistened and glided on in the dark blue depths of heaven, like an army with bayonets and banners interminable.

Meanwhile, by day and by night, our company was evermore growing in numbers; for, as we were continually meeting and passing other groups and individuals moving in every direction, all of whom were greeted by our leader, as I had been, with the same soft and silvery invitation, one and another turned into our course and became part of our company.

"At last we alighted on a bald, rocky mountain-top, on the verge of an immense circular island, which sloped down on every side, in the distant horizon, to the blue waters of the sea. On the face of these waters, which were perpetually rolling in tremendous billows, lay throughout the whole circuit black storm-clouds, on the bosom of which forked lightnings were always playing, and the sharp reports of continuous thunders, like an incessant cannonade, filled the sky with everlasting echoes.

"There was no other access to this island — since the surrounding sea was absolutely unnavigable — than by the rocky mountain pass, whence an enormous staircase, cut in the solid rock, descended from the summit on which we and all others must alight to the broad plain below. But across the head of this staircase rose a lofty iron grating pierced by two narrow gates. Between these two gates and extending backward from the top of the stairs to the brink of the stormy sea, rose also another iron grating through which all could be seen, but with no passageway.

"I now observed, as our company gathered on one side of this impassable barrier, that we were all of my own sex, and I saw that the similar company gathering on the other side were all of the other sex. I also noticed that the most of those on either side were busy grooming themselves, often with great labor and ingenuity; were much occupied in surveying each other through the impassable grating; and occasionally a pair, one on either side, came together and exchanged tender greetings across the barrier. I observed, however, that such conduct did not meet with general approval, but was sometimes made the subject of ridicule and sometimes of frowns and scorn. I saw, too, that this severe rule sometimes caused much grief and shame; and when the delay was long, caused not a few to mope in loneliness and discontent. More than once or twice I saw, with unutterable horror, sometimes one only, sometimes both leap from the rock and disappear in the billowy sea.

"I pressed eagerly forward to our gate, and finding it firmly locked, I stood surveying the sea-bound and storm-bound enclosure through the openings before me. The scene teemed with animated beings. The breezes that swept over it were fragrant with a thousand delicious odors from flowery gardens and fruitful fields; and on their balmy bosom rose a confused murmur of happy voices and varied occupations.

"Shading my eyes from the bewildering brightness, I could discover, by closer scrutiny, men and women walking arm in arm on the shining sands of the roaring sea. Others were reclining on the shoulders of their companions, under the shade of some tree, whose luxuriant foliage drooped about them in solemn majesty or waved high over them with plumes of joy. Others still, in native grottoes, through which ran rivulets, like threads of silver, were embracing with impassioned kisses.

"I observed immediately, that throughout this whole region the inhabitants were in couples, and all were wholly engrossed with their own partners — in this respect, differing much from many of the pairs already alluded to outside the gates, whose tendernesses were of shorter duration, and whose partners were often exchanged.

"I had almost failed to notice, amidst the stirring scenes more immediately before me, in the far distance where the lights and shadows were less distinctly marked, a pair with whitened locks, seated in rustic arm-chairs, under the dancing shadows of a weeping willow, who seemed by their gestures — for the old man would often stretch out his trembling arm in one direction and another, which was followed by the earnest gaze of the ancient dame — to be recalling the more lively scenes which lay in the far distant foreground.

"The attention of our company was now aroused by the soft and rapid notes of a silver horn. Presently we saw three venerable men — whom we understood to be Homer, Plato, and Virgil — taking seats upon a kind of tribune. We began crowding toward them to secure for ourselves each a passport which, delivered to the gate-keeper, would send him quickly to undo the bolts of the narrow gate and usher the fortunate holder into the sequestered paradise.

"We could see that similiar proceedings were going forward on the masculine side of the grated division. The tribune there, however, was occupied by three feminine figures, of a grave and commanding yet surpassingly beautiful presence — the representatives, it was reported, of Fidelity, Philosophy, Passion, namely Penelope, Aspasia, Sappho.

"As each applicant approached the judges, it was necessary to pass through a narrow passage, grated on either side, and of such length that the words spoken while the trial was going on were inaudible, save to the parties concerned — though every movement was visible to all.

"I gladly remained in the background, preferring to see how others would fare, before putting my own destiny at stake. The process in every case was quite uniform, though the results were various. Each candidate, on entering the narrow passage, received from the porter a blank passport to be laid before the judges, each of whom in turn propounded a single question, and according to the answer returned, either signed his name to the document and passed it on to the next judge, or crumpled it in his fist and threw it under the tribune — when the rejected candidate was conducted beyond the tribune and was seen no more. I ought to add that, as each question was asked, the judge raised something like a telescope to his eye, directing it against the breast of the candidate. It was said that the glass revealed the truth whatever the answers might be.

"All the others of my company had passed on, experienced their various fortune and left me in the candidate's lodge alone, when I took from the porter my blank and moved toward the judge's seat. I trembled in every limb. I had seen many a one turned sadly away. What hope could I have to fare better?—for I did not know, in the least, what those three tremendous questions were, on which my fate must turn.

"I was, however, greatly encouraged and comforted, when looking through the grated gate, I saw the fortunate applicants gaily descending the great staircase within. Almost all were busily pairing; or being already paired, were descending, arm in arm, to the happier plains.

"Arrived at the tribune, I laid my blank passport with a trembling hand before the judge who sat on the right. Homer, if it was he, without lifting his glass, and with fixed eyes, as if looking with second sight, demanded:

—'Damsel, swear to me, hast thou rejected a once accepted lover?'

—'No!' I answered with a trembling but emphatic tone.

"He waited for some moments, but without uttering another word, then took the judicial pen, wrote his name across the face of the passport and handed it with the pen to his neighbor. Then Plato, if it was he, lifting the glass to his eye, demanded:

—'Maiden, swear, hast thou scorned the affection of a youth, or encouraged a hopeless passion, or sported with the semblance of the all-powerful sentiment without possessing the reality?'

—'No indeed, no!' I answered with greater emphasis and less trembling than before; and he, quickly laying aside the glass, lifted the pen, wrote his name below the other, and passed the paper on. Then Virgil, if it was he, lifting the glass said:

—'Child, tell me true, hast thou an offer of love?'

"This stung me to the quick. I was ashamed to confess the truth. But seeing the glass aimed at my breast, revealing, I had no doubt, my secret thoughts, I dared not deny, or prevaricate. Hanging my head and with burning cheeks, I said softly:

—'No.'

—'Child,' he replied, while he crushed and threw away the passport, 'these fields are not for thee to-day. Go, and some other day thou may'st return, and if found worthy, enter these gates of delight.'

"The next instant a crash of thunder seemed to burst from the zenith down upon my head. I sprang at the shock and awoke.

"The sash had closed. The next moment *Maria* came flying into the room as on the wings of the the wind. I was sweating with exhaustion and fright."

XX.

O Death you must surely delay;
My beautiful journey is far from its goal,
  I have hardly set out on my way;
Of the o'er-arching elms that emborder the whole,
  I but passed the first columns to-day.

O death, I 'm not ready to rest !
At the banquet of life (yet hardly begun),
  But an instant my lips have been pressed
To the brim of the cup — I have tasted but one —
  Oh, how sweet was the soul-thrilling zest ! [20]

ANDRÉ CHÉNIER.

'OH, *M'amie!*' exclaimed sister, seeing the drops on my forehead, 'you were frightened, were n't you ?'

—'Yes, *M'amie,*' I said. But the truth was, I was yet more surprised at seeing her looking so happy and beautiful.

"Presently she began bathing my face with a soft towel moistened in water perfumed from one of the new bottles on the stand. I was familiar, as I have said, with *Aqua di Felsina,* but this ravishing odor was different from anything I had ever smelled. Years before I remembered something comparable to it though not the same. It came about in this way:

"I once went with Alpine flowers to a great lady who was sick at *Aosta* in the *Albergo della Posta*. Her footman, a few days before, had stopped at our home, enquiring where such flowers could be found for his *padrona* who was ill and longed for some. She used to gather such here in her girlhood; and *Babbo* then promised to send them to her.

"*Maria* and I well knew where to look, and picked a lovely *mazzolino* [little bunch] and put it in a little basket made of small vine-stalks and fir-twigs, with the softest and prettiest mosses cool and damp from the edge of the glacier near our house laid delicately around. It was very beautiful indeed, and smelled very, very sweet when I handed it to the maid, who gave it into the hand of the lady, who was reclined among great pillows and silken cushions on something like a chair and a bed all in one.

"As soon as she saw the basket and the fragrance reached her (for it soon filled the room), she opened wide her beautiful eyes and spoke, in a soft, clear voice:

"'*Ah, che questo è odore soavissimo!*' [Oh, how very delicious this fragrance is].

"Then, as she put out her little hand, as white

as the snow in winter, and the fingers covered with rings of gold and glittering with stones white and red and green, a little *fazzoletto* dropped upon the carpet, being flung by the quick movement of her arm near to me but some distance from her chair. I stooped and handed it to the maid. It was perfumed with a wonderful odor; and I could n't help whispering:

—'*Oh, celeste!*' [heavenly].

—'Is that perfume agreeable to thee, *Piccioletta?*' [dear little girl] said the lady, setting the basket down on a pillow at her side.

—'*Si, Vostra Altezza,*' [yes, your Highness], I said just above a whisper (for I was much frightened at her), 'I do think it must be like the perfumes in *Paradiso*, for it is sweeter than the incense at the Mass for the dead.'

—'*Buona Piccioletta!*' [good, little dear], she replied, 'thou shalt have it then to aid thy prayers.'

"Then she took this from her own neck [here my companion pointed to the pink coral rosary hanging about her neck] and handed it to the maid. The crucifix is a bottle also.

—'*Lappa,*' she said, 'fill this from the green-and-gold flask on the further side of the *credenza* [buffet] yonder, and put it into that Japanese *cassettina* (pointing to a little gold-and-ebony box on the toilet stand), and give to *la buona piccioletta'* [the good little girl].

"Then, talking beautifully to me all the while, she drew a purse from the bosom of her robe, and taking out a bright *zecchino*,[21] beckoned to me to come near her, and laying the shining piece of gold in my hand, which trembled so I could hardly hold it, she said, with a soft, serious voice:

—'May our Lady keep thee as fair and sweet as these delicious flowers, and make thee a dear delight to a good husband some happy day!'

"After the maid had given me the little box the lady raised again to her face the basket I had brought, and said to me, as I curtesied backward toward the door,

—'*Addio, tu bella e buona fanciullina, a Dio, a Dio!*' [Goodbye, God bless you, good little beauty.]

"Certainly, as you will suppose," said my companion, unclasping the rosary from her neck, and offering me to test the truth of her assertions concerning it, "I hold this too precious for daily wear, or indeed ever to be taken from the little table in our loft-chamber under the picture of *Madonna*, where I use it morning and night at my prayers. Except that I take it to the Church three or four times in the year at high Mass, and, as to-day, when I come to pray for my dead. The perfume is n't quite gone yet."

I brought the cross near to my face and perceived a faint but delightful odor; and returned the precious charm to the owner.

"It was with some such highly fragrant water," she continued, "that *Maria* was bathing my face and prattling on with her loving talk, when we heard steps coming up the walk; and presently there came a loud rapping which echoed through the rooms below.

—'*Ecco il medico!*' [there 's the Doctor] cried *Maria*, replacing her implements on the little table and starting for the door. But before she reached the stairs, the steps were already inside the outer door below. Hardly had she begun to descend when she retreated, saying gaily, as she reached out her hand:

—'*Buon giorno al nostro buon dottore!*' [Good morning, good Doctor!]

"Then turning towards me, as a very large man entered the chamber, carrying cane and hat in one hand and a black leathern box in the other, she said:

'*Ecco il medico, M'amie — questo é il dottor Ferrente, il nostro buonissimo medico.*' [Dr. Ferrenti, dear, our very, very nice physician.]

"I tried to smile, but was more afraid than pleased; for he was so tall that he must stoop in entering the chamber, and so broad that the width of the door hardly sufficed to let him in. His big head was covered with coal-black hair, which hung low on his shoulders; and if possible, a still blacker beard wholly unshaven hung in an enormous mass on his breast, and covered his face like a bear-skin mask, except where a broad forehead lay above large, black, yet gentle eyes, and a long Grecian nose ran down between until it reached the tremendous moustache which only failed to conceal the cherry-red line between it and the mountains of hair beneath.

"I really trembled with fear as I looked up and saw him, so big and black and hairy, slowly approaching the bed; but "—here she stopped suddenly short. I turned to discover the cause. She glanced up into my face. Our eyes met. I saw that hers were suddenly swimming and at the same time I was amazed to see that a crimson blush was rising over her whole face. I was utterly at a loss to account for this apparently new revelation, and my curiosity would have impelled me to throw in an enquiry here; but fortunately delicacy and discretion held my tongue, and I instantly turned away my eyes again and made a successful effort to look unconcerned and unsuspecting.

But she evidently felt that she had already gone too far for an abrupt retreat and in a moment, endeavoring to finish her sentence, she stammered:

—'But since — that is — when I learned to — to know him — I came to — to feel — feel differently — toward him. But he looked to me then, so like a great wild bear of the mountains, that I was filled with dislike and fear of him and wished him quickly gone.

—'*Buon giorno, si, si, buonissimo giorno, grazie a Dio, Signorina*' [Well done ! little lady, you look better, I 'm glad to see], he said as he approached the bed, with a soft voice and a sympathetic accent which at once reassured me, 'I 'm so glad to see your *begli occhini* [pretty eyes] at last.'

" Then seating himself in the carved oaken armchair that *Maria* had put at the bedside for him, he went through the motions that all the doctors do — holding my wrist a long while in one hand with his watch in the other, whipping out a glass tube from his pocket and slipping it under my tongue, laying his great head down on one ear upon my bosom, and finally tapping me round in many places and asking me many questions — all which made me feel very queer — for I had never been attended by a doctor before. At last, turning to *Maria* he said:

" '*Tutto è buono. Sicuro, essa sta meglio oggi.*' [She is certainly better to-day — symptoms good.]

Then, leaning back in the armchair, with a grave and gentle voice that soothed my nerves and won at once the whole confidence of my soul, he said :

—'*Signorine*, listen and carefully obey'—

—'We will, we will, *Signor Medico*'—we both in a breath interjected.

—'*Questa signorettina*' [this dear-little-young-lady], he went on, 'must not, for one week more, at least, go out of this room, nor gaze into the sky'—I had told him, in answer to one of his questions, something, not all, of my sky-dream—'nor look down from this window, nor even from the top of the stairs.'

"Then reaching for the black box and taking out a little package, which he laid on the stand, he said:

—'These pellets are to be taken according to the directions within.' Then, drawing out two bottles, he said:

'Here is Mantuan of an especial quality— both grape and make—which I require the Count to keep always by him. Indeed, it is out of the lot which my nephew was bringing when his mishap occurred. I would have it taken quite freely.

'For meals, you will see on the prescription card of yesterday what I still recommend. The game I will send—at all events, the quail and partridge — while I stay at *Martigny*, which will be some days yet.

'Now as to my nephew,' he continued, 'and the Count's waiting-man, who has been here these four days, I shall take them with me to the Hotel to-day. I wish to have *Luigi* nearer to me for more constant examination and for some more frequent surgical applications which can only be executed by my own hand. I wish, also, at this earliest possible moment, to relieve you all here of a burden you have borne too long already. But for his daily airings I will for some days yet have him brought here, for the stay of an hour or two, till the dog shall get acquainted with his new masters, the pastures and the flocks '—

—'Ah, that dreadful dog,' I said. 'will he ever come to obey us and love us?'

—'Most surely he will,' said the doctor, 'I have known him long. He is of the noblest blood and perfectly educated. When once he understands that you are his master's friends, he will give his allegiance to you, and there is nothing he will not do for you. He will work for you and guard you even with his life.'

'I shall have the honor of presenting him to your *Signor Padre*, as a part (if I may call so insignificant a gift a part) of the poor return we shall find it in our power to make for services that have been the price of his life. The tender care, the labor, the suffering, and I may truly add the peril, hardly yet passed, of this *giovanettina* [sweet little young woman], I can never hope to requite, except by the poor tribute of my infinite thanks, and my daily prayers that *Iddio* will bountifully repay her and you all in His own heavenly coin.

'As to the money, *Luigi* shall have the fifty *scudi* he demands for the dog. If it were fifty times fifty, I should gladly give it, for the love of his Mother, now in *Paradiso*—May our Lady comfort her!'

" His voice trembled so as to be almost inaudible. He paused a moment, and I saw a tear standing in the corner of his eye. But he went on:

'I owe, I owe to her all the promotion and success I have attained in the world.'

—'Oh, tell us, *Signor Dottore*, tell us about her,' we both said in one breath.

—'You have heard of the plague that prevailed in the Marches, and especially swept over *Ancona* and the environs forty years ago?

—'*Si, si, sicuro, Dottore*,' I said, 'I have heard *Babbo* say that some of his relations were carried off by it, and there was a little property in the division coming to us—some curious ancient things especially, which he would have been very glad to get; but, at the time, on account of the pest and fear of infection, the *doganieri* [custom-house officers], would allow nothing to pass, and there being nobody there to represent us and care for them, when the disease was over and the fright gone, they were at last sold for expenses, and nothing from them came to us.

—'Sister and I,' he continued, 'were then made orphans. I was eight, she twelve. Our cottage and garden were let for a long term at sixty *scudi*. Sister went to service with the *Parroco* [rector of the parish]. He, for her service, gave me my food and taught me Latin. The sixty *scudi* partly bought her clothes and mine, and part she spun and wove and made; and did it mostly in the night time.

'But when I went up to the University, then came the pinch. She went barefoot that I might have shoes, and in rags, that I might have books. And one thing more—the hardest of all I think for honest maiden-pride to bear—when the summons of my enrollment came and the conscription office must be settled with, she was already betrothed. With my diploma one hundred *zecchini* would free me from going into the barracks. Our patrimony had just been sold for one hundred *zecchini*. One-half of this was hers; and was her only dowry. She gave up to me her share. I went free, and she went to her husband, as we say, 'in her shift.'

'Ah, yes, she was a saint, and finally a martyr, I may say, to her universal charity — to her struggles for me and for others. *Grazie a Dio*, I had the privilege to nurse her through her last sickness. She took in a poor stranger who fell sick at her door. He, through her self-exhausting efforts recovered, and, blessing God and her, went on his way. She was struck by the contagion he brought and died. I took her last kiss and gave her the last. I closed her eyes. Ah, me! I would have died for her. I should be glad to take her chances at the Judgment Day.

'*Luigi* was twelve when he lost her. The dear fellow has a soul so like hers. He has been everything to his father, and I may say also to me,— though my duties have kept me much apart from him. We can see his mother's face, and hear a reminder of her wonderful voice in his. He has had a hard life. I fear a harder is yet before him. The rule of conscription is stricter now than ever. Still I do not despair. I shall do all I can; and *se piace a Dio* [if it please God], I hope to get him off at least from the barracks.'

—'Oh do, do,' we said together; and I think the doctor saw the tears in *Maria's* eyes and mine;

for he gave an understanding look and said parenthetically, yet tenderly,

—'*Buone fanciulline!*' [dear, good girls], and continued: 'And for this reason, I am going to send him home by the way of *Leuk* and the *Simplon*. At the *Leukerbad* I left an old friend, a *militare*. He is an officer of rank and influence on the staff of General *Oudinoto*, the *Commandante* of the Emperor's army in *Lombardia*. He has twice owed his life to me.

—'*Oh, Signor Dottore!*' I exclaimed.

—'How he must love you!' added Maria.

—'What a heavenly thing, I said, it must be to be a doctor—a good and great doctor like you, who can destroy the disease before it destroys the people.'

—'Yes,' said *Maria* softly, 'it makes me think of *San Michele*, the archangel, driving *Lucifero* out of heaven.'

—'Hold, hold, *Signorine*,' whispered the doctor, with a cunning twinkle in his eye, and striking towards us, repressively, with the palms of each hand, 'this is all true enough, at least, I should hope so, but in this case, *Signorine*, it was not *il medico* but *l' amico* [not medicine, but love], that saved him.'

—'Tell us, tell us about it, then, *Signor Dottore*,' we both urged.

COMO. — PUBLIC GARDEN.

—'The first time,' he replied, 'was when we were boys at college in *Milano*. We were both poor and unknown. We had walked over to *Como* the day before. In the morning we had seen many sights; visited the beautiful old marble Cathedral, with its statues, at the entrance, of the elder and the younger Pliny (who were both born in *Como*), and the rare pictures on the walls; spent an hour among the silk-factories; and in the afternoon we went down to the west side of the town near the quay to see the statue of the famous electrician, *Volta*, whose birthplace and home was *Como*, and whose great discoveries we were then studying.

'Later we sauntered on outside the pier and lounged a while in the *Giardino Publico*, beside the lake. The afternoon was hot. My young friend, who was a perfect water-duck, as I also was, proposed a swim. Like boys, as we were, to say it was to do it. In a trice, we had unrobed and plunged in. We were many rods away from the bathers' beach and the guy-ropes which are stretched some distance into the water for their protection. The water in this spot was not of the warmest, and no doubt we had remained in it longer than we ought.

'At all events, while we were floating and turning somersaults, and performing various freaks and frolics, a good way from the shore, I heard a cry and saw him disappear. The distance between us was considerable and I did not at first think of any danger, but supposed that he had called me to observe some trick he was going to execute.

'But after waiting until I became alarmed, I swam to the spot, dove to the bottom, found him fast clenched to some root or log, tore him away, rose with him to the surface, and bore him on my back to the shore.

'At first I laid him on the hot sand. The water poured from his mouth and his nostrils. But his breath was gone, his heart was still, his face was livid. I was frightened almost out of my life. I was alone. The bathing hour was passed and the beach was then deserted.

'I knew well that time was life or death to him. I thought of nothing else. I snatched him up, just as we were, swung him upon my back, and started for a country-seat which stood on the mountain-side, at the end of a straight lane, overlooking the spot.

'I ran with my utmost speed up the gentle acclivity, but the weight of my burden and my fright soon began to tell on my strength. Feeling my load growing heavier, and my energies steadily failing, my alarm increased lest I should not by my utmost effort be able to sustain the strain till help could be reached, and this dread contributed every moment more and still more to exhaust my remaining powers.

'The distance to the villa was a good half mile; but I had not gone a hundred rods when I saw a cloud of dust rising in front of me a good way up the road. I could not tell what it was, but it flashed into me a little hope and I struggled on yet more intensely.

'A few moments afterwards the blessed reality dawned upon me. The coach of the proprietor of the villa was descending for the usual evening drive along the romantic borders of this charming water.

'It did n't need even my cry of distress to explain the situation. The first glance told all. The word was given. The horses were pulled upon their haunches. The reins were thrown to the footman. The coachman leaped from the box. The gentleman sprang from the carriage. The lady descended with a little scream and threw around me a shawl torn from her own shoulders. The little daughter followed and added another. My companion was quickly wrapped in the livery-blankets and lifted in the arms of the two men. In less time than it takes to tell it, the doubly-loaded coach was returning to the house with horses at a gallop, and the footman left to gather up our garments on the beach.

'Five minutes later, the surgeon of the house, with all needful assistants and every suitable appliance, was doing his utmost on the body of my young friend. During a considerable time his life hung in the balance, or rather the balance still turned against it. The whole household stood in intense and painful suspense. The serving-men went about shaking their heads with an occasional meaning snort. The maids kept up a sobbing and sighing over their half-neglected duties. The gentleman and lady sat on the balcony hand in hand, in silence, looking out on the treacherous water, and thinking many sad and solemn thoughts. The little daughter was crouched on a low stool at their feet, weeping.

'It is enough to say that his life was at last found to be in him; and after hours of skilled and tireless treatment, he was quietly sleeping in bed with a watcher sitting at the bedside.

'I was courteously entertained for the night, and, refreshed with repose, returned strong and well to my College duty on the morrow. The place I have never since visited, and these good people I have never since seen.

'My young friend remained to convalesce in the care of the surgeon and under the hospitality of the lovely and motherly Countess. After some weeks he returned to College with strength recovered. But, I may say, that he not only recovered his health, but found much more there, — through this strange introduction of mine.

'That house became thereafter his second home. His vacations were spent there. That little daughter grew larger and lovelier at each returning visit; and he grew manlier and wiser as the years went on. You know the rest. His charming wife to-day, and the mother of his children, was then the sweet child of that household, who first met him under the extraordinary circumstances which so touched her little heart. It has been largely through the powerful influence of her family and its wide connections that he has risen in the military, and indeed into particular favor with His Majesty the Emperor.

'Four years ago, in the battle of *Novara*, we were together on the staff of *Carlo Alberto*. His horse was blown to pieces under him by a shell, and he fell into my arms with a severed leg-artery. His life would have ebbed away in less than three minutes. With thumb and knee I held the hemorrhage back for more than two hours, till an ambulance and assistance came. In the hospital I watched it, I may say, without winking, till the essential tissues had knit.

'He is all in my interest and will do anything possible for me. I hope he will be able to persuade his chief to recommend *Luigi* for the Emperor's relief from the conscription.

'The fact is that he ought to receive a certificate and relief on the ground of incapacity. I find him much injured. I do not know how much. I have great fears both for his head and lungs. It will require time, at the best, to make him sound again. If he were to be put in barracks now, I should fear the worst. But we will try—I may say, we will pull hard—to avoid that.'

"Rising to go, he laid on the stand a purple leathern purse, which contained, as we afterwards found, one hundred golden ducats, saying in a hurried way:

'Will you have the goodness to present this to your *Signor Padre* with my compliments ... I may say ... my most distinguished regard? I shall hope to see you all again during the week. If my directions are followed, I am sure I shall not be needed. But in any emergency, of course you will send for me. . . . *Addio Signorine !*'

"With these words, responded to by our '*Addio, addio buono Signor Dottore,*' he bowed himself out of the room and descended, followed by

Maria. The preparations below, which I could indistinctly hear through the closed doors, lasted a quarter of an hour, and then I heard retreating footsteps outside, and finally the gradually diminishing sound of a *char* rolling away.

ROAD TO MARTIGNY FROM CASA OMBROSINI.

XXI.

"Alive as the wind-harp, how gently soever
If wooed by the Zephyr, to music will quiver,
Is Woman to Hope and to Fear." [22]
SCHILLER, *Bulwer's Translation.*

"AFTER the last sounds of departure had ceased and the lessening rattle of the vanishing *char* had faded out in the distance, and all was noiseless in the house save the monotonous clicking of the cuckoo-clock in the kitchen, and only the tinkle of the mountain rivulets mingling with the soft, sad diapason of the moaning fir-tree tops floated on the bosom of the solemn stillness abroad, and my heart was sinking every moment deeper into a sentiment of loneliness and despair, *Maria* again appeared, and as she entered, stepped briskly up to the little stand at the bedside, saying in her gayest tones :

—'Now, *M'amie*, we must do our best to get you well, and that, too, as soon as we can.' Then, as she took up the package and examined the doctor's pencilling on the label, she added, 'We must obey the orders of the *Medico* very carefully,' and went on reading aloud : "*Per Signorina Marta Ombrosini — Istruzione dentro,*" and began untying the packet. It was elegantly put up. First there was a white wrapper fastened with blue twine. Next, a blue wrapper fastened with yellow twine. When the second wrapper was opened, a pink paper box appeared, and a card dropped on the floor. The box *Maria* handed directly to me, while she stooped to recover the card. Opening the box, I found a phial and two small boxes, one purple, the other white, each separately wrapped in the softest orange-colored tissue paper. *Maria* then gave me the card which she had been closely examining. I had never before seen a prescription, much less one by a physician to nobility. The card had a gilt edge and a gilt border half as broad as the yellow spots on the neck of a pheasant. At the top was a picture of the *Buon Samaritano*, also in gilt, and the letters G. F. curiously wound in together and printed upon it in scarlet ink. Below, it was partly printed and partly written. I keep it still in my treasure-box, and have read it over a thousand times since. It said :

"PRESCRIZIONE NUMERO 51, C.   Ottobre 28, 1854.

'Of pellets in the white box, two every four

hours — but if the patient sleeps, on waking. If nausea occur, intermit four hours, and use, instead, one half-teaspoonful from the phial in a wine-glass of water.

'One pellet from the purple box before retiring and before *siesta*.

'Moderate meals four times daily. Avoid salted flesh-meat or fish and acids. Mutton or venison, game, milk, vegetables, and fruit are commended.

'Use the Mantuan freely at meals.

'Former directions cancelled, except the confinement, the medicated, clinic bath, and the inhalations from the green bottle.

FERRENTI.'

"At that moment the cuckoo in the kitchen sung four. It was the hour for executing my clinic bath. This, according to the orders of the *Medico*, was done in little sections, as I could bear it, and with a medicinal infusion and temperature which, as far as possible, was an imitation of the *Leukerbad*. The medications and the necessary thermometer had been left by the *Medico* on his previous visit."

Being then in my youth, and not largely acquainted with Italy or its people, I was struck by the extreme and seemingly unnecessary extent and minuteness of the physician's orders in a case which seemed to me neither apparently dangerous in its outlook, nor especially amenable to physic. But since I have come to know the practitioners of Italy better, and their scientific and moral standing in the profession — and I believe that, as a class, there is not in the world a more learned, skillful, and painstaking company of professional gentlemen — I find that the great *Ferrenti* did what and only what I must expect, according to the limits of his possibilities, from every humblest practitioner in Italy.

"The imitation of the *Leukerbad* finished, *Maria* dressed my hair anew, and perfumed my cheeks and temples from the *ampulletta* on the stand. Then, having given me the first pellets, and sitting down by the bed, she took my hand in one of hers, and smoothing it with the other — an old habit of ours when alone together — she said, hesitating a little and looking down into her lap, and I thought, blushing slightly:

—'*M'amie*, you are so much better now — I am so curious — I want to know — I am dying to hear it — would you mind telling me about you and *Luigi* — that is, what happened to him — I mean, how you got hurt — what maddened the dog?'

—'Why, *I* don't know, *M'amie*,' I said. 'How did I come to be in this bed?'

—'I don't know exactly,' she replied.

—'But what *do* you know,' I said.

—'Well, when *Babbo* came out to the pasture,— it was the Upper Meadow, you know — and took charge of the sheep, and sent me in, I found you on our bed, wrapped in a blanket. The *Medico* had been here and left instructions and gone away. This cot and stand and easy-chair and some of the phials were in the room. But—'

—'Do n't you know how I got here?' I interrupted.

—'*Babbo* told me,' she replied, 'that as he was coming up the path with the *Medico* and the waiting man, they all heard a very sharp growl, and looking up, saw, through the window, something like a woman's dress flying across the room, and instantly started to run with all their might for the house. When the *Medico*, who was a few steps in advance, arrived at the door of the room, he turned around to *Babbo* and the waiting-man, and exclaiming:

'*Per l' amor di Dio!*' [good heavens], beckoned to them to stop.

'Then, while they stood outside in a great fright and wonder, he flew in. They heard loud thumpings and thrashings and the tremendous voice of the *Medico* rebuking the dog. Then came a hoarse, guttural sound, as if the beast were being throttled. Then there was a silence; and not being willing to remain any longer in

doubt, they opened the door to follow the *Medico*.
But, before they had crossed the kitchen, they
met him coming out of the sick-room with you in
his great arms, wrapped close from head to feet
in his own traveling-blanket, which he happened
to have in his hand. Calling to *Babbo* to show
the way to some other room, he brought you here
and put you, all in the blanket, like a mummy,
into this bed.'

—'Is that all you know?' I asked.

—'About all,' she answered. 'I found your
best holiday gown on the floor, a petticoat, apron,
and other things a pile of rags. I was kept till
dark combing out your touseled hair, washing off
a hundred soiled spots, and patching the long
scratches with the *empiastri* which the *Medico* had
left. I did n't find the rosette till—'

—'When did the young man come to himself?'
I broke in.

—'I don't know,' she replied.

—'Did the *Medico* say anything about it?' I
insisted.

—'Not—not to me, but I think he told *Babbo*
that the patient *era svegliato* [was awake] when he
first saw him.'

'*Mon Dieu!*' I screamed, starting to rise, but
Sister gently laid me down again. My cheeks
burned. I covered my face with my hands and

sobbed : "Then he saw it — he saw it all! — Oh, how can I ever meet him again!"

—'Perhaps you'll not have to meet him,' said Sister, tenderly ; but this was the hardest blow of all, though she struck it innocently. I burst into tears. I could only sob:

—'Pity me, pity me, holy Virgin! — I tended him all day — like a frightened slave — I was bringing him the medicine — I tripped on the rug — (of course, this was a lie, a white lie, but I could n't tell the truth) — and the dreadful dog — the horrid beast, sprang upon me — that is all I know — till I awoke in this bed.'

—'O *M'amie!*' cried *Maria*, gently, yet doubtingly.

—'I swear by the holy Cross,' said I, impatiently, 'that is all *I* know. But why do *you* seem to doubt?'

—'Perhaps I was mistaken,' she replied, 'but I thought I overheard *Luigi* telling the doctor that your face was close to his on the pillow. I thought it likely that in your excitement and pity over the poor fellow, unconscious and moaning so, you kissed his forehead — naturally enough, too.'

"At this I was crazed, and swore an awful oath by the Mother of God. It was only after the worst penance I ever got, that I was absolved.

Maria put her hand lovingly over my mouth, and said :

—'Hush, *M'amie*, it's all right. We all know that it is a true, dear, good girl you are.' Then we heard *Babbo* coming in, and she went below."

Here my companion seemed out of breath, and turning aside to a green bank facing the west, under the shade of an old beach, she said :

"Let us sit down a bit here. The story goes now rapidly to the end. Or, perhaps you do n't care to hear any more. Why should you afflict yourself with my trouble ? "

I entreated her to go on to the end. So we sat down, at a little distance from each other, on the bank. She put her shoes beside her and laid her hat upon them. Then suddenly rising, she went a few steps along the bank, and presently returned with several small, blue flowers in her hand, one of which she gave me, and resuming her seat and raising to her face the bunch which she held, she said :

"*O, Signore, senta ! — che v' è di più dolce ?*"

I brought it to my nose, as she bade me, and repeated her words : *What is there sweeter ?*

"It was partly these," she added, "that I carried to the *Signora* at *Aosta*."

After a little pause, toying with the flowers, she proceeded: "*Maria* returned, bringing a small Sevres vase which had belonged to our *Nonina* [dear grandmamma], filled with these flowers. It had been standing in *Luigi's* room, but now she thought I would enjoy them.

—'*Mille grazie*,' [a thousand thanks], I said, 'and who gathered them for him?'

—'I—I did—I picked them,' she whispered.

—'Did he ask you for them?' I replied, my heart, rather than my head, speaking, and hardly knowing what I said.

—'N-o-o-o—not exactly,' she replied,—'he never asked—never—never asked for anything; but he saw one in my—my hand as I approached his bed one day, and looking up into my face with a smile, drew it from between my fingers, and held it so lovingly, and smelled it and gazed on it so earnestly, that as soon as I was free, you know the spot, *M'amie*, I went and picked this vase full and put it on the little table beside his pillow, where he could look at them and smell them as he lay there so suffering and sad.'

"I made no reply, for I was holding the vase and alternately smelling the flowers and looking at them and thinking. It was so pleasant to me to remember that *Luigi* had gazed on them, and smelled them, and enjoyed them; and indeed I was in full sympathy with her when in a trembling voice she continued:

'And I was so thankful that he did enjoy them — poor fellow! He was so feeble and so lonely and so distressed thinking of his poor *Babbo*, alone at home, but yet so patient and gentle and noble in all he said, and '— here she hesitated and stammered and blushed and added —'he was so grateful for everything I did for him — spoke to me so sweetly — and praised me so tenderly yet so respectfully — I could — I could gladly take care — take care of him — all my life — I mean — I mean if he were sick.'

"As she spoke the last words, she blushed deeply and tears twinkled in her eyes, yet her face beamed with tenderness. The sight put me on a rack of torture. When I thought how her attentions had met with gratitude and praise, with respectful kindness, and perhaps with love itself; while my at least equal devotion had resulted in my shameful fight with the dog, and my unspeakable disgrace before his eyes, and probably in his regarding me with repulsion and contempt; — the bitterness of my reflections, and the stinging sense of my wrongs was too much for my courage and too much for my strength.

"I had no tears, nor did I sob, nor moan. I closed my eyes. There came a strange sensation over my heart. I thought I was going to die. I opened my eyes, all was black. The next I knew,

Sister was stooping over me, bathing my temples with cold water and holding a little bottle at my nose.

"As soon as I came to myself, my breast heaved with sobs which I could not restrain; and a torrent of tears poured over my face. *Maria,* however, very naturally misunderstood the real cause of my emotion. Judging from her own feelings (of which her own swimming eyes were sufficient evidence), she imagined that mine were tears of pity for the young man, mingled with sympathy in her tenderness. Laying away her cold towels and smelling bottle, she knelt at the bedside, covered her face with her hands, and laid her head gently on my bosom. We remained thus some minutes without speaking. Meantime the tumult of my emotions subsided, she arose, pressed her lips to my forehead in silence and descended to prepare and bring my supper; and this subject was not again spoken of between us.

"The second day after, I sat some hours in the easy-chair, during which the *Medico* called, conversed of my health and treatment only, and said his goodbye. In two days more I walked about the room, but did not go below till the full week was over. Meanwhile *Maria,* relieved of constant attendance on me, spent some hours each day with the sheep in company with the dog.

"Every day I heard the *char* arrive and knew that the young man was spending an hour or two in the pastures. His arrival was commonly some hours after *Maria* had gone to the flocks. One day, however, coming much earlier than usual, he found her still in the house. I heard him enter, and heard a small part of the conversation, while she was finishing her housewifery and preparing to go with him to the grazing grounds. I only caught distinctly the words: '*If it is n't yes, I think it will kill me.*'

"You will imagine that I had built up in my fancy every day what *Luigi* and *Maria* might be saying and doing in the pastures. Still, unless it were by that unusual light in her eyes, and a manner and movement rather more gay and merry than her common soft and sober way, she had not shown by word or look, since she knelt at the bedside and wept tears of pity on my bosom, any symptoms, so far as I could discover, of a tenderer interest, or of more intimate relations with him than before.

"To be sure, I observed that she called him '*Luigi*,' and now and then merely '*Lu*.' But I remembered that she had done so ever since I awoke in the little bed. Perhaps it was only her way, for she was always sparing of her breath. Or she might have caught it from the *Medico*.

"Now I was sure I heard something important. For what else could it be, but that he was pressing a suit of . . . ? I did not, I could not pronounce the word.

"My heart fluttered. My head swam. A faintness came over me. I laid my head back upon the pillows of the easy-chair and closed my aching eyes — not for sleep, but for bitter reflection.

"I recalled my fate in the dream. Was not that dream perhaps prophetic intelligence brought to me by my guardian angel from heaven? — or perhaps from my dear Mother in *Paradiso?* — perhaps to warn me of some danger — or to comfort me in coming disappointment. Was I not surely entering now into the darkening atmosphere of that predicted eclipse of my hopes? I must try and learn the mysterious meaning of those ominous words.   All I can see by them now is that perhaps — ah, that dreadful perhaps, always clinging to me ! — perhaps there is still a future for *me* — yes, if all fails now in that quarter, a future of love and happiness for me, for me, for me — and it seemed like a tiny star of hope just twinkling below dark storm-clouds on the distant horizon.

"Presently the murmur of their subdued conversation became mingled with the clattering preparations for their departure. *Maria* opened the door at the foot of the staircase, and in a sprightly tone called to me, as usual:

'*M'amie, maintenant je m' en vais*' [I 'm going now, dear].

'*Adieu, M'amie, jusqu au revoir*' [goodbye, dear, till you come back], I replied, as usual.

" But when the door shut with a bang, it went through me like the report of a cannon aimed at my head. The outer door closed with a deeper thud, and then all was still, except, except an echo in my soul, fading away like the roar of a fallen avalanche.

" I rose and went to the window. Hot tears were running down my cheeks. I saw the two just below me. *Maria* was stepping slowly along in the footpath that led to the pastures with her eyes bent on the ground. By her side a tall figure, also with eyes bent on the ground, was moving with a fatigued yet manly gait.

" The morning was fresh. The sky was cloudless. The frosted dew was hardly gone. A gentle breeze kept the fir-twigs slowly dancing to the solemn music of the tree-tops. The scene was so charming, and so like, that I could not help beginning to hum Petrarch's *canzone* :

' *Alla dolce ombra delle belle frondi.*'[22]

[In luscious shade of witching green, etc.].

"But the scene had also a livelier interest for me. They seemed to be talking of something which stirred their deepest feelings. Often she turned her face in a tender way up toward his, and he looked earnestly down into hers. They were becoming every moment more and still more indistinct in the distance. They came at length to a place where the footpath branches into two—one bearing to the left up the side of the mountain to the spot where the goats were driven—the other turning a little to the right, and gently ascending into that small smooth valley which we called the 'Upper Meadow.'

"At this point they paused. I could trace the outline of their figures completely; but the lower branches of a fir tree veiled my vision with a kind of irregular lattice-work, and the shadows, kept in motion by the breeze, threw a degree of dreaminess and uncertainty over the view.

"I saw him return to her the small pail which he had been carrying in his left hand, while with his right he had been supporting, by a walking stick, his rather infirm steps. As she took the pail, she looked up into his face, he changed the stick quickly into his left hand, and raising his right arm, was bending towards her, when my eyes filled with a new flood of tears. The fir-boughs, also, between us, were at that moment

more agitated by the breeze. Yet I seemed to
see — no, I was not sure — but thought I saw —
at least, I could not doubt — that he clapsed her
waist — that she did not resist — did not even
seem either vexed or surprised — in short, that,
with a warm embrace, he kissed her upturned and
willing face. Then parting, they disappeared.

" I turned from the window and staggered back
to the easy-chair. My heart thumped. My tears
were gone. My cheeks burned. I had broken
the orders of the *Medico* — and how I was punished ! 'Was it then,' I said to myself, 'an occur-
rence that happened daily? Was it to save me
from such a sight, that I had been forbidden to
look out of the window? Did the *Medico* then,
know about it? Did he probably approve? —
Was he helping it on? — No doubt, no doubt,
he was.

'Alas, alas ! Even he then had turned against
me ! — or never cared for me ! — though he talked
so kindly to me — and was so gentle to me — and
looked so great and good — and I thought he was
so noble — and he was so handsome and so grand
— oh, I could have learned to worship him — but
now — now he has spurned me from his foot — he
has seen —'I don't know what he has seen — and
despises me like a toad in the road — what sort
men are ! — it must be that they are all so — so

exacting of us, poor things — and ready to trample us under their feet ! — even the great, good *Medico* is — is — is one of them — but I would n't have thought it — I could n't have imagined it — nor believed it.

'No, no, I cannot believe it — nor will I believe it of the good *Medico* — dear man ! I have been slandering him in my heart. I repent. I beg his pardon on my knees. I will not — I do not distrust him. He has been so kind to me — and he is so lovely to *Luigi* — I almost love him.

'But *Luigi* loves *Marie* — and — and — I — I — love . . . Marie — oh, oh !'"

NICODEMO OMBROSINI.

XXII.

In peace remain : I go : for now
To-day, to travel on with me,
Who guides my fate doth not allow,
But sternly doth forbid to thee :
   Or calmly stay,
   Or take, some day,
   A happier way.[24]
TASSO, GERUS. xvi, 56.

"I REMEMBER," said my companion, after a momentary pause, "I remember nothing more, after hearing the rattle of the *char* rolling away. The fact was, that, my nerves having been overwrought by such powerful excitement, I almost immediately sank into a profound slumber, which kindly extinguished my consciousness of pain and annihilated for me the dragging hours. I had barely awakened, when the cuckoo below sung out four o'clock.

"A glance through the window showed me *Maria* coming down from the Upper Meadow, followed by the sheep, and behind all *Villoso* bringing up the rear with a slow and careful fidelity, as if he were at his lifelong work in his own meadows.

"The far-declined sun was still shining bright and warm on the hillside, and *Maria*, leaving her flock to graze there a little longer, in care of the dog, came to the house and ascended directly to look after me.

"I was leaning back on the pillows of my chair, as feeble as a baby, and the tears which I did my best to keep back, but could not, were filling my eyes. Bending tenderly over me with her happy face, as fresh as a morning rose, she said, with a kiss:

—'*Pauvre enfant!* [poor chick]—you are so lonely.—It is hard to be penned up here, like a sick sheep.—The day has been so lovely.—And you must n't even look at the clouds.'

"Then, stroking my hot brow with her cool, soft hand, she said in the tenderest tones:

—'*Mais n' en t' inquiete point, mia dolcissima* [but don't worry over it, sweetest], you'll soon be well and as free as a lark again.—You are a little better to-day, are n't you?'

"I was silent, and she went on stroking my hot temples with her cool hands, and saying in sweet, bright tones:

—'*M'amie*, I've had the happiest day of my life. I wish you could have been with us.'

"The word '*us*'—ah, what was that?—shall I say it made my ears tingle again?—but I was still, and she went on:

—'*Lu* told me some news—some things, I mean, I did not know before.'

"This startled me, indeed. I was sure, now, that some confessions were coming. But I tried to be calm and to appear unconcerned, and I said, as quietly as I could:

—'Did he?—what were they, *M'amie?*'

—'Oh,' she replied, 'so many things about caring for lambs and kids and about wine-and-oil making and silkworms and straw-braiding and artificial flowers and the musical boxes.

'But, oh, I must tell you, first of all, that he brought *Villoso* to me—we must n't call him *Villoso* any longer—his real name is *Leoncello*, but for short, he calls him *Leo*—he brought the dog up to me and told him, with many signs, that I was his mistress now; and the great, shaggy fellow looked kindly up into my face and wagged his bushy tail and seemed to understand it all.

'Then, also with *Lu's* help, I put him through all his tricks, about sheep and wild game and for fun. He has got twenty of them. I'll show them to you under the window to-morrow; and then—'

—'But,' I interrupted, 'did n't he say anything about himself?'

—'Oh, yes, *M'amie*, he told me everything.'

—'What did he say?'

—'You know what *Babbo* told us. Besides that, he has a sister, *Lappa*, two years younger than he, who—'

—'Oh, I've seen her,' I interrupted, 'I'm certain of it. For it must be it was she with the great lady at *Aosta*. She called her *Lappa*. I never heard that name before nor since. It must be she. Besides, his nose and beautiful mouth and that dimpled chin are so much like hers. It must be, it must be, it was she.'

—'I think so, too,—yes, it's almost certain,' said *Maria*, 'for he told me she had been for several years maid to the *Marchesa di Castiglione*.'

—'Where is she now?'

—'She lives in *Roma* in the winter.'

—'Does he ever see her there?'

—'Yes, two years ago he visited her there in company with his uncle, the *Medico*.'

—'*Luigi* went to *Roma*?'

—'Yes, indeed! and it was then that he learned, oh, worlds of wonderful things, about the pictures and statues there, and he longed almost his life away to be himself an artist. But it was no use repining. He must be content, if God would make him a good vine-dresser and a good man— and a good son—and he hoped some day—a good father and able, if he had such a son, to send him to *Roma* to be an artist.'

—'Is he coming to-morrow?' I asked.

—'No, alas! no. He 's not coming again. He has gone for good,' she replied.

—'For good!' I exclaimed. 'Will he never come — to see — to see *Leo* — nor — nor any of us?'

—'He lives so very far away,' said *Maria* sadly.

—'Did he say he should never come back?' I enquired eagerly.

—'No, he did n't say it exactly so.'

—'How did he say it?

—'He said "*addio*" to *Leo*, patted and embraced the dog tenderly, and when the animal returned his affection with the utmost joy, his voice trembled, and I saw a tear on his cheek, and —' here she stopped abruptly, turned and went quickly to the window as if to look after the sheep.

—'And what?' I said softly, but she made me no reply. I rose and went to the window, and laying my hand gently on her shoulder, said again tenderly,

—'And what, *M'amie?*'

Without turning her gaze from the grazing sheep, she stammered, 'and — and then — he turned — and very quickly — he — he went away.'

"I wished so much to ask another question; for

I was sure some things — just the things I wanted to know — had been left untold. But she immediately put her hands over her face and sobbed aloud, violently.

"It was now my turn to console both *Maria* and myself. I thought I should burst into sobs too, but steeled myself to say:

—'I think he 'll come back, *M'amie.* He 'll want to see *Leo;* and I fancy he 'll want to see *you* much more, *dolcissima.*

"She blushed crimson and said between her sobs:

—'Oh, he — he cannot — if — if he — if he did — want to — ever — ever so much. They won't — won't let a conscript — cross the line — for — for seven years. We — we shall never — never see him — here again.'

"Then she went on sobbing with still greater violence. I wondered greatly how she could have been so gay only a few minutes before and now so sad. I was sure that something more and more important must have passed between them than she had told me of. I knew that what she had said about the conscription was true, and I could think of nothing to say in alleviation of it. In a flush of instinctive sympathy, I threw my arm around her, and we stood looking out of the window in silence, locked to each other, with our now equally moist and heated cheeks leaned together.

"While we stood thus silently, almost vacantly gazing on the grazing sheep with thoughts running far away from ourselves but probably not over fields very distant from one another, there occurred certain rather uncommon evolutions in the flock in which *Leo* was the principal hero and found a chance which he did not neglect to display his quality. A sturdy young ram, which had been for a considerable time slowly working himself apart from the flock, closely watched, however, by *Leo*, suddenly started on a gentle trot in a direction further up the mountain.

"*Leo*, who was crouched with his nose between his forepaws ready for a spring as the ram passed him, leaped forward with his whole force to turn him back. But whether by chance or by the instinctive deviltry of the ram, the two came into a powerful collision in such a way as to send the dog whirling in a sommersault, while the ram started off in a brisk gallop around the edge of the flock, but at some distance away.

"The dog in a twinkling was on his legs again; but the ram had already put the flock between himself and the dog. The latter in a flash took in the situation and started directly for the flock. With prodigious leaps, as straight and swift as a bird would fly, he galloped across their backs, which he hardly seemed to touch, and in less time than it takes to tell it, was face to face with the ram; who, thinking he had outwitted his keeper, was beginning daintily to crop the fresh untrod grass about him.

"As soon as his ramship perceived the dog again *en couchant* before him, he stamped furiously and shook his great, horned head, and started at a run with bent neck directly for the dog, with the obviously wicked intent to send him again flying in the air. But this time the canine keeper was equal to the occasion. Awaiting the terrific lunge, the dog sprang suddenly aside and the ram passed with such force that, meeting no opposition, he fell on his knees and thrust one of his horns into the sod. The next instant the dog was at his side, and at every attempt to rise he was pushed and held down by the strength and weight of the dog, until being quite exhausted he ceased to struggle, when he was allowed to rise and trot quietly back to the flock.

"Evening was now closing in, and *Maria* went to applaud and cheer the dog, and to dispose the sheep for the night."

XXIII.

As in form of butterfly,
At my latest breath, flew I
To the spots I love so well,
On the hill and on the dell,
Paradising through the air,
I surprised a tender pair.
From the pretty maiden's crown
High ensconcèd I looked down.

All that Death had robbed from me
I content in picture see.
Clasps she, with a silent smile,—
And his mouth enjoys the while,—
What the fates in goodness give,
All that mortal can and live,
Flitting from the bosom's swell
To the mouth and hands as well.

Now I start, and flitting by,
Lo, she sees the butterfly.
Trembling for her friend's desire,
And the swiftly rising fire,
Up she springs, I fly afar.
' Dearest, come and catch him there !
Come, let's have his dappled wing —
Yes, I want the pretty thing.'[25]

GOETHE.

"TEN days later I felt sufficiently recovered to undertake, at *Maria's* request, the family errands at *Martigny*," so my companion pro-

ceeded. "The weather was fine and the air brac-
ing, but my strength proved to be less firm than
I supposed and really unequal to the journey.

"When I came to the place where we met to-
day, I was so weary and exhausted that I was
glad to turn aside and sit down on that same
mossy bank, and became busy with my knitting,
but much more so with my thoughts. At last, as
I was on the point of rising to go forward again,
I saw, a little way down the road, a man walking
briskly with a mule before him.

"He carried an alpenstock in one hand and in
the other a long riding-whip with which, at short
intervals, he stimulated the gait of the mule; and
when not using it upon the beast, he lopped off
the tops of the taller weeds and wild-flowers at the
side of the path. Not being in the mood to encounter a stranger, and seeing that he seemed to
be absorbed in his own thoughts, and would probably go quickly by without noticing me, I continued
quietly knitting till he should pass.

"As he drew nearer, however, the figure seemed
more and more familiar. What a few moments
before I should have supposed impossible—I saw
Luigi Donati going toward our home!

"Was this, then, known there? At least, was
Maria probably expecting him? And—oh, could
I believe it—believe it of her—that—that I was

thus innocently sent to *Martigny* — to be out of
the way during his visit?

"I desired now above all things that he should
discover and accost me. I was ready to rush forward and accost him. But the sentiment of propriety restrained me, and perhaps more than all
else, some confusion at the remembrance of the
scene in which he last saw me.

"He was already in front of me. In another
moment he would pass around the corner of the
rock, and I should not see him — never see him,
again. A thought then flashed into my mind.
Had n't *Maria* said to me, greatly to my surprise at the time, and, as I then thought, with a
sort of tremor in her voice and a strange accent,
'Perhaps you will not see him again'? Oh, is
this the meaning of it?

"In an instant my timidity vanished, my hesitation was gone, my resolve was taken. I ran
gaily out from the nook just as he was disappearing beyond the rock.

— '*Come sta ? — come sta Ella*' [How do you do],
I cried.

"Glancing back over his shoulder, he saw me
running after him, and calling to the mule to
stop, in another instant he was approaching me
with uplifted hands, exclaiming :

—'*Grazie a Dio! — tante grazie! — che c' è una tanta Providenza!*' [thank God, what a Providence].

"I supposed he would mistake me for *Maria*. I was willing that he should. I now felt sure that he had; and it was not in my plan to undeceive him. 'How could I do such a thing? Was this a mark of my love for him?' you will ask. 'Was I not ashamed of myself?—ashamed of the thought of it?' To be sure, I was not quite happy on that score, nor did my conscience leave me wholly undisturbed. But then I said to myself: 'It was a desperate case. I should be unspeakably wretched to have it otherwise. Besides, what had I done to bring it about, if he were deceived. And—and—at all events, though it cut me to the heart to think so, was I not, probably, at this very moment, "more sinned against than sinning"?

'Perhaps after all'—for I was ready to believe, or at least to accept the impossible, so that it favored my desires — 'perhaps he was not deceived. He had spoken no name, nor employed any language which would not apply equally to me as to my sister.

'However it should be, it was, as he said, a Providence. *Iddio* had planned and brought it about. He felt it to be so. . It was so. Perhaps my agonized prayers to the *Madonna* were being answered. Perhaps my guardian angel had been permitted to bring me that dream as a prophecy of my coming felicity. Perhaps he had procured this whole event for me and was now reversing my hitherto apparently shattered fortunes. If so, ought I to do anything to thwart his aid?'

"Still I could not deny to myself, that I felt at the bottom of my heart an obscure sentiment of guilt and degradation in being so exceedingly pleased it should be so,— that it was in fact so much to my mind, that I would certainly have brought it about myself, if I could. This sentiment, lying half undefined yet immovable in my breast, did not leave me wholly serene.

"Yet you must remember that I was put suddenly and unexpectedly with the man whom I adored,— the first and only man I had ever been in tender relations with, slight as these were. Every fiber of my body quivered with delighted emotion. My reason was obfusticated. My soul was darkened by sensuous clouds. I did not realize this then, but I see it now, and I often reflect on it with mortification.

"Under a mental and moral atmosphere so hazy, my conscience, with a few gradually lessening struggles, fell asleep. My perception of truth, honor, and right was blurred, and even my real love for *Maria*—shall I say it?—dare I say it?—must I say it?—was in eclipse.

—'This is so fortunate—such a Providence—such blessed luck,' he said again, as he took my offered hand; and then turning we led each other (for I cannot say which was the guide), to the mossy bank and sat down. He enquired whether all was well at home—'the father, the sister, the flocks, the dog.'

Then he asked, with a new sprightliness in his tone:

—'Whither are *you* bound?'

—'To *Martigny* on family errands.'

—'Who tends the flocks to day?'

—'Sister,' I replied, not without a slight twinge in my conscience.

—'Ah, ah!' was his reply. Then looking away down the road, with an abstracted air, and striking the alpenstock into the soft ground several times till it stood alone, he went on, but with much hesitation:

—'I have changed—my plan—a little. I—I ran away—I wanted—I wanted to see—about—to see—you.'

"As he began speaking with his face turned away, I had been looking at him, knitting slowly the while; but when he stammered this out with so much difficulty and stopped, and I saw him turning his great, honest eyes round to look down on me, I could n't bear it, and bent my head over my work, as if attending closely to some difficult part and went on knitting as swiftly as I could. But I dropped stitches continually and was worried and confused, and my eyes were blinded with a mist and my heart rapped so loud that I think he must have heard it. At all events, however, when I did n't say anything he continued, more connectedly, but the words came very slow and trembling:

—'I don't know when I can see you again. I can't come here, perhaps for seven years at least — perhaps I never shall —*you* can tell best about that?'

"I said nothing, but I thought my heart would fly out of my mouth, and after a pause—a dreadful pause, to me at least (I can only guess for him), he went on again:

—'I should n't have come to-day — only — only — to — to find out — to — that is — to see you.'

"I felt most keenly in my heart that, in fact, he was not speaking to me. But I could n't, I could n't tell him I was n't *Maria*. So I was still silent. But, in spite of all I could do, the great tears began to drop upon my work. Between my joy at seeing him again under any circumstances, and the hearing of his dear voice, now for the first time, and my dread at the thought of his going away, possibly forever, and my mortifying consciousness of the dishonest *rôle* I was allowing myself to play — a double crime — deception toward him and treachery toward my 'sister — in spite of all I could do, my bosom was heaving spasmodically, and I expected every moment to burst out aloud into sobs and wailing. But for the present, I so far mastered my emotion as to be able still to work and weep on in silence, and he took no further notice of my excitement, than to go on with increased tenderness in tone and manner:

—'*Grazie a Dio*, that the conscription writ was n't served on me before I left home. They have indulged me to the utmost — or rather I have taken advantage of the utmost limit of the law. For the gentle law of Austria' — he said this with a mingled tone of sadness, irony, and sarcasm, such as I should not have supposed could by any possibility issue from between his gentle, beautiful lips — 'the gentle law of Austria allows to the candidate a choice of the time when the military service, of eighteen years in all, shall begin, from the age of eighteen to twenty-three. I have deferred the commencement till now. I was twenty-three, five days ago — a week after I left home. Further postponement is impossible.

'The old officer at Mantua did n't dream of my being away longer than a night or two, nor did I. It was that ill fortune — or good fortune — at the brook. It is wholly an accident — a providence — this delay — this being free till now.

'But every step toward home is irreversible. I shall get the summons the moment I arrive. No doubt it has been left with my *Padre* already. It will be impossible after that to cross the border on any plea — till my term is over.'

"Without daring to look up, I said, softly :

. —'Could n't you — could n't you contrive to stay this side now?'

—'Of course, of course, of course, I don't forget that,' he said slowly and with an emphasis on every syllable. After a moment's pause, in a lower voice and with a tone half pathetic and half ironical, which I did not securely understand, he added, 'and then — and then, not have to leave you at all — unless — unless *you* — banish me —'

—'*Miserello Esile !*' [wretched exile] I interjected in a whisper and without looking up, but trying to imitate his equivocal expression.

—'It almost drives me mad,' he went on in a more serious tone, 'to think of going back into that Austrian trap. Still, there is another side — yes, several other sides.

'In the first place, my case at least involves a moral question which is the same everywhere in this world — yes, and in the other world as well.

'I will not say anything of my duty to the Government — the Austrian Government. I might say something bitter and wicked. *Iddio* has allowed it "*et definiens statuta tempora et terminos habitationis nostrae.*" [26]

'The old officer is a good man. He is a boyhood friend of my *Padre*. May I tell you, too, he was once in love with my mother ; and they would have been married if the military law had permitted it to them — that is to say, to their purses.

'But he being then only *Sotto Tenente* [second lieutenant], before they could be lawfully married, a dowry of 60,000 *Lire* must be settled on the wife. Mother had but 5,000 *Lire*, her beautiful self, her ancient lineage, her heirloom silver, and the linen which her own hands had created. He was unable to make up one-tenth of the deficit. The prospect of marriage, therefore, was desperate, and was abandoned to their mutual distress.

'For several years she conceded to him *i favori d' un amante* [a lover's favors] ; but to *Babbo* (who had always known and loved her), after his active service was over, she became a wife, and to *Lappa* and me a mother — to us all she was the loveliest and best, till *Iddio* called her to *Paradiso*.

'This being so, it seems so unmanly, so mean — ought I not to be ashamed of it? — to give him the slip in this way. He could have detained me at home. Perhaps in strictness of official duty, he ought. To lose me now might cost him at the hands of the Government very serious trouble.

'At all events, if he had done the safest thing (which is always assumed to be an officer's duty), instead of the kindest, I should n't have been here and never should have seen you. This I owe to his clemency — to his love for my mother and — to his trust in me. Now could I take advantage of his confidence and betray him to the Government? Would it not be almost the same as breaking my *parola?* What should I be worth to myself, or to . . . to . . . to anyone with my truth and character gone?

'But the fact stands that I am at this moment an active member of the Austrian army; and unless I return at the earliest practicable moment and enter upon my duties as such, with a tenable excuse for being caught unexpectedly and by act of God outside the border, I am constructively and really a deserter, and exposed to the disgrace and penalties attached.

'So that if I were minded to sell my soul for seeming worldly gain, save my own skin at every cost, betray and sacrifice my own and my sainted mother's friend, yet the risk is hard and the chance is slim.

'I must at a stroke give up everything there. I should be an outcast in the wide world. All at home would be taken. My *Padre* would become at once a beggar. I should never see him nor *Lappa* again. He would be killed outright, and *Lappa* would break her heart over it.' "I knew he was right, still, intent on my work, I ventured to say: 'Couldn n't you, perhaps, make a home beyond the line not so very far away and take care of your *Padre* there, while he lives; and *Lappa* could come and visit you at least.'

—'I might,' he replied, 'drag on a while so, in terror, but probably not for long, and to be discovered at any moment. No hope then. A deserter must be given up by everybody if found within the border, if not, I should be caught some night, most likely, and dragged over. Then, what of *Padre?*—what of *Lappa?*

'As for me (if I ought to speak of it), the first thing would be a hundred lashes, afterwards would come the camp drudgery in irons, then, to serve out the whole time under surveillance, without eligibility to promotion, or honors and at last, worn out with hardship and disheartened by disgrace to — to —'

—'To marry, I think, the girl you loved and who loved you still all the same,' I interjected again, still without looking up, but intending to give a little cheer, even a little hopeful chuckle in my tone.

—'She would be married, or gone to America,' he said with a heart-broken tone, and I wanted to clasp him to my bosom and say: 'Never, never, never!' but I only said:

—'You are far from well now. Is your strength equal yet to the hard barrack-life?' I said it with difficulty, for a lump was swelling in my throat, and I kept my eyes fast on my work, for I dared not trust myself to look up, and in spite of all I could do, my chin trembled and I felt the tears coming.

—'No,' he said, in a calm, yet sad and solemn voice, 'I fear I could not endure it. I used to be so strong. I never was afraid of any labor, or exposure, or danger. I enjoyed it all — the excitement of it — the power to do it — the rewards of it. Now, it seems so strange, my heart is as weak as my body. I have become a little child again. My strength and my courage have forsaken me together.'

—'You must n't go, you must n't go,' I forced in a hoarse tone from my aching, trembling breast. 'That kind, old officer, your *Signor* uncle the *Medico*, yes, the Emperor, somebody must, will —'

—'Child,' he interrupted, 'you little know how unyielding, how like the polished steel of the cannons themselves are the rules of the military conscription. It would be well nigh as hopeful to countermand the summons of the Angel of death, as to attempt to escape or countervail in one single instance the relentless grasp of that iron hand.'

"I knew it was even so, as he said, but I knew, also, that what he most needed at that moment was moral support and comfort, and I steeled myself to say:

—'There 's nothing like trying, and you know that heaven helps them that help themselves, and perhaps if you pray—and I will pray too—perhaps your guardian angel will somehow—somehow or other—get you off.'

—'*Sicuro, sicuro,*' he cried, impatiently and sadly, 'and I 've done that—all but the praying. I guess the guardian angel don't meddle much in such matters. If he did I 'll wager he'd find a match in the Austrian Government, or in *Lucifero* behind it'—

—'Oh! Oh! don't say that,' I whispered, under my breath, and he went on:

—'However, Uncle *Gulielmo* has already written, with the strongest endorsement of his patron, the Count, laying the case, with every argument, before the Government —

—'*Bene, meglio, ottimamente*' [good, better, best], I interrupted in glad surprise, but he went on:

—'But the answer is doubtful — very doubtful. He only petitioned for my relief from barracks for two years. This as the best policy, for he dared not ask for more, lest it should preclude all hope. We shall certainly hear from it in a day or two — perhaps to-morrow. That will settle my fate. As I said the other day, *if it is n't yes it will kill me.*'

"These last words brought a load of intelligence to me far beyond the meaning of the syllables, and a revelation which he little dreamed of. They were the very same he had used in conversation with *Maria*, and which I assumed to be a part of his suit to her. It was now plain that this supposition was a mistake. He had explained them now unconsciously; and in how different a way! Had he then made any such advances at all? Dare I think, probably not? It was possible — oh, that it were certain that he had not!

"It was not certain, but I felt it was probable, very probable, and my conscience was much relieved by it. A heavy weight was lifted from my heart. A strange, vague comfort came into my soul, such as I had not felt for many days. Yet if I had been asked, I could not have given any sufficient or satisfactory reason for it. But the sentiment — the repose and content, such as it was — was there all the same.

"He had ceased speaking. There had been a few seconds of silence, save the soft sighing of the fir tree-tops above our heads, and the faint and fainter echoing roar of one of the *Jungfrau's* unceasing avalanches. My own thoughts were now beginning to flow smoothly, I know not of what. I think I was partly dazed by my sudden discovery.

"At all events, I folded up my work and laid it in my lap and ventured to look up into his face. Our eyes met for the first time. Although I had seen him and done for him so much — and far more than he knew of and had undergone all that unexplained misfortune with him and for him, yet I had never looked into those eyes before.

"Oh, where was I then! I seemed to be in an ocean of tenderness. I seemed to be swimming in a sea of love. My whole being seemed to be sinking down and melting away in his. I was greatly agitated and trembled from head to foot. He took my unresisting hand gently in both his own and said:

—'*M'amie*'—he had caught our family pet name, a part of our dear, sainted mother's own language, it sounded so queer yet delicious in his mouth—' M'amie, if I would go to America, would you go with me?'

"The blow had come—come at last so suddenly, though not wholly unexpected, and certainly not by any means undesired. Yet unfortunately, or fortunately, I had never been in a more unprepared state to receive it. The restraint which I had been so long using on my feelings while he was saying so much which stirred my emotions to the lowest depths, had quite exhausted my but half-restored physical strength. The feebleness of my nerves and of my whole frame decided the issue for me.

"Perhaps it was for the best. Perhaps it saved me from deliberately stealing for myself my sister's happiness. For I longed—oh, how irrepressibly!—to throw myself into his arms and bid him do with me as he pleased. Yet I saw the forbidding wall between us. I knew, I was morally certain, that this proffer was not mine—that it had not been made to me, but to . . . . .

I dared not finish the thought. But in a flash, I thought of a hundred consequences—of the coming desolation of my sister's heart—of poverty, loneliness, and shame in an unknown land— of the ever and everywhere pursuing curse of avenging fate in a thousand forms. The strain between such opposing forces was too much for me. I sank speechless and unconscious in his arms."

THE TRYSTING-PLACE.

XXIV.

" Under a tuft of shade, that on a green
Stood whispering soft, by a fresh fountain-side
They sat them down . . . . .

PAR. LOST, iv, 325.

" WHEN my consciousness returned, I found myself safe and sound, to be sure, but in the funniest plight I could have imagined. I was laid upon the mossy bank. *Luigi's* folded blanket, taken off from the mule, was under me, rolled at the end for a pillow.

"His red and yellow handkerchief, which had been dipped in the spring, was laid across my temples. My hands were crossed upon my breast, as if laid out for burial, and wrapped and tied close in the corners of the gray shawl which I wore upon my shoulders. *Luigi*, without hat or coat, was kneeling at my side. He was fanning me with my great straw hat. His own, of soft, whitish wool, was on my head. He was gazing into my face with a pitiful look of pain and despair.

"I felt confined, and looking down, saw my shoes (for, as a half-invalid, I had on shoes and stockings then) — I saw my shoes at my side and my feet drawn into the sleeves of his coat, which was wrapped around the bottom of my dress and closely buttoned. At the moment I opened my eyes, I had heard his desponding wail, keeping a kind of measured time with the fan:

'*Ahi, mia carissima, ritornami!*' [alas, my dearest, return to me] repeated over and over continually.

"The dolorous rhythm of these words, ringing in my ears as monotonous and solemn as the antiphon in the obsequies for the dead, at the very moment when I caught the first glimpse of my ridiculous plight, was too much for my disordered nerves, and brought upon me a fit of hysteria.

"Notwithstanding the seriousness of the occasion — which, in truth, I realized but too deeply,— and my heartfelt gratitude to him for his kindness, I burst into irrepressible laughter, to the greatest discomfort of the good fellow, and to my own profound mortification. In fact, my shame and anger at myself, over my inability to control my nerves, aggravated my infirmity; and the consciousness of my apparent yet irrepressible ingratitude threw me again and again into an agony of tears, which (as he understood them no better than the laughter) were not less distressing to him.

"Meantime, in the intervals, I told him that I was neither weeping nor laughing about him,—that there was no reason for either, except the weakness of my nerves, and that I thanked him from my heart for all his care.

"Then another fit of laughter would take me, and he could not believe otherwise than that in all my protestations to the contrary, I was really and truly making fun of him. He bore it bravely through several of these alternations, though his lip often trembled and he looked very sad.

"At last, as I broke out still again (after a considerable period of calm, and against every effort I could make to prevent it), into a low titter, he threw himself on his knees at my feet — my feet still deep in his coat sleeves,— I close fettered by the buttoned coat, crowned with his woolen hat, decorated with the red and yellow handkerchief across my forehead, my hands demurely pinioned across my breast by the corners of the old gray shawl,—

'*Mon Dieu!*' thought I, 'what a tableau! — the sylvan grotto — the dancing shadows — the mossy bank — the murmuring waterfall — an original, ornamented mummy — a noble lover at her feet, pushing his laborious suit, without hat or coat!'

"I thought I would have given or suffered anything then for the power to control myself. But though I was in the deepest distress at the seriousness of the occasion and the wicked levity of my conduct, yet an overpowering, irresistible sentiment of the comic, involuntary and meaningless though it was, seemed to be underlying and mingled with everything, so that I was as utterly and helplessly at the mercy of the tempest within me, as a tiny skiff on a stormy sea.

'*O M'amie! mia cara crudelissima!*' [my dear, my cruel darling] he sobbed, 'you will kill me — you are so beautiful — I think the holy Madonna looked like you —'

—'Not like me just now,' I murmured; and doing my utmost not to go off into another fit of hysteria, I succeed this time, and he went on:

—'*O M'amie*, I have loved you — I have adored you — you will kill me — I would have died for you — I shall die for you — oh, oh!' all in the tones of a wounded, crushed, broken-hearted soul.

"This was more than I could bear. Like the heroic treatment of the doctors, it cured my hysteria, but it carried me into madness. At that moment I was as if re-made—as if I had not existed before. I had no longer any scruples, for I had no memories of the past. I had no fears, for I existed only for the present moment and for him. I had no other sentiment in my soul, but my boundless, unreasoning love of him. All the forces and activities of my being were as if concentrated in that sentiment, and this was uncontrollable.

"I sprang forward, bound hand and foot as I was. I would have thrown my arms around his neck, but they were tied. Naturally, I went helpless toward the rocky ground. But his great arms caught me, before I fell, and, my head resting on his shoulder, I wept there convulsively in sobs of real passion intensified by shame, like the gusts of a summer shower. He remained silent and motionless till my external agitation was over. Then he said, softly:

—'Would you like me to put you in a seat on the moss?'

"I had, in truth, no choice, no wish, but, as to a request to me indifferent, I assented. Then he put me at the foot of the tree where I was sitting when you passed me to-day. There is a mossy seat there, wide enough for two, with a large root bending round at the back, and a flat rock projecting like a footstool in front.

"Having settled me there, he proceeded to readjust my attire. He transferred the woolen hat from my head to his own. Untying the shawl which was about my hands he arranged it upon my shoulders and set my own *Livorno* on my head. Finally he removed the queer leggins and replaced and tied my shoes.

"Then, having wetted the red and yellow kerchief again in the brook, he gently bathed my temples and wiped the tear-marks from my cheeks, hung the damp muslin on a bush to dry, put on his coat, and — did n't do . . . what I then . . . most . . . I will only say . . . expected.

"I closed my eyes waiting for it — for I thought it certain to come when he had arranged me to his mind — but as it did not come — not even on my forehead — I opened them again, and only in time to see him vanishing around the corner of the cliff where the mule had passed out of sight. A succession of new emotions, each different from the preceding, chased one another in a rapid train through my bosom.

"At first, I felt defrauded. No word, no kiss. This was so different from what I had read of accepted lovers, that I should not have believed it possible. For surely he was as good as such. At all events, I had not rejected his love.

"But presently a thought suggested itself,

which, if it did not quite wipe out my sense of wrong, went far to modify and mollify it. 'Might he not have suspected — for what is more incredibly suspicious than true love? — may he not well have suspected that my rather unusual performances were mere performances over his intense but honest passion, performances of girlish pride or fun; and that I had best be punished a little for it at the outset? — the rogue! — but, after all, did n't I deserve it?'

"This feeling, again, soon changed into a sentiment far more distressing. Reflecting now more calmly on my behavior, I saw things in a more serious light. 'Was it not possible, yes, quite as probable as not, that, no matter how involuntary, it had gone too far? — had shown him (he must believe), the levity and cruelty of my character, and suddenly extinguished, like water on fire, the flame of his love? — or at least, shown him his peril in yielding to it, and in a moment of returning reason given him strength and courage to tear himself away and flee as for his life? This would explain the abruptness of his going and — and all the rest. Yes, very likely — and the more I thought of it the more likely it seemed — that I should never, never see him again.

"Still I tried not to believe it, and used every

means to calm my mind. But the fact stood that I had found myself suddenly, unaccountably, painfully alone. I was very uneasy. I was really alarmed.

"In the midst of my tossing anxiety I became conscious of delicious notes, ringing like silver bells, or the pearly droppings of some exquisite guitar issuing from among the boughs of an overhanging tree. My attention was engaged for a considerable time in searching for the source of this liquid melody. At last I discovered, far out from the trunk, swinging on a slender bough, the well-known nest of the 'Hermit' thrush; and on two still slenderer twigs, overhanging this nest, I saw its two feathery owners.

"I knew the habit of this bird (which returns, if undisturbed, to the same nest, year after year), and I saw that they were taking a last look at the home where their little ones had just been reared, and were giving it a farewell song, before departing for the winter to warmer regions.

"It was the male bird, in his gaudy, glossy coat, from whom the principal stream of melody proceeded, but at certain intervals, his partner, who sat close by, on another twig, looking demurely down into the empty nest, dropped two or three soft and plaintive notes into his strain, which seemed to close the measure. Then the same melody was repeated, in the same order, with the same intervals and the same additions.

"This repetition executed again and again and again, with so much gentle pertinacity and earnestness, struck forcibly on my attention, seemed to be addressed to me, and aroused a sort of self-application in my soul. They seemed to be endeavoring to make me understand some thing hidden — was it some prophetic meaning?

'Was it,' I thought at last, 'was it, perhaps a requiem over the corpse of my hopes. Who knows, if it were angels in the form of birds, sent by my guardian or the blessed *Madonna*, to comfort and strengthen me against my coming sorrow?' I was surprised to feel the tears again running down my cheeks, and to find myself murmuring half aloud:

'*O cantatori innamorati!* [enamored songsters] — exquisite lovers, exquisite artists! Beautiful souls must be yours, to pour from your breasts such strains! Pure and tender sentiments only could modulate such a melody. Lovely emblems of chaste and simple affection, teach me your innocence and your peaceful joy, I will try to understand your song'—

"Bang! bang!—two sharp reports in quick

succession, made me jump with fright. The next instant, both the birds fell bleeding and lifeless at my feet; the next, a trained dog came like the wind, and bore them away in his mouth; the next — oh blessed relief ! — *Luigi* appeared flying round the corner of the cliff, and in my own bliss, I forgot the murder of the innocents.

THE RETRIEVER.

XXV.

Of the judgments of woman, full often the best
Is suddenly formed and as quickly expressed —
'Tis a part of her dower from bountiful heaven.
This intuitive wisdom to men is not given ;
'Tis not their allotment — far oftener they spoil
Conclusions not wrought out with time, care, and toil.[27]

ARIOSTO.

"WHAT a dream," said my companion, "I had been dreaming! — so sweet, but, alas, cut so suddenly and so terribly short!

"*Luigi* came bringing a cup which I knew contained wine that he was carrying with his luncheon. When he arrived in front of me, he knelt on the flat rock and handed me the cup, saying,

—'Drink, *mia cara !*' [my dear one].

"I brought the cup to my lips, tasted, and returned it to his hand. He took it, drank, and gave it again to me, saying,

—'Drink, *carissima !* [dearest] — drink it all.'

"As I obeyed, he said, softly, and very solemnly:

—'Like this blood of the grape, receive my love, which, as if it were my life-blood, I give you.'

"I had many times heard this formula of the 'loving cup,' and knew it was a part of the usual ceremony and contract of betrothal between parties of our rank in Tuscany. I always thought it beautiful both in words and meaning; and looked forward, like all maidens, I suppose, with ardent hopes to hearing it some day said to me, and pictured to myself that moment as the fulfillment of eager anticipations, and the crown of earthly joy; yet now, when the case came to be indeed my own, and I felt, almost without thinking it in words, that from the moment the cup touched my lips, it would bind me, soul and body, to him, with a vow that was irrevocable in the sight of God and man, and would, according to the common custom of our country, give him a husband's rights, though the sanction and benediction of the Church should be delayed — my rollicking sentiments were instantly altered.

"Dread took the place of reckless joy, and mingled with and mightily restrained my former longing. It sounded so much like the Sacrament, in spite of my dread, and that almost involuntarily, I slipped down upon my knees and said 'amen,' as if I were indeed receiving the Communion. Then, wondering in my soul to hear *Luigi* speak the words and in such a way, I whispered:

—'*O Luigi*, it sounds like the Sacrament.'

—'Yes,' he said, as we seated ourselves side by side, 'is n't Marriage a Sacrament?'

—'Surely, the *Catechismo* says it is,' I answered.

—'Is n't a Sacrament an oath on life-blood?' said he.

—'The *Padre* has often told us so,' I said.

—'Is n't life-blood the sign of deepest, truest, strongest love?' he asked.

—'*Sicuro*,' said I, 'what could be more so?'

—'Then Marriage,' said he, 'is the oath of deepest, truest, strongest love?'

—'I think so, certainly,' I said.

—'And the wine stands for life-blood?'

—'I know it does.'

—'Then the oath of love by wine is an oath of the deepest, truest, strongest love?'

—'It seems so.'

—'And Marriage, we said, is an oath of the deepest, truest, strongest love?'

—'We said so.'

—'Then is n't an oath of deepest, truest, strongest love, made and sworn to with wine, really and truly Marriage?'

"Now, indeed, I was alarmed. Had I not willingly drank with him the cup of love, while he pronounced the solemn words? Was he going to take that for Marriage?—'*Mon Dieu!*' thought I, to the very brink of what a precipice has my indiscretion, or at least my inability for guidance, brought us both!

"His love was plain, I could not doubt his honest purpose, his character I even revered; but I remembered, with terror, that love, like wine, could intoxicate; and where the power of both should be united, what an inebriation—both intellectual, moral, and physical—might result; and what might not a man thus triply drunken, think or do?

"I had hoped to lead him to a certain point; but he had led me to wholly another. I must endeavor at once to bring him away from his thought. Springing to my feet and pulling him to walk with me on the mossy bank of the brook, I said:

—'Ah, *Luigi*, I do not understand all about this, but certainly love is holy, and Marriage is holy, yet in some way I am sure they are not the same. Marriage must be something more than love—however ardent, deep, and true.'

—'Not more, not more,' he said, 'but, I grant you, something different. For our Immaculate Lady and the holy Angels are loving and lovely, and God Himself, we are told, is Love itself. I spoke only of mortal men and women.'

—'Can, then, this holy love you speak of be exclusive between two only?' I asked.

—'Surely, Adam loved Eve with holy love in sinless Eden,' he said.

—'There were n't any other women there then,' I said.

—'Of course not,' he said, with a shrug of his shoulders, 'what then?'

—'Why, just this,' I said. 'Suppose there had been other Eves in the garden, all just alike, could he love them all alike?—and if he did, would this make this love to be like that other holy love we spoke of?'

—'I do n't know whether he could love them all alike at the same time,' he said.

—'Well, then,' I replied, 'if he loved one very much more dearly than the others, would it still be the holy love you spoke of that he would be loving the dearest one with?'

—'If it had become Sacramental love, it would surely be holy,' said he; 'for does n't the Sacrament make it holy of course?'

—'Then the Sacramental love is holy towards one and the Angel-love holy towards more, and this is the difference between them?' I said.

—'You have stated it exactly.'

—'The Angel-love and the Divine love we know is everlasting and cannot change,' I remarked.

—'Yes, we know that certainly,' he said.

—'But the love between men and women, we know, is sometimes very short and changes often.'

—'Alas, we know that,' said he, 'it is too true that men and women are very changeable creatures.'

—'But Sacramental love,' I continued, is between men and women, can that then be sometimes short and change often?'

—'Surely it must not,' he replied.

—'How so?'

—'Tell me how love becomes Sacramental,' he said.

—'By putting it under the Sacramental oath, I suppose.'

—'Precisely so,' said he. 'And how long then is the time for a Sacramental oath to last?—can it change?—I do not say, often—but ever?'

—'Then Sacramental love is everlasting?'

—'How can it be otherwise?' he said.

—'Conjugal love,' said I, 'is by the sacred oath Sacramental and therefore perpetual, is it not?'

—'It must be in its nature so,' he said.

—'But is it not sometimes broken off and destroyed?'

—'Apparently so,' he replied.

—'How is that?—how can it be?'

—'Why simply this,' he said, 'it must be—it is, in every case—the story of a crime.'

—'Do you mean,' I asked, 'that in every case, the sacred oath both ought to have been kept and might have been?'

.—'Yes,' said he, 'undoubtedly it ought and undoubtedly it might—if the parties had willed it.'

—'Can we love by willing it?' I asked.

—'No, I think not,' said he.

—'How do you mean, then?'

—'I mean this,' said he. 'Without first the living spark, of course you can have no fire. No arranging of material, and no fanning of the cold pieces will kindle a flame. But when the spark is already kindled, judicious arrangement and fanning, will be that which will ensure and hasten the flame; and after this, continual care and addition of fuel will perpetuate and enlarge the fire, so that it need never wane.'

—'But yet it often does wane,' I said.

—'True,' said he, 'I mean that too. I mean that the fire actually burning, and at first as likely as any other fire, under proper conditions, to go on and spread and last indefinitely, may, by the opposite treatment, be as certainly put out. The two in whose charge it is—and perhaps either of the two, in spite of the best efforts of the other—may easily quench it, by pouring on such floods that no fire could survive it — or even by letting it burn out of itself and die of neglect.'

—'But,' said I, 'I do n't like the simile of fire. I do n't mean the heat and blaze of passion.'

—'Very well,' said he, 'let us take then the common yet sweet and beautiful emblem of love — *la rosa rossa d' amore* ['the red rose of love ']. I will grant, nay, I maintain that love is an exotic in many latitudes, so to speak, of human existence. It is a flower originally brought from the celestial paradise, but nevertheless it will grow and bloom in terrestrial gardens. It will do it, I say, but it requires a careful, constant, thoughtful, and sometimes an ingeniously thoughtful cultivation —

—'Ah, *Luigi!*' — I interrupted, but he went right on:

—'It requires, in fact, a double culture — as they tell us that two angels, a mighty and a gentle one, an angel of power and an angel of grace, were set to take care of Eden together, till the charge was given over to the human pair. The culture of the 'red-rose-of-love,' I say, requires the strong, bold strokes of manhood, and not less the soft, shy, subtle touch of womanhood. Beyond every other laborious culture, the precious yet tender thing must be shielded from every rude encounter, every chilly blast, every uncongenial storm. Neglect on the one hand will cause it to wither away, on the other, unprotected winter will freeze it to death.'

—'It is safe, then,' said I, 'if we are willing to labor for it, to promise "till death"?

—'Most surely,' said he, 'for it is in our power.'

—'But now, *Luigi*, said I, suppose again, that there had been two Eves just alike in the garden; and that Adam had found and loved one, and their love had become Sacramental love together, and by and by when she has gone out of his sight, he meets the other, but does not know it is another, and loves her; and this love becomes Sacramental love between them;—would this *his* love then be holy love? I do n't speak now of *her?*'

—'Only, I should think,' said he, 'before he knew they were two.'

—'But what if he came afterward to know that they were two loves?' said I.

—'You know the *catechismo* says he must have but one,' said he.

—'We are supposing it was a mistake,' said I.

—'Of course,' said he,' 'for otherwise it could not have become Sacramental love.'

—'And a mistake must be corrected, when it is found out, must it not?' said I.

—'It seems so,' said he.

—'Then he must break the Sacrament with one,' said I.

—'It seems that it must be so,' said he.

—'But is n't it a dreadful sin to break the Sacrament?' said I.

—'The *Catehismo* says so,' he replied.

—'Then he would break the *Catehismo*, if he were to keep both, and if he should put away one, he would break it again?' said I; 'is it not so?'

—'Of course, that cannot be denied,' said he; 'but then the second is to correct a mistake, and a mistake must always be corrected, if it can be, when it is found out, must it not?

—'I do n't know,' said I. 'That 's the very thing I am asking you about.'

—'How is that?' said he.

—'Why, if I understand you, it is that he would do wrong at first by mistake and afterward correct it by doing wrong on purpose.'

—'That is about it, perhaps,' said he.

—'Which, then, is better,' said I, to do wrong by mistake, or do wrong on purpose?'

—'Ah, *M' amie,* said he, you are too much for me. Perhaps I 'm wrong.'

XXVI.

"Then is there mirth in heaven,
When earthly things made even
Atone together."
As You Like It, v, 4, *Hymn.*

"AS we seated ourselves again under the tree, *Luigi* continued:

'Why, *carissima*, do you talk of Eves and of Divorce, as if any such thing were possible between us?—Do you think I might be unfaithful?—at least in America?'

'I think,' said I, 'you are noble and good, *Luigi*. I'm sure of that.'

'Then do you think I would ever—ever—oh, I can't say the words, "cast you off"—it frightens me to think of them—do you think I would ever—ever—let you go—give you up, under any circumstances?'

'But what if I were what we were speaking of—not the first, but a second Eve?'

'*O carissima!*—how can you say that? Do you think I have had another love?—a short-lived flame?—and forsaken her?—and will do the same by you?—'

—'I think,' I interrupted, 'that'—but he went right on:

—'Can you believe I would deceive you?—seduce you?—even if I did not believe your holy virtue were impregnable?—and adore you for it?—'

—'*Luigi*, dear *Luigi*'—I tried again to interject, but heeding me not, he still continued, in a passionate stream:

—'I swear to you, by the Blessed Sacrament—'

—'Do n't, do n't!' I cried, but in vain.

—'That I never loved another—no, nor never will.'

—'How few men could say that, and a great deal less, oh, a great deal less, I fear, from what I've heard,' I found room to say, while he paused an instant. Then he continued:

'*Carissima delle donne ch' esistano!* [dearest woman alive] I never knew what it is to love, till, I looked into your angel face, and all my soul was full of light, and I "knew good and evil." When now I see your blessed figure sail along, I think it ought not to touch the dusty earth, but swim in the soft air, as the clouds and the angels do. When I look down into the awful loveliness of your deep eyes, my head swims, and my body and soul seem to be dissolving in a warm sea of love. *O mia adorata!* could I ever give you up for another?—would I ever give you up at all?'

—'Would n't you, though?' I said, in a tone of affectionate irony. For such very sweet "taffy" as he had been proffering, though it was delicious to hear it, I knew well enough was superhuman stuff, like the ambrosia of old Olympus, and just as mythical; and I did n't know how much was due to the fumes of that strong wine he had been drinking, and the effects of which I felt, with some alarm, to be rather warm and lively around my own palpitating heart at that moment; so that I was in a very anxious state both of thought and feeling.

'Would n't you, though?' I repeated, in that same semi-affectionate, semi-quizzical tone, 'would n't you, though?—not if you found out that my hair was partly blue, or that there was an ugly scratch or scar, or spot on my arm, or neck, or somewhere?'

—'Cruel, cruel girl!' he uttered, in a mingled tone of sadness, anger, and love, 'why will you talk so? I could n't give you up if I would, for have n't we taken together the Sacrament of everlasting love? But, most surely, I would n't if I could, for I love supremely your dear soul and dear body through which it shines in every feature. I say once for all, I love you just as you are. I would n't have you changed — not even to make you more beautiful, if that were possible. I would n't have your hair a single shade lighter or darker, nor one of your fingers a hair-breadth shorter or longer. I want everything as it is. I want you, *mia cara, cara, carissima* [my dear, dear, dearest] — you and not anything else — even better than you.'

—'*Santa Madonna!*' I exclaimed, 'you are, indeed, a lover worthy of the chivalric days of my ancestors! What girl of to-day is worthy of you? What girl in the whole world might ·not well be crazed with your love? But then, you feel sure you'll never be put to that trial. Yet you may — you may be put to the test, *Luigi, carissimo.*'

—'Well,' he said, 'let it come. *Per l' amor di Dio*, let it come ! '

—'Ah, *Luigi*,' I said, ' do n't swear any more. I swore a dreadful oath about our Lady, in my distress and despair ; and when I went to duty, I got the worst penance of all my life. I only got absolution yesternight.'

—'It's long,' said he, 'since I went to confession, and I shall eat much bread before I go again, unless —'

—'But you'll have to go,' I interrupted, 'before you eat the bread of a good Marriage —'

—'Marriage ecclesiastical,' said he, 'you mean to say.'

—'Yes, of course, I mean that; and is n't that a good, even the best Marriage? For did n't the Saviour say we could judge the good and the bad of such things by the fruits?—and what other thing shows more clearly that the Church is a kind, good Mother, than her lovely, holy, everlasting Marriage?—unless it is, by contrast, the dreadful Divorces and wicked doings about it, we hear of in those wretched countries where she and her holy rules are rejected?'

—'I shall go, then,' said he, 'for your dear sake, just as for that I would go to any other punishment.'

—'But the penance,' said I, 'whatever it should be, will be made up for in the future. God forbid we should be separated in Eternity! Rather would I go with you, *Luigi*, to the *Inferno*, like poor *Francesca da Rimini;* but how much better to go together to *Paradiso!*'

—'I was n't thinking of the penance,' said he. 'I dare not tell you — it's of no consequence — what I think.'

'May our Lady and all the Saints and Angels keep you,' I said, 'from saying, or thinking any wicked thing of the Church; or of her sacred priests. The Church is our Mother and theirs;

and they are mostly holy men, in hard poverty, who are toiling under every kind of self-denial, for our salvation. We owe them, all men owe them, not suspicion and ill will, but trust and affection. But I, too, dare not tell you what I not only think, but know; and not about the church and the reverend priests, but about—myself— my own poor self. Yet I must tell you. For "*can you believe I would deceive you?—would seduce you?*"

—'No, *Carissima*, ten thousand noes. I would trust my life, and my eternal life, too, in your hands, as quickly as a straw.'

—'Ah, *Luigi*, do n't say it!'

—'I mean it all,' said he.

—'*Luigi*,' said I, now, in a voice that hardly came out of my throat and which I felt quivering in the center of my heart, '*Luigi*, you do n't know me.'

—'Do n't know you!' he exclaimed, 'do n't know you! by the holy Confirmation, do n't begin that cruel sport .again, I pray.'

"As he said this, he slapped me gently on the cheek (as the Bishop does in that rite of the Church), then threw his great arms around me and pressed me unresisting to his bosom, imprinting kisses on my cheeks—I know not how many, and saying as he did it:

—'I'll mark you, then, and seal you for my own

— there — there — there ' (with every kiss) 'mine!
— eternally mine !'

"This overwhelmed me. I was conquered,
crushed, trodden in the dust, till there was no
more strength left in me for choice or resistance. Utterly broken up, I burst into sobs.
Under the stress of an invincible propulsion
within, yet with the utmost physical difficulty,
I ejected from my bursting breast these four
dreadful words, syllable by syllable :

—'You — think — me — *Maria*,' and then sobbed
on, hanging down my head in delicious pain and
shame.

—'Or rather,' he interrupted, ' *mia donna Maria
carissima* [my dearest love Mary] —'

—'No, no, *Luigi*, it's false ! — all false !' I cried
or more truly screamed, I suppose, for I
was indeed beside myself with the conflicting
emotions of time and eternity, desires and
fears, hope and despair, surging in one blind
turmoil in my distracted soul. 'No, no, *Luigi*, it
is not so, it is not so,' I repeated many times. 'I
am not *Maria*. Would to God and our Lady I
were ! — were smooth, fair, sound, unscratched,
loved *Maria !* — but I am not. I am only
scratched, banged, spotted, sad, uncared-for,
forgotten *Marta*.'

"Then I could hold in no longer. I put my

hands over my face and burst into a paroxysm of tears. He slowly gave up my hand (which he had been holding, bringing it from time to time to his lips), returning it to my lap, and I heard a soft but piteous groan that made me shudder. Then for a few moments all was still, except my sobs which I could not control; between which I heard him murmuring under his breath, and the first words I caught were :

'Is she out of her head?—or am I dreaming?—oh, I can't endure this!'

"Then it was still again for a little, and then he took my hand and said, quietly :

—'*Carissima*, I can't bear to have you sob so, but I know —'

—'O *Luigi*, you do n't know,' I interrupted; and with a great effort I now succeeded in checking my sobs, and was resolved to stake my all at one throw. So I said, with the most quiet and earnest tone I could command :

—'Dear *Luigi*, believe me, for really and truly I am serious now and am in my right mind. You do n't know, because you never saw *Marta* before — unless — it was — was when —' here I choked again, and for my life, I could n't force out a word more, but gave a great sob, covered my face with my hands, and was still. Then I heard him murmuring to himself :

'*Per Dio!*—Is it possible !—It must be so.—I had forgotten.—I had forgotten.'

"Presently, very tenderly and with much hesitation, he began :

—'Then—you know—about that—that time. I thought nobody but me—and uncle—knew much about it.'

—'Of course, I know—I know,' I stammered out, 'for—for it was I—and—and it was—was something—something dreadful—but—but I—I do n't know just what.—Tell me—tell me, *Luigi*,' I said, still keeping my face covered with my hands. He made no reply, and I repeated:

—'Tell me, tell me, *Luigi*. I must know—if it kills me—I must know.'

—'It's no matter, now,' he said, 'I have never told anybody. I never should have spoken of it, and I never shall. It's no matter to remember, it's no matter at all.'

—'You must tell me,' I said. 'I ought to know—and—and I think I have a right to know—from you—from you, *Luigi*.'

—'I'm almost ashamed,' he said, 'to tell my dream. I was so weak and light-headed, then—and—and it signifies nothing.'

—'Oh, was it only a dream?—was n't it true, then?' I cried, catching at a straw, drowning as I was, in terror ; and being thus comforted for an instant, by this idea, I raised my head and looked up into his face.   He was looking far away down the valley.

—'Something was true, of course,' he said.

—'Tell me *Luigi* — tell me all — tell me quick.'

—'If I should, it would be only to obey you,' he said. 'I should never speak of it except at your command, for it is nothing, nothing, nothing.'

—'Tell,' I said, 'tell everything.'

—'If I must, then,' said he, 'I was dreaming about the river behind our Mantuan home.   I used often in summer to go there to swim.   My little sister, *Lappa*, before she went to live with the *Marchesa* used to go there for berries in summer and for nuts in autumn.

'There were raspberry bushes and hazel bushes, and chestnut trees all around, and two high rocks which had a narrow opening between them like a gateway on the side toward the house.

'The opposite bank was a very steep, bare rock which came down from the mountains, and nobody ever went there. In the night, we sometimes heard wolves barking there; and once when Uncle was with us — it was clear moonlight — he shot at one across the river. The next morning we found it lodged in the bushes further down, but I never knew of any swimming across the river.

'It was a very hot day. I was at work among the vines. The *Babbo* was still in his siesta. Nobody was near. *Lappa*, after finishing her tasks in the house, had passed toward the river, telling me where she was going.

'This was a common thing; and I did n't think of it again, till I heard the wolves barking, and, looking up, I saw *Lappa* running towards me, like a frightened sea-nymph, her long hair streaming behind her and a great wolf yelping at her heels. She rushed directly into my arms, her wet locks flew into my face, and she came against my breast with such a blow that I awoke.—You know the rest.'

—'No,' I said, trembling all over, 'I do n't know it at all.—Tell me—tell me all—every worst thing.—If it kills me, let me die now— with nobody here but you.'

"He hesitated, but I urged till he proceeded:

—'When I first opened my eyes, I thought, for an instant, that the dream was real. You (if it was you) were lying partly on my breast. My arm was under you, and your cheek was on the pillow. You seemed asleep.

'Then I wondered where I was. Of course, I wondered to see her there, and was at my wits' end what to do, when I heard a voice outside, and in an instant more a step at the door. I looked, saw Uncle, and heard him exclaim something — I do n't know what — then saw him throw his blanket and take her in it quickly away. The dog, too, was growling fiercely around the room. Uncle soon returned, but we have never spoken of the thing.'

—'But did n't you observe,' I said, 'anything on her neck or anywhere?'

—'Yes, I saw a red rosary and crucifix hanging there,' he said.

—'Tell me, *Luigi*,' I persisted, 'was that all you noticed?'

—'Well, there was a dark spot below the crucifix,' he said.

—'Did n't you despise and hate her?' I said, in a trembling whisper.

'No, surely not,' he said, 'why should I? — I've hardly thought of it again. I was too weak then to mind it, and afterwards too worried, and since too happy — unless,' he added, after a pause, 'when thinking of the future.'

—'Ten thousand thanks, dear *Luigi*,' I said, putting both my hands in one of his, "I have forced you to tell, now I will compel you to listen. You must hear me. If you despise me, I shall die, but I will die here with you.'

"I looked up into his face. It looked so noble and true, yet so worried. His hand trembled, but he did not take it away from mine. I went on :

'*Luigi*,' I said, 'I must tell you all. You must know all.' Then, with a spasm, I seized the pink shirred rosette, and tore it from my heart-shaped dress-front. I closed my eyes; and while I seemed to see a shower of shooting stars before my fiery eye-balls, I pointed with my trembling finger to the pink crucifix and to the dark seal of my identity below.

'*Eccolo!*' *eccolo!* [See it, see it], I stammered on. 'I am she — I am she. I was watching — all day — by your bed — of pain. Oh, so dreadful — it was. *Maria* was with the sheep. *Velloso* — *Leo*, I mean — would not go. I was alone — with him and you. I was trying — trying to be good — to you. My heart ached — to hear you — moan, moan, moan — so hoarse and low and trembling — and *Leo* was always rolling his eyes — toward the bed — or me — and growling — and sometimes — grinning and gnashing his teeth '—

"Before I had said half of this, he had gently taken my hand away from my bosom, and brought the shawl that was about my shoulders closely around and fastened it in front, and when at last I opened my eyes, he had his arms folded across his breast and was looking down on me with his great, soft eyes so tenderly; yet his face wore a look so solemn and so sad. I was a little comforted by that look, but it was with my heart beating very fast that I dropped my eyes and my hands in my lap and went on with my story:

'At last there was a moment when there came a sudden and a frightful change. The flushed face grew ashy pale.—O *Luigi*, I loved you. I thought then you were dying. It put me out of my head with grief and fright. I thought of the *acquavite* [brandy]. I rushed to the little stand. I snatched up a glass and poured in. Holding it in one hand, with the other I tore away my *camicinetta* and seized the crucifix—and was flying to the bedside— to make you swallow the liquor—and to pray —to pray on the crucifix for your life—or, at least, for your passing soul—'

—'Angel from heaven!' I heard him murmur, but I went right on:

—'I heard a horrid growl at my ear. My foot tripped on the wolfskin rug. I felt a sharp pain on my shoulder and knew I was plunging forward—upon—I know not where—and—and I know no more—'

"Here I broke down, and could say no more, only to sob out, word by word,

—'Except—that—I found—found myself—alone—in the cot—in the loft-chamber—and—and the phials—of the *Medico*—around—around me—and—and—I could not—could not raise my head—nor think—nor guess—what—what had happened—happened to—to me—and *Maria* said—said that the *Medico* forbade—forbade me—to look—even to look out—out of the window—and—and so—so—I've kept—kept away—away from you—and—and I thought—thought I should—I should never—never see you again—and—and I think—yes, 'I'm sure—you—you love—love *Maria*—and—and I love—love—*Maria*—oh dear, oh dear!'

"He did not speak, but I saw great tears roll over his cheeks, and looking up through my tears into his swimming eyes, I said softly, yet earnestly :

—'You do love *Maria*, do n't you?'

—'I will not deny it,' he said, tenderly.

—'You kissed her when you said "*Addio*," did n't you?' I persisted.

—'No, never!' he said, earnestly.

—'But you embraced her then?' I urged.

—'My soul? Yes!—My arms? Never!' he said, still more earnestly.

"Then, with a nervous spring, he bounded from the sofa-bank, holding his temples with both hands, ran to the little brook and walked hurriedly up and down many times on the mossy brink of the prattling stream, stopping again and again to look down into the sheeny water, where schools of tiny fishes were frolicking over the pebbly bottom, but during what seemed to me a long, long hour, he did not once look toward me. He seemed to be absorbed in an agony of self-consultation.

"At last the conflict appeared to be ended. His extreme nervousness ceased. He came and stood again at my side, and took both my hands in his, but said nothing. There was now a long silence between us. I dared not break it, and he did not. He closed his eyes, but still held my two hands in his, which trembled yet.

"But he now became ever more and more calm. The tears which had been from time to time shooting across his cheeks flowed no longer. The trembling in his hands passed off gradually, and was presently gone. A look of peaceful satisfaction came over his face. He opened his eyes, and looking down on me with a noble gentleness, in soft but faltering tones, he said:

'It is so — so — so. Duty — my duty is . . .'
He did not finish the sentence, but stooping

and raising my hands to his lips, kissed them fervently and laid them again in my lap.

"While he was speaking, I had closed my eyes in a sort of dreamy content; and when his voice ceased, I did not immediately open them, for I was dazed with my own thoughts. When at last I became conscious of the silence and raised my eyes to look about me, *Luigi* was gone — gone for the second time, and was it not surely now forever? I sprang up with a pang of alarm, and flew to the turn in the path around the great rock. I was only in time to see him disappearing in a distant turn of the high road toward *Martigny*.

"I was frightened indeed. A hundred uncanny explanations suggested themselves to me in a moment. 'That last unfinished sentence to begin with — did it bode good or ill? Was that discovered and overpowering duty going to give him to me — or carry him to *Maria* — or — or — was it not more likely, from his behavior, driving him, in his distraction and wretchedness, to drop us both and vanish from the scene, in the army, or in America? I think he has dropped us both.'

"But there was no human help for it. The mule was gone. I could not overtake him. Even if it were possible, what good would it do? What else could the result be, but to have my love (already proffered under such mortifying conditions) again, and in still colder blood, rejected? My maiden pride fought fiercely with my distracting love. Piercing thoughts crowded upon me from every quarter. My poor heart sank under a hundred stabs. I felt as if I were dying, and for the moment, I wanted to die.

"Then I reviewed his conduct again and again. He had been so intense in his love, and so decided in his choice, before; and so calm, so gentle, so tender, since the trying ordeal which revealed my indisputable identity and reversed his hopes —'was not this a good omen for me? —was it not almost a proof that he was surely settling back into my arms?—and would not all our future life together be so much the more indissolubly welded, by these recast joinings, these cicatrized wounds, the reaction of these shocks and strains securely outridden?'

"But then it flashed upon me in another light. 'Was n't that last tenderness meant to soften the final blow?—to mingle the gentlest possible memories with the coming shock which duty—what he felt to be his inevitable duty—he knew would give me at the moment of my awaking to the dreadful fact—memories which to my dying day also would sweeten the bitterness of it?

'What if that silence was what he felt to be a better thing than words — indeed the only thing to be endured — at such a parting? What if that pressure of both my hands, the imprint of his impassioned kisses there, were the native language of an unspeakable love and an unspeakable anguish giving an everlasting farewell!'

"One moment in hope, the next in doubt, the third in despair, with a heart swiftly palpitating under conflicting emotions, I crept slowly back to the mossy bank, my eyes dim with tears and my limbs trembling in every nerve; and throwing myself on my knees I prayed to the dear *Madre di Dio*, to pity me and send my *Luigi* back to me.

"So I prayed and wept and prayed again, until, from excitement and exhaustion, I fell asleep on my knees. After this, it may have been longer or shorter, the touch of *Luigi's* hand on my shoulder was the first thing I remember; and in an instant more, almost before I was aware of it, he had lifted me from my knees, and we were sitting again side by side on the sofa-bank.

"Half-way between silent hope and silent despair, I looked up into his sober face and he immediately began:

'Most surely *Iddio* or our guardian has decided our lot.   Unquestionably you are "the first Eve"; and yours is the Sacrament of love.   I did, unknowing, and as I think, innocently, wander after the second.   Yet, *grazie a Dio*, I did not become entangled with any bonds of duty there.

'But if any tender sentiments must now go unreciprocated, which may have sprung up in the heart of the other Eve — the dear girl — my heart bleeds to think of it — through my ignorance or indiscretion, we must do every-thing in our power to soothe and console her gentle heart and make up for the wrong — involuntary wrong — by our lifelong kindness.

'Between us the Sacrament was and is sole and true, although clouded then by ignorance in my intention.   By proxy, at first, as it seems, I was charmed (such was the will of heaven), by the beauty of thy body.   I was also ravished by the sweetness of her spirit which was an image of thine.   Now clouds have vanished, and all is reality.   The proxy has served its heaven-sent purpose; and is now as a dream of the past.   We stand already in a union, invisible and spiritual, yet indissoluble.   If thou art will-ing we will be made outwardly and lawfully one, by the arm of the State and the benediction of the Church — and what we are to do we cannot delay.'

"I buried my face in his bosom and said nothing."

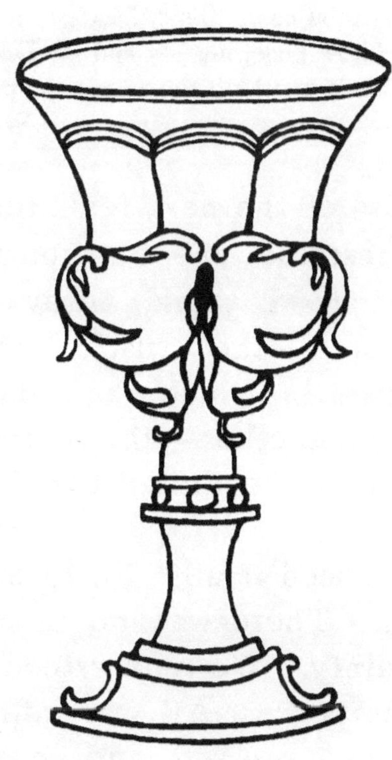

XXVII.

"I have waited so long for thee, Love!
Art thou come to me, Dearest, at last?
Oh, bless Thee, my Joy and my Dove!
This is worth all the wearisome past."

F. W. FABER.

"THE bliss of the next few minutes!—who can describe it?—but you will guess it aright, for it is, I think, always and everywhere the same—the trustful embrace—the long, long kiss, in which the very souls commingle with one another—the conscious blessedness that drowns the united two in one sea of oblivious joy.

"We experienced it all. No lovers were ever more blessed. There was no more doubt, no more uncertainty. We understood each other now. All was peace. All was infinite joy.

"But our time pressed, and in five minutes we were on our way to the town. I was seated on the mule, the bridle-rein hanging loose in my hand, dreaming dreams that were all to be reversed. *Luigi* walked at my side, with eyes lowered upon the ground, apparently absorbed in watching the shambling steps of the mule.

"After a pretty long silence — it seemed long though delicious to me — *Luigi* began, as he said, with 'a story — if it was a story.' The substance of what he said was this:

'Good old padre *Gilberto di Pastrengo* is prior of the *Convento* of the *Benedettini* at *Mentova*. He has been an intimate of our family and my father's friend from childhood. On my eighteenth birthday, I went to the *Convento* with some choice wine, and a letter from my father to the *abate Gilberto*, asking him to accept the present on the score of old friendship and to give me not only the usual *natale* [birthday-blessing], but also a general benediction upon my opening manhood.

'He received me most lovingly, took me to the High Mass (for it was the feast of St. Luke, my patron), and made me receive the Communion in the Chapel with the *padri* and *frati* [cleric and lay monks], and afterward brought me to their midday meal.

'This was eaten in the great *Refettorio* [monastic dining-hall], which, with its furnishings, was a curiosity to me. A rather narrow table of uncovered and unpainted wood ran through the whole length of the hall on either side, with a bench behind immediately against the wall. Across the end opposite the entrance hung a very large picture reaching from side to side of the room. It was a Last Supper — a beautiful copy of the *Cenacolo di Foligno*, so long of unknown origin, but then lately discovered (to the infinite delight of the owners), to bear the sign-manual of *Raffaelle* himself.[28] This was interesting to me every way, and by far the most beautiful thing of its kind I had ever seen. At the side of the entrance door, was a kind of pretty high pulpit for the brother who read from the lives of the Martyrs or from some similar book of edification. The *fratri* sat on the benches, at a distance of more than a *metro* apart, and in front of each was a complete set of all the very plain eating and drinking vessels and utensils which they allow themselves to use — exactly the same before everyone and never removed from the table. The long sides of the hall were also hung with religious pictures and busts of famous members of their order — none of especial interest to me, except a Crucifixion by *Fra Angelico*.[29] This was wonderful. The impression it made on my soul I shall never lose.

'The *Abate* could not speak to me there and then, for, by the rule, one brother must read aloud during the meal and all the others must be silent. But when this was over, and the *padri* and *frati* had gone to their cells, and all was still in the house, the Superior took me again into the *Refettorio*, and standing in front of the wonderful *Cenacolo* of which I have spoken, talked to me beautifully of it — both in an artistic and in a religious way. Then he led me into the garden, and brought me to an arbor at the farther end, where he was accustomed, he said, to sit during the hotter afternoons and study and write. We sat there together till the *scampanata* [hurried ringing] of the *Convento* sounded for Vespers.

'The place, the hour, my errand, and my reception — all conspired to make it seem Paradise to me. A soft breeze swept over the garden and the banks of flowers and the sweet-scented shrubbery and through the lattice-work, above and around us, which was densely covered with climbing roses of many varieties. All was beauty and stillness; and the perfumed air, the murmur of the central fountain, and the faint melodies of flute and violin which were wafted to us from the windows of the *Convento* (for it was the hour when these *religiosi* allow themselves such innocent recreation), created an environment into the like of which I had never before been admitted. I was, in fact, almost bewildered by the exquisite fascination.

'But what shall I say of the conversation of the *abate?* In its gentle earnestness, in its affectionate sweetness, I forgot the loveliness of the surroundings. A desert, a dungeon, would then have seemed to me *Paradiso*, I listened — as *Dante* says of *Virgilio* — with such rapture to his discourse. He talked both of religion and of the earthly life, and even — would you believe it of the old, severe, emaciated ascetic? — he talked with the tenderest sympathy of human passions and youthful love. What he said I shall never forget; it is engraved on my memory as with a pen of steel.

'Omitting now many wise and beautiful things which he said of love and marriage — which I will tell you at another time, dearest — when he came to speak of the choice of a wife, he began somewhat like this: "My son, child of my choicest friend, *Francesco Donati*, heir of that princely name, though shorn, in the Providence of God, by the wickedness of men, of their ancient fortunes, listen to my words. Remember that they come, not only from your true friend, and your noble father's friend, but from an old man who has seen and known much of human life, in every station, from the king to the beggar; and who for scores of years has sat in the stall of the Confessor, and heard there, from the privacies of ten thousand lives, unspeakable things which it is not lawful to utter into any ears but those of the Almighty."

'Then he proceeded with a very particular and minute yet most delicate description of the feminine qualities of both mind and body — noting which were to be sought, and which avoided. He spoke of concordant and contrasted peculiarities, of stature, complexion, and temperament; and of the best adjustment of these, in a pair perfectly assorted for the highest felicity. He described many signs of character, in the *tout ensemble* of the countenance, in the particulars of the face, the brow, the nose, the lips, the chin, and even in the ears, hands, palms, fingers, etc., etc., and told ways of judging in regard to important things which could not be seen nor spoken of. I might say, in short, that he gave a whole science of testing the dispositions of the mind and the constitution of the body; and added many wise and weighty conclusions, which were the fruit of much reflection, under extraordinary opportunities for observation.

'But what surprised me most was the last item of his counsel; and this was also the point on which he insisted with the greatest earnestness and at the greatest length. It was after he had canvassed the whole nature of woman, and sifted her celestial aptitudes, and opposite disqualifications, in respect to marriage, that with a gentle laugh he quoted the words which *Leopardi* puts in the mouth of *Tasso* and of his familiar as they converse together in *Tasso's* cell during his seven years' imprisonment at the *Ospizio di Santa Anna.*"

'The substance of it was this: *Tasso* says, "Oh that I could once see my *Leonora* again! Every time she comes back to my mind, a thrill of joy spreads over me, from the crown of my head to the tips of my toes. There is n't a nerve or vein in me that does not quiver. And if it were not that I have no more hope of seeing her again, I should not believe that I have yet lost the faculty of being happy."

'To which the familiar replies: "Which of the two things do you consider to be the sweeter: to see the beloved woman or to think of her?"

'*Tasso* replies: "I do n't know. I am sure that while she was in my presence, she seemed to me a woman; away, she seemed and seems a goddess."

'The *genio* retorts: "These goddesses are so obliging that when one comes up to them, in a trice they fold up their divinity, detach their effulgent rays, and put these things in their pocket, so as not to dazzle the mortal who places himself before them."

' *Tasso* replies: "You speak only too truly. But does n't that seem to you a great sin of the ladies that, at the proof, they turn out for us so different from what we imagined them?"

' The *genio* answers: "I am not able to see that people should be faulted for being made of flesh and blood, rather than of ambrosia and nectar. What thing in the world has a thousandth part or even a shadow of the perfection which you think has to be in the ladies? And yet it seems strange to me, when, of course, and no wonder, the men are men, that is to say, creatures little praiseworthy and little lovely, you then cannot understand how it happens that the ladies are, in fact, not angels."

' After this, the genial old abbot rose, and, taking me by the hand, led me to that side of the arbor which was the most profusely overhung with roses, in every stage of advancement, from the wilting and scattered charms of overpassed maturity to the scarcely discernible opening of the finest bud. Here he stopped, and, turning toward me with an expression of mingled anxiety and tenderness, not only suffusing his countenance, but overspreading his whole figure and bearing, he said, for substance (for I cannot pretend to remember every one of his beautiful and exalted words):

"My son, son of my friend of such revered memories, heir of the unknown future destinies of a most noble house, what, after all, are the purity and perfections of the body, otherwise considered, incomparably important—what are they in comparison with the purity and perfections of the soul?"

—"Nothing, nothing," father, I said, half under my breath, and looking up reverently into his stern but intellectual face, now aglow with earnest and tender emotion.

—"Whatever, then," he continued, "may be the other qualities of the woman (*Iddio bene-dicala*) [God bless her], whom you would take for the partner of your life, see to it, above all else, that she comes to you with a virgin heart. Assure yourself beforehand, beyond question, that the affections she has to offer you are fresh and untried", (and plucking a cluster of unopened rose-buds, as he handed them to me he added,) "like these unfolded buds."

'I received them in respectful silence, and he proceeded:

—"What should your fresh, innocent soul have to do with the gleaning of fields where others (whether guileless or not), have harvested, or trampled the first fruits before you? What partnership should the snowy whiteness, the unbounded wealth, the infinite yearnings of noble, untried affection contract with the withered residue which time has left", (stretching his hand toward the discolored clusters whose faded petals were falling in showers and floating, on the inconstant wings of the zephyr, to the ground, he added,) "like these past-blown roses, once indeed the joy and the glory of the scene, now pouring abroad those exhausted petals which have attracted the notice and displayed their charms to a thousand passers by, and disbursed their fragrance upon a thousand flying breezes?"

—"The simile is striking, father," I said in a hesitating tone, not wishing to seem to contradict, or even to doubt his teaching, though, I confess, I was not then so fully impressed with the truth of it.

'He observed my hesitation, and conjecturing rightly the cause, replied: •

—"It is true, that a simile, however striking, is no element of proof, as I think you meant to say. But, notwithstanding, the doctrine is true. The virgin freshness of first opening love, once unfolded to the air and light of day, can never be restored. Once dead it knows no resurrection."

—"Ah, father," I said mournfully, "how little, then, there must be in the world, of love under its best conditions!"

—"Doubtless," he replied, "the confessor's seat has taught me that. If it were not so, this present world, poor as it is, would be a paradise indeed."

—"It is much, father, to hear you say that, —that a paradise is possible here. It may, then, be mine."

—"Yes, my son, thanks to God, more than this is possible. For I will not deny that a heart *blaséed* by coquetry, or even having fallen under the anathema of a broken vow, may yet, perhaps, perform, perfunctorily at least, and with an honest scrupulosity, every apparent office of the united life. I will not deny that innocence may follow, and bring with itself a certain satisfaction and rest, which, by the merciful law of heaven, is always and everywhere of innocence and duty the exceeding great reward. But this, my son, is a lower than love's highest benison. It is at its best, like *Dante's* discovery concerning the second-rate happiness of the inhabitants of the Moon:

> ' Then was it clear to me how everywhere
>   In Heaven, is Paradise; though yet the power
>   Of goodness doth not in one measure shower
> Always its highest delectations there '.[31]

"But why, my son, stoop to the lower estate, when the highest heaven of love is open to your possession? Let, then, the lips which are for all future time to distil away your griefs be spotless as the descending snow, of any former stain, whether of folly or of untruth. Let the bosom, where for all future time you must seek the oblivion of your cares and the solace for your fatigues, be not only like a garden where you will move alone in the peerless fruitions of love, but also a garden whose bloom and fragrance has not been ravished by bygone blasts, has not been opened to the roaming access of preceding approaches."

"Some of this talk of *Luigi's* made my bosom flutter, but I was dazed in the acquisition of my great treasure and remained silently devouring the dear fellow with my hungry eyes.

—'Such a heart,' he continued, '*M'amie*, I know I have found—and what is more, have acquired'—

—'It is—it is that'; I interrupted, 'in whatever else it may be wanting. If my poor heart is a garden it is yours, dear *Luigi;* and I swear to you by the Blessed Virgin that it has never been entered nor. approached by living mortal before.'

"He did n't say that such was his; how could

he? But he came nearer to the mule, and walking close at my side, took my hand in his, brought it fervently to his lips, and then returning it to my side, still held it in his own, as we went on for a time in silence."

LONELY TURN IN THE ROAD TO MARTIGNY.

XXVIII.

Not two miles traveled when they hear
  Such rattling, rumbling danger sound,
As made the encircling woods appear
  To rock and tremble far around ;
And quickly rose upon the sight,
  O'er twinkling stream and bush and tree,
A charger housed in trappings bright,
  And dashing onward furiously.[32]

ARIOSTO.

"AS he discoursed thus and we moved quietly along toward *Martigny*, how delightful had the way and the whole world now become to me ! — The autumnal sky was so bright, the breeze was so soft, the trees were murmuring such a silvery cadence, in reply to the unceasing prattle of the laughing water which danced so gaily on with many a tumble and many a frothy whirl, in the brook at our side. But above all, emparadising all, at my side moved tall and handsome *Luigi*, noble in every limb and look, and yet more noble in soul — and he was now mine, my affianced husband, my own forever and forever ! — hallelujah !

"Such a load of joy, such a blissful transition from my late distress and despair to this miracle of my present infinite good fortune, was almost too much for my poor, overwrought heart to bear. It seemed as if my bosom must burst open and my fluttering heart spread its wings in the upper sky.

"I suppose *Luigi* had similar feelings, but the outward deportment of us both became quiet — very quiet indeed. Now and then we spoke of some pleasant thing in prospect; but much of the time, also, we were silent and busy with our own sweet thoughts; often and often *Luigi* came nearer and pressed my hand without speaking a word; and then sometimes our eyes met, and I felt a thrill like the bliss of Eden.

"Yet boundlessly happy as I was, there was one sore spot in my soul; and when, ever and anon, my dancing thoughts struck it, I was compelled to groan within myself at the momentary yet heart-cutting pang. These moments of shuddering pain came when I thought of *Maria*, — dear, dear *Maria* — the shock that was to fall on that poor, deceived, deluded heart — the storm of agony that was about to burst upon that so gentle, so loving, so trusting creature — the cup of bitter anguish which, all without her thought, was now prepared for her to drink.

"I would gladly have persuaded myself to be-little her coming grief. I tried to think of every soothing consideration — of every hopeful relief — of any possible remedy. But I could discover nothing; I could invent nothing. The cold, crushing fact remained. It could not be miti-gated, and it could not be exaggerated. 'She had been robbed! — waylaid and robbed, robbed, robbed — of her heart's treasure — her hope — her life — her all!'

"I could not doubt that she had regarded *Luigi's* love as surely and securely her own. 'Was she not, probably, at this moment, reveling in rosy fancies, never to be realized? Was she not a victim on the way to the altar decked and gar-landed for the sacrifice? If, under every disad-vantage, I had so fully and so far built the whole superstructure of my happiness upon it, and the thought of losing it had desolated my future with a rayless despair, what, with everything in her favor, must not she have done? — what structures of hope must she not have reared! — and how tremendous might be the consequences of their instant collapse! Would she probably sink in sickness? — Could she survive it? — Might she not, perhaps, become a maniac? — how much less than a fratricide should I be?'

'And then' — oh, the pang! momentary, indeed, yet ever returning to stab me, again and again, in the most sensitive fibre of my heart of hearts — 'what of my *Luigi* himself?' I knew, beyond the shadow of a doubt, that the sentiment of duty would always bind his judgment and control the conduct of his life. 'Had he not, however, confessed that he loved *Maria*? — that his soul had embraced hers? Was his a heart to change its affections in a twinkling? Was it, then, to be, that I should, indeed, possess his hand, while *Maria* still kept his heart?—and who shall say it did not belong to her? — oh, oh, oh!'

"But in the midst of such reflections on my part and of much silence on his, suddenly, we both discerned in the distance before us, a horseman coming furiously along from the town. Very soon *Luigi's* sharp eyes recognized the white face and feet of the largest of the Count's saddle-horses, and a little later, he made out the tall figure of the waiting-man who had attended him while he lay at our house. Coming on at full speed, the man was presently so near as to recognize *Luigi*; and then drawing up suddenly, he leapt from his horse and came running toward us, while the trained animal trotted gently along in the track of his rider. Lifting his cap, without further salutation and holding a letter in his outstretched hand before him, when hardly within reaching distance, he began :

'*Il Signor Medico* sends this to your worship in the greatest haste; and I am to mount your worship on this horse and myself return with the mule.'

—' Has something happened, then?' exclaimed *Luigi,* in a tone of much concern, while my poor heart began to palpitate furiously.

—'I do n't know what it is,' said the man. A *messagio,* in a green and silver livery, came this morning from *Leuk,* bringing a letter to *il Signor Medico ;* and very quickly after, I was sent in all haste to bring your worship back.'

"*Luigi,* receiving the letter, examined the superscription a moment, then opened and perused it in silence. But I saw, with increased anxiety, that his hands trembled violently, and the color came and went on his face, and his brow wore a look that was new and strange to me.

"When he had glanced through the lines, he lifted his eyes, and looking far along the road toward the town, said to the man :

'Do you remember, *Felice,* the old beech-tree, just beyond that farthest turn in the road, where the chair-rock is and there is a little fall in the brook?'

—'*Si, Signor,* I know the place,' said *Felice.*

—'Well,' said *Luigi*, 'go forward thither with the horse, and wait till we come up. We won't be long after you.'

"*Felice* remounted and in another moment was out of hearing; and then *Luigi* read the letter to me. It was from his uncle and enclosed the reply of the Government to the petition for a reprieve from the barracks. The substance of the answer was, that 'upon his returning to *Mantova* and reporting to the Military bureau there, and receiving the allotment of his regiment, etc., and signing his solemn *parola* that he would not leave the country, and at the end of twenty-four months would report for duty, he should receive (out of regard to the special recommendation which the Government had received for him) a furlough from the barracks for that time. But his seven years of active service would begin from the day of entering the barracks; and a breach of the *parola* is punishable with death.'

"The good *Medico* said in his note that the enclosed paper had been that moment received, and that the messenger had been dispatched with it, on the back of *Adolpho* the swift, in the hope of overtaking him before reaching his destination and perhaps the using of some expressions or even making some promises which, under the new circumstances, he might afterward regret, or find it hard to fulfill. 'At least,' the uncle went on to say, 'I thought you would prefer to return and reflect and consult, before completing the purpose of your visit ; and I shall be awaiting you during the day, to give some further informations which I have received from other quarters, and to help by the best counsel I can command, in view of the various aspects in which your difficulties and advantages may be viewed.'

'I must, of course,' said *Luigi*, 'respond at once to this invitation of Uncle. I must meet him as speedily as possible. I must get his counsel, for really I do not know what is best to be done.'

—'Ah, *Luigi*,' I exclaimed, 'that dreadful *parola!*—you must n't give it—never—never give it. If you should ever go—if you were found one *metro* beyond the line—if your father or your wife were dying—or if your clock were wrong—or if you forgot—and should be one hour behind in reporting—oh, horror of horrors!—the punishment is death!—death! *Luigi*. They will lead you out and shoot you!—Oh, *Luigi, Luigi!*—never, never do it!'

—'But we could live together in love and peace for two years,' he said, mournfully.

—'How could it be peace, on such conditions?' I said.

—'We could keep the cottage and the land and comfort each other and be a great solace to dear old *Padre*,' he said.

—'For two years,' I cried, with impatience and grief, 'and what then?'

—'If my *Padre* should still live,' he said, 'you could take care of him; and if the barracks were in *Mantova*, I could often have an hour or two with you and often a Sunday.'

—'But more likely by far,' I groaned, 'your regiment would be quartered elsewhere, God knows whether in Austria, Hungary, or Poland.'

"He did n't reply, but we were now come up to *Felice* who was awaiting us with the bridle on his arm and the stirrup in his hand. *Luigi* said to me in a loud and cheerful tone:

'Now *Marttetta*, *Felice* will attend you and bring you to the hotel with a gentle gait. We 'll talk over everything there together and with Uncle.'   •

"Then beckoning to *Felice* to bring the horse nearer, he exchanged places with him, sprang into the saddle, and kissing his hand to me, saying:

'*Ecco la mia parola a Lei!* [Here is my parole to you], he started off with a gallop and was almost in a twinkling out of sight.

"*O Santa Maria!* pity me, pity me!—*Ecco la*

mia parola a Lei! — these were the last words I ever heard him speak. If ever they are verified, will it be in *Paradiso?* While they still rung in my ears, he passed around a turn in the road, and — *Oh, Dio in cielo!* — when I saw him next, his arm was clasped around *Maria*, and they both were flying, swift as the wind, forever, forever, from me.

"*Felice*, at the words of *Luigi*, committing me to his care, made a *berretta* [cap-salutation] in silence and took up his station behind the mule where he remained as we moved slowly on.

"When *Luigi* was gone, though I expected to meet him again within an hour, a sentiment of unutterable sadness came over me. My spirits which for the last hour had lifted me to the highest heaven of earthly felicity, now carried me down to the nadir of moral depression. I busied my uneasy thoughts by contemplating the conditions of the offered *parola*. I tried to look at it wisely and unselfishly and especially in every favorable light. But in fact, the more carefully I considered it the more alarming the prospect became. He might be tenderly nursed for a few short months towards recovery and vigor; but I was sure it would be, only to be afterward offered up a precious sacrifice to horrid *Bellona;* and then to leave a widow crushed with sorrow, and perhaps dependent orphans to drag out a whole life of desolation and distress.

'What a career,' I thought, 'would his dear life have been?—begun in motherless sorrow—pursued in a continual struggle with destiny—closed at the opening bloom of love and domestic joys, by a pitiful martyrdom!—Alas, the dear, dear fellow!—it was pitiful, so pitiful.'

"I could not endure to think of it. I burst into uncontrollable sobs, and the hot tears poured over my face. *Felice* came immediately to the side of the mule, and with cap under his arm, and with a very solemn face and mournful voice, said:

—'*O Signorina, Signorina, che cosa ha?*' [O dear Lady, dear Lady, what is her trouble?]

—'*Non importa molto, Felice*' [Nothing of much consequence], I said.

—'*Si, si,*' he replied, '*Ella sta solitaria e timida ma Felice è forte e fidele.*' [Yes, yes, she is lonely and afraid, but Felice is strong and faithful.]

—'No, no, *Felice,*' I said, 'it is not that. I am not lonely, nor afraid.'

'*Ogni donnettina sta sempre ben timida*' [every nice little lady is always much afraid], he replied. '*La mia Signora la Contessa,* is very timid when she rides in the country, if our *Padrone,* the *Signor Conte*, is not along. Often and often when the coachman is on his box and the footman has mounted to his seat, *la Contessa* makes him dismount and run and get me to come and sit with the driver in his stead, and as soon as ever I come to the carriage, *la mia donnettina* [my dear little lady], says to me: 'Come *Felice, il mio guardiano* [my bodyguard], get thee on the box with *Stefano*. My heart beats so fast to-day. I forebode some danger or accident. I shall be calm when I see thee there. I trust to thee next to *il mio Signor Marito il Conte.*' Oh, never fear *mia Signorettina*, I will go here close at her side. *Ecco, ecco!* [look, look].

"With the word, he lifted his *casacca di fustagno* [long fustian waistcoat], showed two great *pistole d' arcione* [horse-pistols], and a huge sheath-knife hung in his belt. I had not thought of fear before. I had often passed over this highway alone, and had never heard of any robberies or dangers there for anybody, at least in broad day. I believed now that *Felice's* words were only empty talk. Yet in spite of myself, the sight of these grim weapons, and the excited looks of the dusky giant who wore them, standing so near me, and the remembrance of the crooked way through a lonely valley, a little way before us, filled my heart, already so worried and worn, with fear, indeed.

"But this fear, which became a terror greater than I had ever felt in all my life before, did not come from any prospect of dangers from roaming robbers or highwaymen, which seemed to me practically impossible; but rather (and I could not but feel they were real), from far others which lay in the character of my so-called guard.

"He was absolutely unknown to me, and not much better to *Luigi;* who, in his excitement and anxiety, I thought, might have failed to remember this. Nor did we know how much, or how little, the Uncle, even, knew of his antecedents.

"The fact stood, that I was absolutely in his power. I could n't but think: 'What might not such an opportunity tempt this giant monster to do! Who would ever know what had happened?—or what had become of me? He could throw me into the chink of a glacier, a *chilo* deep—and the mule into another—and make up a story about robbers—or about me—that I had run away with another man — gone, probably, to America—or he might go to America himself—or enlist with a false name in the army, and never be seen or heard of again.' My heart began to flutter and I was in an agony of terror.

"*Felice* rattled on praising his prowess. He entered now upon a description of a terrible scene, a few miles outside of Naples; where four *malandrini* [roughs or highwaymen], who were really escaped convicts, sprang from a concealment at the roadside, and surrounded the coach in which his mistress the Countess and her two young lady daughters were riding.

'They tore the reins,' said he, 'from the trembling hands of the driver, unhitched the traces from the carriage, stripped the coachman and footman and dressed themselves in their clothes, throwing their own discarded prison-rig to the poor naked fellows to put on if they chose (which of course they dare not do), then they robbed the ladies of their purses, jewels, rings, and every movable thing, turning their pockets inside out, leaving them half dead with fright and terrible expectations, sitting *abiti disordinati* [tumbled and tousled] in the empty carriage, which the villains had drawn aside behind a broken cliff, where, with the horses, their prisoners and booty, they were out of sight from the beaten track of the road.

'At that very moment, itself, by the goodness

of heaven, I came then around a sudden turn of the way. I was flying on the back of *'Dolfotto*, having been unexpectedly sent by my master to recall the ladies, because a noble stranger had arrived from *Francia* whom it was important for them to meet, though his stay was limited to the two or three hours during which the passing steamer on which he came would delay *al sbarcatojo* [in the harbor].

'I was passing at a gallop, for the *padrone's* last words were, "*Giuseppe*, thou hast *Adolfo*, show thy metal and his." At the instant, I heard a woman's moan, followed by a volley of course blasphemy commanding silence. I looked down and saw on the ground the marks of a scuffle and a trail leading away to the spot.

'To leap from *'Fotto* and have flown around the cliff, was the work of two seconds. What a sight! — The ladies clasped in each others' arms, kissing one another and weeping in silence! — all in the empty, unhorsed carriage! — the poor, naked fellows crouched on the ground beneath and trembling like olive leaves in the wind! — The four *ribaldi* — two bareheaded with our long livery coats on, and two uncoated but hatted and breeched with our livery, having distributed as best they might between them the spoils of our coachman and footman — were squatted on the

MER DE GLACE.

ground with their backs towards me, wholly absorbed in their quarrel over the division of the
gold taken from the ladies' purses, which lay
empty on the ground between them.

'*Ella* [the lady] may be sure that I used these
weapons lively, and with such effect that the
scoundrels did not get on their feet again, till
we had pretty roughly replevied our property
and with the little aid of the ladies returned
them bound to the serjants of the law. I suppose they are more useful now in the mines of
Sicily.— But, *ola !* — who comes here?'

"I looked up and saw a strange-looking fellow
emerging round a turn in the road not a hundred
steps in front of us. He was coming on a dog-
trot, and held a coil of small rope in his left hand.
His clothes were a semi-mixture of flashy civilian
and military undress, and he carried pistols and
knife in his belt. His head was surmounted by
a black woolen hat with a broad brim and a black
plume drooping low on one side. Huge boots
came far above his knees, and from the once
white but now soiled tops hung tassels once
gilt, now equally faded and soiled. He wore
gauntlet-shaped gloves and carried in his right
hand a heavy polished cane.

"When within a few steps he stopped, removed
his *chapeau* and saluted me with several profound

bows, bringing his head at each inflection almost into contact with the stupendous boot-tops. Then flourishing his bonnet in a very extraordinary and telling manner, he said to me — *Felice* had stopped the mule when we came abreast —

'*Prego molto! — la Signora melo perdonerà — ho due parole da dire col suo staffiere*' [I beg the lady will pardon it, but I must have a few words with her *staffiere* "].

"Then taking *Felice's* arm, who stood silent, and, as I thought, not at all surprised, he led him a short distance aside, and began in a low tone an animated conversation filled with excited gestures on both sides, with occasional references to the rope.

"I could not catch the drift of their discourse, for it was only occasional words spoken in a higher tone that I could make out, and of these, some were in a patois such as I had never heard before. But I caught *la femminetta* many times, and such phrases as:

'*Ella non può*' — '*Essa sta modestissima*' — '*la sua vita disonorata*' [She cannot — She is extremely modest — her disgraced life], etc. I knew they were talking of me, and my imagination filled out the sentences with a fearful meaning.

"The parley was soon ended. *Felice* returned,

and taking the mule by the bridle, said to me, with a respectful touch of his cap:

'*Questo è di necessità, molto necessario, mia Signorina buona*' [This is, of necessity, very necessary, my good little lady].

"Without saying more, he turned the beast around and began leading it back toward my home. I was dumb and powerless with fright. The stranger followed in silence behind us. When we came to the rock from which I had started, he turned into the by-path and led us away from the road further than I had ever been before. We passed my old seat on the left hand and penetrated, by a winding path, into the dense firs and undergrowth, gradually ascending the mountain, till we came to a kind of grotto which had a mossy bank like a bed, and was thickly overhung. Then he said a few words in patois to *Felice*, who came to my side, and making a *berretta*, as always, said:

'*Prego, Signorina, Ella debbe scender adesso dal mulo.*' [Pardon, the lady now must dismount and go from the mule].

"From the moment the mule was turned about, I was so astonished and confused that I had not spoken a word, and now I was so frightened that I made no resistance, when he stretched out his great arms and took me, like a baby, from the saddle. Preceded and guided by the stranger, he carried me quickly into the grotto, and laying me gently on the mossy couch, spread a shawl over me very cavalierly. Then I heard him lead the mule away through the crackling bushes, till the sound died away in the distance. The stranger did not come into the grotto, but remained just outside, where, as I lay, I could see his gigantic bulk passing solemnly to and fro before the entrance.

"When *Felice* returned, the two men stood for some minutes conversing together in a low tone and in a strange patois, sometimes turning to look or gesticulate towards me, of whom I was perfectly sure they were talking. I thought *Felice* said something which meant:

—'How dare you?' To which the stranger replied:

—'I will risk it.'

"Then I thought *Felice* said:

—'What if you were caught with her?'

"I could make nothing out of the rather long reply, into which there entered much gesticulating and the drawing and brandishing of the weapons. But I surely understood *Felice* at last saying:

—'What then will become of *her?*'

"Without making any reply, the giant stranger

turned and came in, and, kneeling down before me, said in a half intelligible patois:

—'She will go with me — she will not fear — do so in *Tirolo* — the *contadine* [country-women] like it.'

"I was paralyzed with fright; and as in a nightmare, I could not speak a word. The stranger, however, did not wait for a reply, but immediately rose from his knees and proceeded to undo the coil of rope, winding it, as he did so, around me from my feet to my shoulders, leaving my arms free. Then he kneeled backward and fastened the rope to himself in such a way that as he rose he carried me with him on his back. To steady myself I instinctively grasped the rope where it passed over his shoulders, and so I rode out of the grotto whither and to what fate — what must I think?

"Issuing from the grotto, and flinging a few words more of patois at *Felice*, which I did not in the least understand, and throwing one of his great arms back around me, he started rapidly up the woody mountain-side, through thick underbrush which made me hide my face under the shelter of his great shoulders, and which would have torn me and my clothes to tatters if they had not been closely bound down.

"When, at last, we emerged into an open place — it was a dark and dreadful spot — he stopped. He was panting audibly, and my whole body rose and fell, as on a wave of the sea, with his every breath. But he did not lay down his load.

"I remained in instant expectation of every-thing and anything; and the time he stood there seemed to me an eternity. I could not escape, I dared not speak or move, and all around was still.

"Suddenly there came a sound of many horses' feet clattering on the road; and inter-mingled with the steady and increasing noise of the horse-hoofs, and with the intermitting roar of the tree-tops, seemed to rise the mur-mur of many excited voices. Louder and nearer and clearer every moment the alarming uproar became. Was it an army, an avalanche of men and horses, sweeping on to overwhelm us? But nothing appeared. After a few mo-ments of suspense, agony, and terror, the up-roar began to decline, the sounds became less and less distinct, and gradually faded away, till all but the unending song of the forest had died again into silence.

After the stillness had lasted for a short space, a shrill whistle echoed among the rocks and bushes and was answered by another from my giant guard or jailer (I knew not which he was), who immediately started to descend the mountain again; and the same experience as before was undergone by me on the passage.

"Arrived at the grotto, we found *Felice* and the mule waiting for us there. I was quickly transferred from the back of the giant to that of the mule, having been delivered from my mummy-bonds during the transition. The office of the giant seemed now to have been finished and he ceased from further attentions to me. After a few hurried words with *Felice* (which were unintelligible to me), spoken while he was recoiling his rope, he made, precisely as when he first arrived, a profound *inchino*, then a salutation *di cappello*, and then with an emphatic '*addio a Lei*' [adieu to Her], he quickly turned and went off "with God," falling into a sort of dog-trot, and in a few seconds had disappeared.

"I was now again in the hands of *Felice*, badly frightened indeed, but unhurt. He began at once to lead the mule down to the road again, but without a word of inquiry or explanation, instead of taking up again our journey toward the town, he turned backward and led on toward my home.

"I was too much confused with wonder and uncertainty at this as well as at all that had happened to make any resistance or enquiry at first, but after we had moved on in silence for many minutes, I at last recovered strength and courage enough to call *Felice* back to my side and say:

—'What does all this mean, *Felice?*'

—'Ah, *la Signorina*,' he replid, 'she must not ask *Felice*. He does n't know anything. *Il Signor Luigi* will tell her.'

—'But who was that strange man?' I asked.

—'*Il Signore* will tell her,' he replied.

—'But why are we going home,' I persisted, 'and not doing as we were ordered by him?'

—'*Questo è anche commandato*' [this too, is commanded], he answered.

"Nothing more was said, and in silence we climbed along the road toward my home. My busy, restless thoughts leapt forward and dwelt upon the evening when *Luigi* would have returned to me; and I consoled myself with the prospect of the pleasure it would be to hear it all from his own dear lips. But the promise of *Felice* was not fulfilled. '*Il Signore*' never had the opportunity to reveal to me the mystery of these strange events. Whether on meeting a detachment of French troops going to guard

the Holy Father at Rome, *Luigi* had sent back
to shield me from the shock of passing them
(really no trifling affair for a girl like me, and
especially in the then so feeble state of my
nerves); or whether the troop was a recruited
squad on the way to join the Austrian army in
Lombardia; whether, perhaps, *Felice* were an
escaped conscript, and would hazard a recogni-
tion and even some insult might befall me, if
found in his company; whether the stranger
were a fellow-fugitive with *Felice*, or some
friendly officer or bravo even;— these and
many other possibilities and conjectures were
never satisfactorily cleared up, and the mystery has always remained.

"What is certain is, that after accompanying
me to my home, *Felice* immediately set out
with the mule on his return. The mule wandered back to the hotel during the night, without his driver, or any marks of his fate or
flight, and he was never afterwards heard from.
Luigi's parola to me, alas, was but too sadly fulfilled.

XXIX.

"`. . . . . My theme
Has died into an echo ; . . . ."
CHILDE HARROLD, 4, 185.

"IT was long after midday when I arrived at home with *Felice*. *Maria* was in the pastures. *Babbo* soon came from his trip to the *Hospice*. When he had finished his chocolate and bread, I cuddled at his side and told him all my story. The tears of the dear old man dropped many times on my head, and he drew me again and again to his bosom. When I was done, he said :

'*M'amie, Luigi*, I trust, is a good youth, and I'm glad for thee, if thou shalt be happy, and I believe thou wilt be. Thy mother and I were happy together. You, my dear girls, are a sweet solace to me. But since she has gone, I may say that I live no longer. I only work and sleep, and go on my way alone, waiting till my time shall come to follow her. Yes, every woman must have a husband's strong arm to encircle her timid and fluttering heart, while her soft arms hang about his rejoicing neck. In the struggles and sorrows that none can avoid, his hairy breast is her bulwark of peace, and her soft bosom the pillow for his tired and worried head. *Iddio* has willed it to be so; and otherwise, there is no happiness in this world. Therefore I rejoice for thee.

'But, *M'amie*, I mourn that it will take thee so far from me — perhaps, thou sayest, even over the sea — to free and rich America. Bright stories, indeed, are told of that wonderful country, but, *M'amie*, there must be another side. There's no perfection anywhere. There's compensation and loss everywhere, here below. I do n't know what it is there; but I know and thou knowest, that there is a reverse to every picture. I should never, never behold thee, again; and besides, I should have deep forebodings for thee there.

'Perhaps, thou sayest, thou wilt go to sunny Italy — to the vine-clad hills of *Mantova* and the green banks of the *Po*. Dear, dear country! It would be an earthly paradise to me. For thee, it will be more. Thou wilt be the brightest sunbeam there to the other *Babbo* — happy man!

'True, *Maria* will be with me here still — poor thing! — and be my comfort — my only comfort — while I stay. But how she'll miss thee!—and when I go!—ah, my child!—and the summons must come soon—what will that tender lambkin do? Go to her now—and tell her all—and comfort her—thou canst do it best—before thy betrothed returns—he'll then absorb thy time.'

"I obeyed at once, and went rapidly along to seek *Maria*, towards the Upper Meadow. I passed now for the first time since the accident had occurred to the young man and these great events had transpired in our home, over the foot-path where Sister and I from our earliest recollection had so often trod. How familiar was every *metro* of the ground, every rock and bush and turn! Yet, what was that strange glamour now overspreading them all? It was as if I were moving in a dream. I knew every object perfectly, yet each one seemed to look at me as a stranger—as a sort of intruder, I thought. Had not our infantile feet toddled over this space, clinging to our dear mother's dress? Had we not gamboled here hand in hand in the careless innocence of childhood? True, for so many days, just passed, my feet had not trod that path; but it was the first time in almost twenty years that the ground had not felt their pressure daily, and often many times a day; and had I not once and again, in the days of my banishment, stolen forbidden glances, and seen—oh, what through my tears had I seen?—*Maria* tripping gaily along here under *Luigi's* smile?—Could it be these memories that now threw this startling strangeness over the scene?—or was it, perhaps, yet more the sentiments that were boiling in my own soul?—the glamour of my dazed perceptions,—for what was my mission now?—whither and for what was I bound?—to look for a stray lamb?—ah, yes, a lamb condemned to the slaughter. I thought of it under this very similitude, for I knew that stranger things had happened, than it would be, if, at the first comprehension of the truth, her poor heart should break, and she should fall a lifeless corpse upon my breast. When I saw this image in my mind's eye, a cold shiver ran over my whole frame.

" By an extraordinary effort, however, I shook myself at last out of this mental distress, and felt again a sentiment of profound peace and happiness bubbling up from the bottom of my heart. The fact stood, however, do what I would, that my heart was convulsed and, like a boiling caldron within me, overflowing with a confused fullness of content and anxiety, of lively hopes and deadly fears of a melting sisterly sympathy and of a self-absorption that seemed at other moments so brutal.

"The thought of living as his wife with *Luigi*, anywhere in the wide world, much more, if it might safely be so, in his own Italian home, and of helping him among the vines on the sunny Mantuan hills, made my heart dance for joy. But the only too sure apprehension of there being no escape from the conscription, no respite without the dreadful *parola*; and the certainty of the long separation beyond, with the dangers of life in the field, and hardly less in the sickly barracks, perhaps in the most distant part of the Austrian empire—or as the grim alternative, a life-long exile in unknown America—these were spectres which danced like scowling demons in my mind's eye.

"Then my reflections over *Maria* would return, still more conflicting and tumultuous. 'The poor girl!—how I loved her!—so good, so loving, so gentle, so beautiful! Was not her sweet innocent soul, at that moment, paradising in pictures of love and life-long happiness?—alas, never to be realized!—alas, to be erased in a moment before her eyes! Alas, the bitter draught of sorrow that she must drink!—and am I to be the cup-bearer? Must I, alas, press to her dear lips the chalice of misery?—Shall my breath perfumed with the bliss of Eden blow out the light in her soul?—Worst of all—shall my conduct, which I might have altered, stand the active cause of all this mischief?

'Why did I intermeddle in her affairs?—Why did I do anything in this matter?—Why did I tell *Luigi* of myself?—Why did I not act the proxy for her to the end?—Shall I talk tender words to her now with my lips, and with my right hand go on driving the iron into her soul?

'Why not renounce all from this moment? — I — self-absorbed — selfish — unsisterly — unnatural — inhuman — wretch!—Shall I say I love her?—and go on breaking her heart-strings?

'But hold!—this is not so. Another thought comes into my mind. Did not the *Padre* teach us at our Confirmation that each of the seven Sacraments is a triple mystery; and is made up of three elements—the operation of the mind, that is, the intention; the operation of the heart, that is, the affection; and the operation of the body, that is, the various outward actions by which each of the seven is consummated? Did he not tell us expressly that the Sacrament of Marriage was really and truly enacted by these three things, even before it

should be blessed and registered by the Church?
So that, although not yet religiously completed
(as it ought to be and must be, before it is
secure from mortal sin), yet it cannot be drawn
back from, or violated, without equally mortal
guilt.   Did not Jesus Christ say as much in
the Gospel, of one who should put away his
lawful consort?

'*Sta bene!* [very well].   Have n't these three
things enacted the union—the infrangible union
—of *Luigi* and me?   Has it not been done really
by Providence — by *Iddio* Himself.   Is n't it,
then, almost like the first marriage in the
Garden?

'It must be right of me, then—yes, it must
be kind of me to .... or rather not to .... to
tempt—yes, not to allow them to go on—yes,
indeed, not to permit them, in their blindness,
to rush into mortal sin—as I am sure, I am
perfectly sure they would have done, unless I
had told him—that is, if I had carried out
the beautiful theory—had remained the silent,
sweet proxy for her!

'But, hark!—what voice is this that I hear in
my soul?—Oh, I am afraid the Gospel is against
me. Would I like *Maria* to have done so by
me?—She loved him so—and he loved her—
and she hung her life on being his—and he

had set his heart on her — ah, what a work have I been doing ! — what a temple of bliss have I been tearing down ! — and that from *Maria*, dearest *Maria* — so innocent and so gentle ! — and — and he — so good and handsome and noble !

'But then they would have to burn for it — at least in *Purgatorio.* — No ? — What angel or what demon is filling my soul with voices ? — Is there a remedy ? Speak, mental visitor, whoever thou art ! — Ah, I see it now. Why did n't I comprehend it before ?'

"Up to this moment, the consciousness of *Luigi* being securely mine had been a constant, an ineffable, an inextinguishable joy welling up in the bottom of my soul, preserving a degree of peace and sweetness there, notwithstanding the ever-present bitterness of a sympathy, not to mention an intermittent twinge of shame, over *Maria's* heart-breaking loss.

"But now a third element of disquiet — yes, of desolation and unbearable misery, was borne in upon my fevered imagination. It was a gloomy doubt (if it ought not to be considered a moral certainty), which was able to empoison and destroy, with a remediless wretchedness, the happiness of us all.

"It was flashed upon me now, with a distinct-

ness and intensity such as I had not felt before
—the memory of the fact, with all its possible
consequences looming up in my fancy—that
Luigi had never declared, not even at the supreme moment, any, the least, passion for *Marta*,
but had plainly confessed, over and over again,
that he loved *Maria*. Although so powerful
and perfect was the purity and self-control of
his manhood—oh, how I adored him for it!—
that even under those extreme temptations, his
arm had never once been thrown around her;
yet their souls—ah, yes, their souls—were
united—as he confessed, 'had mingled in the
most intimate embraces of love.'

'Could that foregone result ever be undone?
—that soul embrace between the two—each so
loving and so true—could such a pair ever be
unclasped, much less such a union ever be
transferred to another?' My reason answered,
'Never,' and my Conscience, with an emphasis
that made me shudder, added an awful 'Amen.'

'What a foreshadowing of woe, then, lay
before us all—certain in this world and hardly
less so for the next. For were we not human?
—and how could human nature bear up, either
in peace or sinlessness, under such conditions?
—his hand mine, his heart hers?

'But what, is this whisper in my soul?—

"divide, share his love"?—Never, never!—I can renounce—yes—I can—but divide—share—give up half to another woman—I cannot—no, I cannot—not even—not even with *Maria*—sister, darling, angel that she is—no, no, no, I would sooner—if I must—if I must—I would sooner—give her the whole—and—and leap into Hell outright.

'Ah, now I see—I comprehend. It is I—I only am in the way—I am the Jonah in their voyage. If I were only gone—how sweetly it would bear them to Eden now—and after—to *Paradiso!* There would be no *Purgatorio* in the question. It is I who am *Purgatorio.* Oh, oh! Why do I not leap from this precipice—there is no happiness for me here—and take my chances for the other world? Would it not be a deed of charity?—and perhaps save me, too, from the fire? Oh, pity me, *Maria Santissima!*'

"Crazed with my thoughts, I wandered on, and was already far away from the accustomed track, and rushing forward with the nearly-formed purpose of sacrificing myself for the happiness of the two and the honor of us all, when, at the moment that I was approaching the brink, I heard, in quick succession, two piercing screams. Springing back instinctively, and turning to my left — oh, horrors ! — horror of horrors ! — what did I see ? The whole cliff on that side was giving way, and — oh, merciful God ! — *Luigi* and *Maria* locked in each other's arms, were descending into the abyss, a *chilometro* below !

"It was only an instantaneous glance, but the horrid vision is photographed — no, branded as with a red-hot iron — for eternity in my soul. Her head rested on his bosom. His eyes were upturned toward heaven. Their right hands were clasped together. Her left arm was raised as if in the act of prayer ; his encircled her in the closeness of a spasmodic embrace.

"There were two or three seconds of a rattling, rushing, roaring sound somewhat like the wind in the fir-tree tops in a storm. Then came an awful and prolonged crash, the grinding of rocks one upon another, then unearthly echoes rebounding from mountain-side to mountain-side, through all the branching valleys, which pounded and pierced my whole frame with continuous shocks of indescribable terror. As the horrible uproar, like the world tumbling into ruins, gradually ceased, and a silence, equally dreadful, succeeded, there uprose a vast cloud of yellow dust into the sky, as if hell had opened her gates and sent forth into the upper world a puff of her infernal atmosphere.

"For an instant only, I was fixed to the spot. The next, I was flying at my topmost speed toward home. It had become alarmingly late; and none of us having returned, *Babbo*, greatly worried, had started out in search of us all. I met him, peering in every direction, already at some distance from our home. The meeting was unexpected and instantaneous. I was rushing swiftly around a clump of hazel bushes, where the path made a sharp turn to avoid an angle of rock, and in fact fell into his arms, my breast almost striking upon his and my hands coming down on his shoulders, nearly felling him to the ground, as well as rendering him senseless with amazement. At first, I could not speak, but for some minutes wept hysterically on his bosom. When my voice and self-command returned, in reply to his agitated enquiries, I told him, in the fewest words, what I had seen. Without speaking a word, *Babbo* gently lifted my head from his breast, and taking my hand in his led me swiftly and silently down the mountain-side. He did not speak, only a sigh now and then escaped him, and his hand trembled greatly.

"When we arrived at the house an unexpected good fortune, which greatly relieved our first perplexity, awaited us there. Two stalwart men who had spent the day at work in the forest below us were passing on their way to their homes. *Babbo* called to them and in few words explained our unspeakable trouble and imperative need of help. It was while *Babbo* was thus talking with the men that I now for the first time heard how *Luigi* had come, as he promised, and in searching for me had found *Maria*. The two believing that I should, by this time, have returned to the house, came back together. But finding me still absent, in great alarm, they started together in search of me. It was, it seemed probable, in the apprehension that I might have fallen over the cliff, and possibly (as the despairing heart will fashion to itself and cling to the slenderest thread of hope), might be still hanging, by some root or twig, over the yawning destruction below — impelled by such a thought they had ventured too far, and paid with their lives for their fidelity to me.

"The men, though tired with the long, hard work of the day, and supperless, entering into the case with all the warmth of sympathy and excited abandon which is native to our Italian peasantry, eagerly consented to help us, in our dreadful distress and need. The utmost haste was necessary. It was possible — we thought so — we hoped so — that by some miracle of escape — they might still be — one or both — safe, or at least alive. We must bring all the help we could command and fly to their rescue. Within two or three minutes the three men with our two mules, and ropes and axes and spades, a bottle of strong wine and a lantern (though the moon was full and the night clear), were hurrying up through the gorge to the base of the dislodged cliff.

"Dazed with horror I began mechanically preparing a supper for the helping men, when they should return (for they had two miles to go to their home and could not be sent off exhausted and famishing), and this occupation was a buffer to the first shafts of the thunderbolt. When these preparations were over, I set myself to making such arrangements as ·in my ignorance of the facts seemed to be most suitable; and the uncertainty and perplexity of my thoughts again absorbed for the time much of the terrible anguish of the blow. The accommodations of our house were limited. If one only were living, could they be put in the same room? If both should be found alive, *Maria* would be taken to our loft-chamber; and

important changes would have to be made —
which would not be necessary, if — I did not
clothe this thought in words — but an awful
picture was painted in my soul.

"At last all I could reasonably do was done,
and then the terror of agony began to grow
greater and the time to pass slower. As the
long minutes and the long, long hours went
by, I became ever more and more sadly certain that they would not be brought home in
life; and if their lips were forever sealed, a
question I yearned to know could never be
answered. My thoughts were glowing at fever
heat, and revolved and re-revolved and gradually became fast closed about this problem,
which I could not satisfactorily solve; and yet,
in my enforced idleness, I could not dismiss it
from my mind. The query would not down:
'What had they said to one another — *Luigi*
and *Maria* — during the opportunities that were
offered by that first and second walk together
in the search for me? Did *Luigi*, probably,
communicate to her the facts of our interview?
— and explain the changed relations which
must, henceforth, exist between them — so unlike what both of them had hoped for and
surely expected?

'If he did,' I reflected, 'it is also certain

that he did it so gently, and opened to her a view of his transparent soul so sweetly, that all was done that could be done — and infinitely more than I could have done — to reconcile her to the inevitable change from a lover's and a husband's to a noble and tender brother's love.'

"But considering all the circumstances, recounting them to myself a thousand times, endeavoring to weigh, with the utmost carefulness, every scrap of evidence that could be discovered in fact or deduced by reflection, I was constrained — I need not say how happily constrained — to believe that he divulged none of these matters to her.

'The occasion,' I thought, 'was inopportune. It was a time of hurry from the first; and of increasing alarm as the hours wore on. There was, also, much else to think of and speak of. It was me that was the great object of concern, and they were both the most unselfish and generous of beings. My danger and my fate would so absorb their thoughts and feelings that their own concerns and interests would be for the time forgotten.'

"Besides, *Maria* would, as usual, be quiet and happy in her shy and trustful love; and no one was more sure than *Luigi* to be slow in approaching a matter of such prodigious and tender interest to both. In fact, he might very properly escape the pain of making the disclosure at all, by leaving this duty for me.

"Above all, I thought it conclusive to reflect that, if he had disclosed it, the effect could hardly fail to have been evident. The shock of such a discovery on her affectionate nature would, for the time, at least, have so prostrated her strength as to forbid such an expedition as she undertook with *Luigi*.

"It also corroborates this conclusion, that, at the unexpected moment of the fall, they were so near together that, at the first alarm, they clasped themselves in each other's arms, and she, seeing herself going with him to death, instinctively executed the last and profoundest act of trustful love, nestling her head on his bosom.

"It has been a great comfort to me to think so — that she was spared that cruel pang. She never knew of a rival for his affections. She quaffed the cup of love — ecstatic, undisturbed by a doubt, undashed with a drop of bitterness. In a moment, and encircled by the arms dearest to her on earth, she went with him through the shadowy gateway."

BERNESE ALPS.

XXX.

" Spirit no fetters can bind,
No wicked have power to molest,
There the weary, like thee, the wretched shall find
A haven, a mansion of rest."

MOZART'S REQUIEM.

"IT was very late in the night when, at last, from the window of the front room which I had passed several of the earlier hours in preparing, I saw torches coming down the path and *Babbo* leading the way. The two mules came next, one at a little distance behind the other; and as they wound along the spiral track, I could see that there was a single lit-ter of fir-boughs swung between them, and the two helpers walking close behind brought up the rear.

"My heart seemed then to rise up into my mouth and try to utter inexpressible things. Among these I said to myself, 'Alas! one lit-ter — then one is lost, — buried in an awful grave — beyond recovery till the judgment-day! — ah, which? — which is that one? — which dear body, at least, is it that is coming?—oh, dear! which would I wish it to be?—shall I never again see—him—or—her!—which can I part with—forever!—she would marry and leave us some day—but him—if he is gone!—my life is gone!—I wish I were in the other world with him!' In my distraction I went on thus suffering an unutterable anguish in my thoughts, as if it rested with me to decide this horrible question, quite forgetting that *Iddio* had decided it already for me, and that my office was that of fortitude alone and uncomplaining resignation to His will.

"It was fully a quarter of an hour that that dreadful procession, laden with such awful certainty, overshadowed by such horror of uncertainty, was slowly winding its mournful way down the circuitous track of the mountain-side in full view of my almost maddened vision. Oh, the untold agony of those never-ending minutes! Oh, the rebellious, wicked things I thought!—even the selfish, unsisterly sentiments that passed through my bitter soul! Oh, the dreadful hopes which I would not cherish, but could not banish, which hovered, like shrieking, ill-omened birds, in my mental sky!

"At last the suspense was over. The horror was revealed in its dreadful, unchangeable reality. I stood in the open door when the heart-rending procession arrived. As it wheeled in silence up to the step, what a sight!—what an astonishment met my frenzied eyes! That vision was branded as by a lightning-flash on my soul, and will not be erased from the tablets of my memory for eternity. There they both lay—the two bruised and stiffened bodies lay entwined together in the indissoluble embrace—the wedlock of death!

"The full blow had come. I knew the worst. I was amazed at myself that I did not swoon at the sight. I felt instead a strange calm overspreading my troubled spirit. I seemed to have passed into another sphere. The glitter of dazzling hopes had been left behind. The fever of determined expectations was cooled. I accepted the allotment of the Omnipotent Will, and under all this shadow of death, a sentiment of peace and content poured into my soul, the like of which I never before felt. 'What is this?' I said to myself in new astonishment. 'Whence are these strong comforts that now encircle my soul? Why am I not now rather standing in the darkest dungeon of despair?'

"I immediately answered myself, or rather the answer seemed to come like a floating whisper into my soul. 'They are praying for you now on the other side, and your guardian has been sent to you with his arms full of comforts and strength.' Then it came over me, too, that this was evidence that they were safe—that they were surely where the blessed are.

"Such thoughts filled and steadied my soul while my hands were busied with the last earthly duties to the dead. According to the custom of our country, being the only matron of our home, though so young, it was my office to prepare their bodies for the grave. No mother bathes her darling infant with tenderer hand, or with heart more thankful that she still has the precious form to expend her care upon, than I prepared their dear bodies for the tomb. I had them laid side by side in one coffin. I had dressed her in her white muslin gown, like a bride. I put blue violets in her hair and her own blue and white earrings in her ears. I hung her blue rosary around her beautiful neck with the Crucifix lying on her spotless bosom. I put her white dancing slippers on her feet, which were tied with a blue rosette. I laid her left hand on her breast below the Cross. I put his left arm around her, and laid his left hand below hers under the Cross. Their right hands I joined together.

So that they looked in their coffin, as nearly as could be, as if they were standing before the *Padre* in the act of taking the everlasting vow and receiving the benediction of Holy Church.

"Thus they lay for four days in our home —the weather, which was unusually cold for the season, favoring delay of burial—and while the fragrant candles grew shorter, many people, both neighbors and strangers — for the news spread quickly and far—came and looked into the coffin; and many silent tears were shed. Of course the uncle *Medico* was among those who came, and he came not once but many times; and what shall I say of that dear, good man!"

Here she went on to expatiate on the amiable *Medico* — detailing with a noticeable zest his hundred little attentions to her in her sorrow, and his unnumbered acts of kindness to her *Babbo* in this crisis of his affairs. It was, I thought, at the time, a very pleasant theme for her thoughts, and succeeding events, I could not but hope, would justify my worldly and wicked suspicions.

"So—just so," she said, "they lay before the high altar while the Requiem Mass was sung. So, just so they were buried. So, just so, they lie in one coffin together in that double grave. So, just so, I have them in my fancy when I kneel in the *Camposantino* [dear little cemetery] and tell my beads and say, '*Requiem dona eis Domine!*"

She ceased speaking. I walked on in silence with her to the path that led up to her cottage. Then with many thanks and many expressions of sympathy and many an adieu, I parted from my interesting companion, sadly and forever. But, to use her own expressive words of her sister and the youth with whom her fate was so tragically entangled, very often since, 'our souls have conversed together'; and I will not deny that at a revival of these memories, I have often found the world growing dim around me, and felt a hot stream rolling across my cheeks.

GRENOBLE — QUAY.

CONCLUSION.

IN the summer of 1868, I found myself again in Italy, and at the moment of which I now speak, at the *Hôtel du Montblanc* in *Aosta*, whither I now arrived by the same route that I had traveled fourteen years before.

While treating with the *Directeur* at the office, I observed in fair letters on the end of a large *baule* [in American speech, "Saratoga"], which was bound with a cord, like a package from a retail-shop, and sealed at every crossing of the string with huge patches of red wax, the name FERRENTI. Then, running my eye up the list of names on the register where I had just set my own, I read with a heart-quickening surprise which I think the reader can well imagine: '*Dottor G. Ferrenti e Moglie e Figlio e Bambinaia*' [Dr. G. F., wife, son, and nurse].

On enquiry, I was told that the Doctor and his wife were gone for a few days to *Martigny*, but that the child was left there in the care of his nurse. Where they were at that moment was unknown. I pursued my enquiries to the

limit of propriety, of every maid and serv-
ing-man I met, but in vain. They had been
seen here, and seen there, a few minutes
before, but were everywhere invisible now. I
learned, also, that they sometimes strayed into
the country, and in this case might not appear
again till evening.

This distressed me much, for my arrangements compelled me to leave for the south by
a late afternoon train, and I felt an infinite
curiosity to see the child, if I could not see
the good Doctor, and especially to learn, after
my old suspicions, also who the wife and
mother might be.

However, I could only wait and hope; and
having heard much, among other objects of
antiquarian interest in the suburbs of this old
Celtic stronghold (which gave the great Julius
so much trouble in keeping open the passes of
St. Bernard to his provinces in Gaul, and which
was only cleared up by Augustus extirpating
the whole tribe of the *Salassi*, selling 36,000
men, women, and children into slavery), of the
Church of *St. Orso*, with its tomb, in the choir,
of old bishop *Gallus*, who had been sleeping
there more than 1,300 years; of the old Roman
Crypt, and various other objects of similar
interest contained in it, all of which I had

AOSTA — TRIUMPHAL ARCH OF AUGUSTUS.

never seen — I now happily bethought myself that I could not better spend the time I had on my hands, than by making such a visit. I left my hotel and sauntered along the principal street through the ancient *Porta Prætoria* to the Triumphal Arch of Augustus, and across the *Buthier*, stopping to examine the still remaining arch of the old Roman bridge, half buried in the ground, and wandered on and around to the said Church of *St. Orso*, and entered.

I immediately observed the kneeling figures of a young female and of a boy apparently about ten years old before a shrine of the *Madonna*. I could not doubt that I had thus unexpectedly found the objects of my search.

They at once became of more interest to me than any other object of my curiosity, and I kept them constantly under my eye. The time I had to wait seemed long to me, but at last they rose from their knees, curtesied and bowed toward the altar, went to an alms-box and deposited their offering, and hand in hand walked silently and rather rapidly toward the *uscio*, which was in this case a side-door closed by the usual leathern curtain.

As soon as I saw them ready to leave the church, I issued first and contrived, by crossing a little open space, to meet them face to face. The girl was a pretty maid of some sixteen summers, with great black eyes, and a bright, serious face. The child was a finely-formed youngster, very dark, with curling black hair, which seemed never to have been cut, and hung waving far down his shoulders. His face! — My heart leapt for joy. It was indeed one I had seen before — could not mistake — could never forget.

I made the customary salute, which was instantly and gracefully returned by the little gentleman, but instead of passing, I stepped in front of him, and after a hasty apology, told him I believed I was an old friend of his parents, and if he would assure me that it was so, by giving me his name, I would like to make some enquiries about them.

Without any hesitation he replied: "*Gulielmo Luigi Maria Donato Ombrosino Ferrenti.*"

This, of course, in effect, told me everything. But in fact I could have read it all in his face and figure and manner; for he was, in every feature, an unmistakable copy of his mother. Besides, had I been blind, his tones — that never to be forgotton *timbre* — would have reproduced hers in my ears beyond the possibility of error.

I walked back with them to the hotel, telling him something about my long ago acquaintance with his mother and drawing from him all his little head could tell of her history since — which was not much — but was of the most important kind. 'They lived in Naples. He was born there. His *Babbo* made the Prince (he did not know his other names) to get well when he was sick.'

He showed me a picture of his mother which he wore in a gold locket around his neck. It was the face I knew. Age had added something, years of life in a wider and more exalted station had added more, and all was in a manner glorified by the dress and pose of a lady instead of the young and interesting yet undeniable *contadina* whom I had met fourteen years agone.

I gave him a visiting card with my address for the next few weeks in Rome, and a small photograph of myself for the mother.

During the day I parted from him with a kiss, and went on my way toward the south. I never saw him nor his parents again. Some weeks later, passing through Naples, and making enquiry for the family, I found that the Doctor was well known in upper circles there, but had not then returned from the north.

One word more finishes this history forever. Being again in Naples at the end of the eighties, I sought there for my interesting friends, and found that during the season of the cholera which visited Naples with such violence" in the summer and autumn of 1884, putting in so much anxiety even the life of the amiable and self-forgetting King of Italy, the faithful Doctor Ferranti was struck by the malady and died; and within a few days was followed, from the same cause, by his wife and son. In short, that the family which had been of such interesting concern to me was now extinct in this world.

AT NAPLES.

AOSTA.—TOWER OF BRAMAFAM.

NOTES.

NOTES.

PAGE 7.   NOTE 1.

"*Now the Sunday-morning Bell.*"

Schon klingen Morgenglocken,
Der liebe Gott nun bald
Geht durch den stillen Wald,
Da kniet' ich froh erschrocken.
BARON VON EICHENDORF.

The allusion of *the poet* is, of course, to the *Ave Maria* bell, echoing around the world at dawn the daily call to prayer.

PAGE 10.   NOTE 2.

" *The grave is still and deep.*"

Das Grab ist tief und stille
Und schauderhaft sein Rand ;
Es deckt mit schwartzer Hülle
Ein unbekantes Land.

Das Lied der Nachtigallen
Tönt nicht in seinem Schoos ;
Der Freundschaft Rosen fallen
Nur auf des Hügels Moos.

Verlass'ne Bräute ringen
Umsonst die Hände wund ;
Der Waise Klagen dringen
Nicht in der tiefe Grund.
SALIS.

379

PAGE 30. NOTE 3.

" Oh, do not dry, etc."

Trocknet nicht, trocknet nicht
Thränen der ewigen Liebe !
Ach, nur dem halb-getrockneten Auge
Wie öde wie todt die Welt ihm erscheint.
Trocknet nicht, trocknet,
Thränen unglüchlicher Liebe !

GOETHE.

PAGE 49. NOTE 4.

The cruel political strifes between the Guelfs and the Ghibelines, and between the *Bianchi* [whites] and the *Neri* [blacks], parties into which the Guelfs were divided when the Ghibelines had been overpowered, is known to every reader of *Dante*, whose mournful history is almost a monologue upon these XIII and XIV century quarrels.

The *Piagnoni* and the *Palleschi*, in a certain sense heirs of the more ancient strife, come into view most prominently two centuries later, in the times of the great political preacher, *Savonarola*, and revolve about the successful struggle of the Medici for supreme power in Florence. The dreadful story is graphically outlined by Massimo D'Azeglio in his famous historical novel, *Nicolò de' Lapi*.

The word *Piagnone* properly means a person who weeps easily and for trifling cause. It is commonly used of the 'weepers' who accompany, for pay, a dead body to the grave. It was a nickname given in Florence to the followers of *Savonarola*, who were hostile to the Medicean faction.

Pallesco properly means a 'ballman.' It is a comical adjective formed from *palla* [a ball], and was a nickname given in Florence to those who belonged to the party of the *Medici*, whose arms were six balls.

PAGE 69.   NOTE 5.

" But night for each, etc."
. . . . *Sed omnes una manet nox*
Et calcanda semel via leti.

HOR. CAR. i, 18.

PAGE 71.   NOTE 6.

As is universal in Continental Europe, it is to be supposed that *Signor Ombrosini* had several Baptismal names, among which was *Jacobo*, which his wife had chosen for her own affectionate use and Gallicized into *Jacques*, while he himself used *Filippo*, which appears, also, to have been that by which he was generally called in his youth.

PAGE 80.   NOTE 7.

La Compagnia della Misericordia is the Italian name of a Charitable Brotherhood, found in most Roman Catholic countries, whose office is to render assistance to those who are overtaken by sudden sickness, or serious, especially mortal accident, and to bury the dead — chiefly the very poor and strangers.

PAGE 80.   NOTE 8.

Miserere mei Deus.

The 50th Psalm of the Vulgate. It is numbered 51 in King James's Version.

PAGE 81.   NOTE 9.

Ostende nobis Domine.

The 84th Psalm of the Vulgate, 8th verse.   It is numbered 85 in King James's Version, 7th verse.

PAGE 101.   NOTE 10.

" Gave the *tu* to each other." That is, in addressing one another, used the second person singular instead of the common second plural, or the still more formal third person singular. It is an expression of familiarity common to all the Romaic languages, and to some others, but quite unknown to ours, and the subtile sentiment carried by it, it is difficult, perhaps impossible, for us fully to realize, since it is strictly reserved for such as stand to one another in the most sacred, or personal, or intimate relations.

PAGE 109.   NOTE 11.

The tower of *Bramafam* was built in the XII century, and is that in which Count *Challant* is said, out of jealousy, to have starved his wife to death.

PAGE 123.   NOTE 12.

"*What if I choose to weep alone.*"
Und hab' ich einsam auch geweint,
   So ist's mein eignen Schmerz,
Und Thränen fliessen gar so süss
   Erleichtern mir das Herz.

GOETHE, Trost in Thränen.

PAGE 128.   NOTE 13.

The *scudo* [shield] was until recently in Tuscany a nominal piece of money representing a value of $5\frac{80}{100}$ *Lire* [about one dollar]. In the Pontifical and some other Italian States it was, at one time, a real piece, but of various values.

PAGE 139.   NOTE 14.

"*Why now Casella mine, etc.*"

Casella mio . . . . . .
  Diss' io ; ma a te come tanta ora é tolta?

PURG. ii, 91, 93.

PAGE 146.   NOTE 15.

St. Francis of *Assisi*, founder of the Order of the Francescan monks, is said to have retired to a desolate mountain for the purpose of passing forty days in fasting and prayer.   On the day of the Elevation of the Cross, while he was engaged in intense devotion, and was agonized in contemplation of the pangs of the Crucified, Christ Himself appeared to him in the form of a Seraph, and imprinted on him, under crushing pains, the scars of the five wounds of His passion.   This vision and miracle is said to have occurred in the year 1224.   Benedict XII, an Avignon Pope, granted to the Order the Celebration of the Feast of the ' Imprinting.'   The festival occurs on the 17th of September.

PAGE 152.   NOTE 16.

" *Rosolio* " [oil of roses] is an Italian wine of exquisite flavor and perfume, called also by the natives *Rugiada del sole* [sun-dew].

PAGE 167.   NOTE 17.

" The Siege of *Firenze* " [Florence].   She alludes to the final and successful attempt of the Medici to grasp the supreme power, in 1530, when, under a coalition of the Emperor Charles V with Pope Clement VII, of the house of Medici, Florence was invested by the Duke of Orange, and both the name and form of the Republic were quenched in the best blood of the city — most stirring pictures of which abound in D'Azeglio's novel alluded to above.

PAGE 167.   NOTE 18.

" Views in old *Siena*."   It has rather justly been called ' the Pompeii of the Middle Ages,' since no other city of Italy has taken on so little of a modern appearance, and retained so much of the medieval — so that its wolf-topped pillars, its queer *Palio* [horse-race], its fountain *Fontebranda*. its *Mangia* tower, and many other things there, are almost or quite as curious and interesting sights to an Italian of to-day as to a visitor from foreign parts.

PAGE 197.   NOTE 19.

"*And suddenly upon the day arose.*"

E di subito parve giorno a giorno
   Essere aggiunto, come Quei che puote
   Avesse il ciel d'un altro Sole adorno.
Beatrice tutta nell' eterne rote
   Fissa con gli occhi stava ; ed io, in lei
   Le luci fisse di lassù rimote.

.   .   .   .

Non dèi più ammirar, se bene stimo,   .
   Lo tuo salir, se non come d'un rivo
   Se d' alto monte scende giuso ad imo.
Maraviglia sarebbe in te, se privo
   D' impedimento giù ti fossi assiso,
   Com' a terra quieto fuoco vivo.

PAR. i, 61, 136.

PAGE 208.   NOTE 20.

"*O Death, you must surely delay.*"

Mon beau voyage encore est si loin de se fin !
Je pars et des ormeaux qui bordent le chemin
   J'ai passé les premiers à peine.
Au banquet de la vie à peine commencé
Un instant seulement mes levres ont pressé
   La coupe en mes mains encor pleine.

LA JEUNE CAPTIVE.

PAGE 211.   NOTE 21.

"A bright *zecchino*."   A golden coin of several countries.   In Tuscany it had the value of $11\frac{20}{100}$ *lire* [about \$2.25].   It is no longer coined, but the phrase is common, '*oro di zecchino*' [zecchino-gold] for finest gold.

384

PAGE 228. NOTE 22.

" *Alive as the wind harp, etc.*"

Aber, wie leise vom Zephyr erschüttert,
Schnell die äolische Harfe erzittert,
Also die fühlende Seele der Frau.

WURDE DER FRAUEN.

PAGE 241. NOTE 23.

" *Alla dolce ombra delle belle frondi.*"

This poem, which is such a favorite in Italy, owes something, at least, of its popularity — it is hard for a *forestiero* to say how much — to the exceedingly mellifluous flow of the rhythm, united to a sentiment of wonder at the miraculous skill with which the stanzas are constructed.

These are technically known as the unrhymed *sestine* [sixes] — the most artificial of all poetical handiwork, and hardly known or possible outside of the language of Italy. The number of syllables in a line is eleven, as is, also, for the most part, the rule for all unrhymed verse in Italian.

But the number of stanzas in the poem is six. The number of lines in a stanza is six. The six line-ending words of the first stanza are the same in each of the six stanzas, but in a varied order : and the last word of the first line of each succeeding stanza is the same as the last word of the last line of the preceding stanza.

At the end of the poem there is a *coda* or refrain of three more lines, ending with three of the same six words.

The first stanza, which will give a fair idea of the whole, is :

> *Alla dolce ombra delle belle frondi*
> *Corsi fuggendo un dispietato lume*
> *Che 'nfin quaggiù m'ardea dal terzo cielo;*
> *E disgombrava già di neve i poggi*
> *L'aura amorosa che rinnova il tempo,*
> *E fiorian per le piagge l' erbe e i rami.*

TRANSLATION.

To the sweet shade of the beautiful tree
A disquieting heat compelled me to flee
From the third heaven descending on me ;
While the amorous breeze strips the snow-covered hill
And the primrose is born on the banks of the rill
And the grasses and flowers their fragrance distill.

The substance of the rather obscure thought is this : He says it was Springtime when he fled from the heat [of natural passion], *i. e.*, when he became enamored of his *Laura* and found solace in her presence. This is a pun on the name of Laura, a laurel-tree. The third heaven, again, is the sphere of Venus, who enkindled this passion. The 'amorous breeze,' *l' aura amorosa*, love-inspiring Laura, who melts the snowiest heart, is another pun on the same dear name. And so on and on.

PAGE 245.   NOTE 24.

" In peace remain : I go : for now "

Rimanti in pace : i' vado : a te non lice
Meco venir : chi mi conduce, il vieta.
Rimanti, o va per altra via elice.

GERUS. LIB. xvi, 55.

PAGE 253.   NOTE 25.

" As in form of butterfly "

In des Papillons Gestalt
Flattr'ich, nach den letzten Zügen,
Zu den vielgeliebten Stellen
Zeugen himmlischer Vergnügen
Ueber Wiesen, an den Quellen,
Um den Hügel, durch den Wald.

Ich belausch' ein zärtlich Paar ;
Von des schönen Mädchens Haupte
Aus den Kränzen schau' ich nieder ;
Alles was der Tod mir raubte
Seh' ich hier im Bilde wieder,
Bin so glücklich wie ich war.

Sie umarmt ihn lächelnd stumm,
Und sein Mund geniesst der Stunde,
Die ihm güt'ge Götter senden,
Hüpft vom Busen zu dem Munde,
Von dem Munde zu den Händen,
Und ich hüpf' um ihn herum.

Und sie sieht mich Schmetterling.
Zitternd vor des Freunds Verlangen
Springt sie auf, da flieg' ich ferne.
" Liebster, komm, ihn einzufangen !
Komm ! ich hätt' es gar zu gerne,
Gern das kleine bunte Ding."

SCHADENFREUDE.

PAGE 262. NOTE 26.

" *Et definiens statuta tempora et terminos habitationis nostrae,*" VULGATE, *Acts* xvii, 26 [And has determined the times
before appointed and the bounds of our habitation]. It is not
uncommon for the better educated peasantry in all Catholic countries, to which Italy is no exception, to know, at least by rote, the
more important parts of the Bible in the Vulgate version, as well
as large portions of their great Poets, being familiarized with them
in childhood in the Parish-school.

387

PAGE 281.   NOTE 27.

" Of the judgments of woman."

Molti consigli de le donne sono
Meglio improviso, ch' a pensarvi, usciti ;
Che questo è speïzale e proprio dono
Fra tanti e tanti lor dal ciel largiti.
Ma può mal quel degli uomini esser buono,
Che maturo discorso non aiti,
Ove non s' abbia a ruminarvi sopra
Speso alcun tempo e molto studio et opra.

ORLANDO FURIOSO, xxvii, 1.

PAGE 314.   NOTE 28.

" A beautiful copy of the *Cenacolo di Foligno*."   The original is now treasured in Florence (in the secularized *Convent of S. Onofrio* in the *Via Faenza*).   I quite agree with *Luigi* that this ' Supper' is by far the most soul-satisfying to me of all I have ever seen — not the *Leonardo da Vinci* at Milan, in this r espect surpassing it.

Besides the great advantage which, of course, *Raffaelle's* picture has, in its excellent state of preservation, over *Leonardo's* in its ' deplorable condition,' and setting aside a comparison of artistic merit between two supreme artists, the work of either of whom is unapproachable, the comforting *motive* of *Raffaelle's* picture goes home to my heart with a joy which I do not find in the same degree from the painfully pleasing shock which *Leonardo's* famous work was designed to give and does give to every sensitive soul. *Luigi* had only seen *copies* of either of these, and I think, no doubt, *Leonardo's* also loses more by the best attainable copying than *Raffaelle's* does under the same conditions.

PAGE 314.   NOTE 29.

The Crucifixion, or Christ upon the Cross with more or less additional figures and environments, was several times painted by

Fra Angelico da Fiesole, with great success. Into each of these he infused, perhaps in a higher degree than any other artist has done, the peculiar type of his own character, and especially of his own religious emotions.

Luigi, no doubt, refers to a copy of his Crucifixion in the Chapter House of the Monastery (at that date not yet suppressed), of *S. Marco* in Florence. Into this are introduced many saints gazing up at the Saviour in wonder, sorrow, and ecstasy, and around is a framework of prophets and sybils, and beneath, is kneeling *S. Domenico*, from whom springs a Tree of the Order branching into many distinguished saints. And it seems to me that *Luigi* was quite right in his homage of the depth of sentiment and sense of beauty, as well as of deep and devoted piety, which reign in that picture — and perhaps I ought to say in all the products of the pious and peaceful genius of that lovely Christian soul and Dominican friar.

PAGE 318. NOTE 30.

The curious reader may find the whole dialogue, full of *Leopardi's* most subtile thoughts, in the *Le Monnier* edition of *Leopardi's Opere*, Vol. I, page 221 *et seq.*

Of *Tasso* himself, I think it may be said that he leads the whole celestial-terrestrial choir in the infantile purity and *naïveté* of his sentiments towards the sex.

Is it not possible, then, that this very absence of the grosser sensualism of love in his soul, was a feature which brutish *Alfonso* could not conceive; and that he in consequence imagined and believed what was not and could not be true?

Still, after all that has been said and written, by great and small, it seems to me that the true reason for his emprisonment is to-day as uncertain as it was to poor *Tasso* himself, and has been ever since.

Of course, in addition to the fact of his long and painful incarceration, it is certain that, as *Dante* had his *Beatrice*, and *Petrarca* his *Laura*, so *Tasso* had, as the inspiration of his erotic muse, his

Lucretia, and that there was a lady of such name, sister to the reigning Duke, and that the poet must often have met this lady at the court of *Alfonso* and in the Ducal Palace at *Ferrara*.

How much of the rest is, in fact, the glamour of poetic frenzy, every reader must, I think, determine for himself.

PAGE 325. NOTE 31.

" *Not two miles traveled, when, etc.* "

> Non furo iti duo miglia, che sonare
> Odon la selva, che li cinge intorno,
> Con tal rumor e strepito, che pare
> Che tremi la foresta d'ogni intorno ;
> E poco dopo un gran destrier n'appare,
> D'oro guernito e riccamente adorno,
> Che salta macchie e rivi, et a fracasso
> Arbori mena e ciò che vieta il passo.

ORLANDO FURIOSO I, 72.

PAGE 340. NOTE 32.

The *staffiere* [stirrup-man] might be roughly translated 'esquire,' but it has no really exact name in English, because the English have never had precisely the thing. Where it has a use it means, properly, that servant of a prince or great lord who goes on foot beside the stirrup of the riding lord.

PAGE 376. NOTE 33.

It is of record that in one night of September, 1884, nearly 2,000 persons in Naples were attacked with the cholera and about 1,000 died. King Humbert spent a considerable time in the city during the prevalence of the scourge, when nearly all who were able to flee had fled, not only lending his influence and authority to the measures for combatting the disease, but visiting the hospitals and giving his personal sympathy and large sums of money, from his not over-full private purse, for the relief of the suffering poor.